SEARCHING
for BILLIE

a novel

FREDA JACKSON

VICTORIA · VANCOUVER · CALGARY

TouchWood Editions
#108–17665 66A Avenue
Surrey, BC V3S 2A7
www.touchwoodeditions.com

TouchWood Editions
PO Box 468
Custer, WA
98240-0468

LIBRARY AND ARCHIVES CANADA CATALOGUING IN PUBLICATION
    Jackson, Freda, 1942–
    Searching for Billie: a novel / Freda Jackson

ISBN 978-1-894898-53-9

    1. Home children (Canadian immigrants) — Fiction.   I. Title.

    PS8619.A243S43 2007   C813'.6   C2007-901158-6

LIBRARY OF CONGRESS CONTROL NUMBER: 2006907469

Edited by Marlyn Horsdal
Proofread by Lesley Cameron
Cover and interior design by Jacqui Thomas
Cover images Glenbow Archives NA-836-4 (photograph) and iStock/Amanda Rohde (background)

Printed and bound in Canada by Friesens

TouchWood Editions acknowledges the financial support for its publishing program from the Government of Canada through the Book Publishing Industry Development Program (BPIDP), Canada Council for the Arts, and the province of British Columbia through the British Columbia Arts Council and the Book Publishing Tax Credit.

This book has been produced on 100% post-consumer recycled paper, processed chlorine free and printed with vegetable-based dyes.

To the memory of Heather Vogt

I would like to thank Terilyn Paulgaard
for her constant encouragement and sound advice

The boxes were new. So were the contents: a brush and comb, a change of clothes, serviceable underwear, a Bible. Labelled simply with a child's name and a destination, many of the boxes have been lost or deliberately destroyed. The records of some of the 100,000 children sent from Great Britain to Canada between 1869 and 1930 have similarly been lost or destroyed.

The British Child Emigration Movement was born of the social upheaval of the Industrial Revolution. The migration of workers from the country to the city, combined with no compulsory education and no social-safety networks, resulted in fractured families and orphaned or abandoned children.

They were commonly called "street urchins" or "guttersnipes," and the city streets of Great Britain teemed with them. They begged, stole, prostituted themselves and formed gangs in order to survive, offending the sensibilities of the recently formed middle class of merchants and manufacturers. Not surprisingly, this nuisance gave birth to a new movement among the same middle class. Philanthropic organizations were a perfect outlet for the energy and zeal of the wives and daughters of the newly moneyed.

Most were well intentioned, convinced they stood on solid moral ground. Fresh air, food, school attendance and, most importantly, hard work, were the ingredients needed to produce a sound, upstanding adult. All were available in Canada.

The motives of the governments that encouraged the movement were not so noble. The New World was in desperate need of labourers, and employers, especially farmers, were not averse to indenturing children as young as six or eight to the most arduous of labour, work for which city children — street urchins — were ill-suited.

Accounts of neglect, physical and sexual abuse, torture and even murder haunt the stories of Home Children. Not written in court records, and not easily measured, are the damaging effects of loneliness, emotional deprivation and total isolation from anyone or anything they could rely upon. They were on their own.

It is a testament to the dauntless spirit of a child that many Home Children not only survived but flourished. They grew to adulthood, married, had families and contributed to their new country in every way possible. Their descendants, estimated to number 4.5 million, can be found throughout North America. The boxes may not have survived and the clothes may have been taken away by greedy sponsors, but the children left a legacy of strength and fortitude they can all be proud of.

For more information on Home Children, or to register a family member who was a Home Child and/or search for a relative, visit http://www.collectionscanada.ca/02/020110_e.html.

ane Priddle spread her feet to brace herself against the wrench and roll of the train, holding onto the backs of the seats on either side until her knuckles turned white. Outside the window, a coyote kept pace with the train, tongue lolling, like a dog chasing a milk cart.

Soon she would feel nauseous again, but for the moment, standing in the aisle relieved the ache in her hips from sitting on the slatted seat of the C & E line from Calgary to South Edmonton for—what? Nearly eight hours.

The train clanged into a small ravine, so the coyote sped up and, intent on staring in the train window, crashed into a small tangle of brush. It flew head over heels and landed in a disgraceful heap on the brown plains. Jane bent her knees and saw it pick itself up and slink off into the sunset before the train carried her farther northward. She chuckled aloud but no one paid attention. She could have burst into song and not caused the least stir.

Three hours later, staring out the same window at the glimmer of a few weak street lamps, she could as easily have burst into tears. Every part of her now ached, especially her head.

"End o' the steel!" the conductor called for the third time, and with such satisfaction in his voice that Jane knew he took personal comfort in the fact that, when the train turned around in two days' time and went back to Calgary, he would be on it. Perhaps she would, too.

From Calgary she could retrace her steps east, across the empty grasslands where antelope bounded beside the train. In Winnipeg she would not even disembark. She had no more business to attend to in that city. Inside the mahogany-lined luxury of one of the Canadian Pacific Railroad Company's passenger cars she could enjoy the great rocks and green forests of Ontario one more time. And when the vista threatened to become monotonous, she would remind herself that she was actually living an adventure, not just reading about it.

But for now, she joined the crush of unwashed bodies that pressed toward the door as the train squealed to a stop, then clattered down the metal steps to be part of the weekly spectacle that entertained the locals on the crowded platform. The motion of the train stayed in her legs so that she wavered like a drunk in front of the conductor.

"That-a-way," he said in answer to her question about a newspaper office. "Charlie Taylor will be running late tonight. The paper is due out in the morning and he always waits to see what news the train might bring in."

She staggered "that-a-way" through the horse manure and baked ruts, her alligator club bag jammed under one sweaty armpit and her writing case under the other. A strapping lad with a dilapidated child's wagon offered to cart her small trunk across the street to the Princess Hotel for five cents and she didn't seem to have any choice but to take a chance on him.

Twenty minutes later, Jane tossed her simple straw sailor hat onto the narrow bed in her hotel room and eased her feet out of her boots. Her trunk sat safely at the foot of the bed, so she dropped her writing case on top of it. She searched through her bag for a packet of headache powder, dissolved it in a glass of water from the jug on the washstand and downed it with a grimace before padding to the window, where she lowered the olive-green blind. She unfastened buttons and tapes until she stood in a puddle of soiled clothes, then poured tepid water into an enamel basin and proceeded to wash every inch of her body, finally bending her knees to dunk her heavy mop of hair in the water.

The room felt close and stale, and the stink of fried garlic and sweaty bodies from the train lingered on the heap of her clothes. She pulled the chain to turn off the lone light bulb that hung in the middle of the room, then raised the blind on the window so the breezes could lift the lace curtain.

Across the dark outline of the railroad tracks, she saw a cluster of tents and shanties similar to those she had seen in countless other towns across the frontier. Canvas triangles, grey in the moonlight, appeared to shimmer and move in the haze of smoke from all the campfires. Dim shapes drifted idly from one tent to another in a familiar kind of way.

She shook her damp hair and shivered. "Unseasonably hot for the beginning of October," she had been told at the newspaper office. Was it really October? Time and distance had become distorted for Jane, but the ink-stained calendar on Mr. Taylor's desk had been circled at October 8, 1897.

This late at night the air turned cool, a hint of things to come perhaps, and Jane realized again that she had stayed far too long. She needed to return to Ontario to help Suzette, then make her way back to Halifax and hope to find a berth on a ship headed home.

She moved back toward the bed, stopping long enough to

check the lock and, as an added precaution, to prop the lone chair under the knob. She felt the motion of the train return as she lay between cool, sweet-smelling sheets, grasping the narrow bed frame to steady herself, wondering what tomorrow would bring.

From the street below the open window came the rattle of harness, then the profane bickering of drunks, which announced that the taverns had closed for the night. As a deep silence settled on the town and sleep overcame her, she held onto the bed and the fact that tomorrow her advertisement would appear in the local paper, along with the hope that it might bring results.

Where on earth was Billie Thomm?

It was the quiet that woke Billie. He lay perfectly still in a shallow spot dug into the dirt at the back of the lean-to that he shared with a couple of railroad workers. Billie hated the quiet, preferring the bedlam of a city that never slept. Most of the noise out here didn't make sense to him, but he'd heard the train whistle a while back and felt that longing in his belly again, the way he did every time a train passed through. Later, he'd been aware of a fuss and a stir as a crowd of newcomers added a bulge to the shanty town that squatted a few blocks from the train.

Now he narrowed his eyes to adjust them to the dark, then shifted soundlessly onto his back, easing closer to the snoring bulk that blocked his way. Taking a deep breath against the stink of whiskey, Billie fumbled his way over the limp body.

"What the hell ya doin'?"

"Need to take a piss," Billie muttered as he sprang to his feet, already on the move. Three tents down, he checked the coin he'd palmed from the drunk's vest pocket—only a five-cent piece— then struck a match with his thumbnail and lit the loosely rolled cigarette that he'd managed to get at the same time. He dragged the hot smoke into his lungs and cut silently across the tent camp toward the train station.

Wide awake, and alert to the possibilities of the night, he felt a tingle of excitement. Passing the last tent, he snagged a tin of something that had been left on a packing crate. The station looked deserted but he knew from a couple of recent scrapes that there was usually someone around at night. Billie crawled under the luggage cart, back out of the light of the full moon.

It was an unnatural thing, that moon, so big and bright it lit the whole settlement. Flipping open the blade of the biggest of his two knives, he wondered if this was a different moon than the one back home. Using the heel of his hand to hammer the knife, he stabbed again and again at the tin until he felt something wet and sticky spill over his wrist. He licked at the syrup. Peaches. Leaning against a tarry-smelling post, he sucked the fruit from the jagged hole in the tin, flinching when the cool sweetness hit his broken tooth. He tried to remember the times he'd been collared and hauled off to school. Might they have talked about moons and all? He stopped eating as footsteps echoed down the platform.

"... all these crates of fancy wine and grub?"

"Aw, we got a bunch of big shots in town—hunters mostly. And then there are the ones headed north, hoping to find gold."

Billie held his breath. The men stopped directly beside him, laughing at the antics of those with more money than brains.

"Some of them are staying at the Princess," one said as they moved away. "No room left in any of the hotels on the other side of the river."

Billie had been to the other side of the river, where there was another dirt-pile of a town, no better than this one. Edmonton and South Edmonton—couldn't even think up two names.

The sound of the men's boots echoed inside Billie's head along with a notion that had struck him as quick as a swipe from Ma's hand. He dropped the empty tin and wiped his mouth. The Princess. That two-storey hotel across the way that didn't lock the back door on its second floor at night; it had a boardwalk to a double-decker privy for the special use of its fine guests. He could shinny up the back of that easy enough. Have a bit of a look around. Maybe find enough money for a train ticket.

On Thursday the train would go back to Calgary and from there he could catch a westbound train to Vancouver. He crept from under the platform, searching for shadows to hide in on his way to the back of the hotel. Stupid moon. A fellow could actually see it move of a night, casting long ribbons of light up and down the alleys, showing his every step.

Vancouver. It was a real city; at least that's what he'd heard from more than one bloke, so perhaps it was true. But he'd made a big mistake in trying to get there. In his hurry to leave Calgary, he'd hooked up with a rowdy bunch of drovers who were headed out with some cows. He hadn't paid much attention to where they were going; he'd just known he had to get away from a Frenchman called Langevin. Turned out the cows were headed north and Vancouver was west.

A dog barked over near the livery. Billie hunkered down and waited a minute before trying to climb the clapboard siding on the lower privy. His new boots slipped with each effort so he took them off and hid them under some loose planks on the ground. They cost a pretty penny, a lot more than good boots back home, and he was determined to take care of them. He liked the thought that he could have new things now, and the boots were sort of a promise to himself that he could make it on his own, didn't need anything from anyone.

He took one of the loose planks and propped it against the lower privy, then, with his bare toes curled on the splintery wood, crawled up far enough to get his fingers on the walkway above. Inside the hotel, he stopped long enough to pull his frayed sleeve over his bony wrist and hand so he could reach up and unscrew the bare light bulb. The long corridor flickered into darkness. He took a bit of twisted wire from his pocket and began, nervously at first, to work his way down the line of doors.

His luck came in small packages. He pocketed a few dollars here and there; watches and jewellery he left behind because he didn't know how he would flog them in this stupid little village.

Like a ruffle of night air, he moved in and out of rooms, soundless on bare feet. He pressed his ear to each door before working the lock, his eyes accustomed to the dark, sweeping the length of the hall for movement. Instinctively, and because he lived mostly at night, he knew the sounds of deep and unsuspecting sleep. He worked quickly. One door resisted his efforts with a grating sound. Must have a chair propped under the knob. Probably some old maid without much worth stealing anyway, and he sure didn't need her to wake up and scream.

With only two rooms left, Billie tried to guess what the night's take might be. Lots. Enough to catch the train, maybe all the way to Vancouver. At the second-to-last door he stopped to listen. Time had stood still in his mind, but it sure seemed like he had done well in short order. He eased the wire into the keyhole and turned gently; a few jiggles, a quick turn and he could press the door back a crack and slip through.

By the combined light of the moon and the street lamp, he made his way easily around the room. They were all arranged the same way, which was good of the hotelkeeper. By now he knew there were four steps from the night table to the single dresser

and five across to the wardrobe. He palmed a heavy bill clip —
probably gold—but empty. Good leather luggage, but where
was the money?

Billie pawed through a heap of shirts, making no more noise
than a cat in a laundry basket. He considered taking one of the
shirts because his was getting too small, but the stink of them gave
him a creepy feeling. Moving away from the suitcases, with his
back to the bed, he gently opened the wardrobe door.

He didn't hear a sound. And he hadn't made any himself, he
felt pretty sure about that. But a hand tangled itself in the hair at
the scruff of his neck and the breath was strangled out of him. He
was jerked backward out of the closet, landing with a thud on his
rear in the middle of the room. He grabbed his throat where his
collarless shirt cut into it like a snare, squinting and blinking as
the light came on.

The little man, in tatty grey combinations, had a splotchy
yellow face and wrinkled neck, like fruit left out to rot.

"So, lad. Been a good night, has it?"

Before Billie could scramble to his feet, the man yanked a
chair over, placed it squarely in front of him and then sat with his
legs spread. The sickening smell of body odour drifted into Billie's
face. He felt the peaches he'd nicked turn sour in his belly, the
acid rushing up to burn the back of his throat. He shifted his eyes
toward the door, despair rising with the bile in his chest.

The man responded by sliding forward in his chair. "I think
we could be good for one another. Take care of each other, as it
were," he said to Billie in an oily whisper.

Billie felt a liquid rush in his bowels. He was back home, hurt
and scared and—Denny—poor little Denny. Billie wondered
how he always managed to stumble into the likes of this, especially when he thought he was taking such good care of himself.

He kept his eyes averted, not just from the shame, but because he knew well enough by now that he couldn't let them see what he was feeling.

"My boots," he said in a voice that only this morning had cracked to an almost grown-up pitch. Now it sounded whiny and thin, even to his own ears. "I need to get my new boots."

ane woke to a commotion that came from out-
side her door. The angle of the sun told her she
had slept late and her first temptation was to roll
over and have a nice long lie-in; then she remembered that her advertisement would be in the paper this morning.
She gave herself a generous stretch instead, feeling the need for
exercise. Then she rose and shook the wrinkles from her last clean
costume, a fawn-coloured walking suit with a dainty ecru shirtwaist. The first order of business would be to find a laundry.

The voices in the hallway grew more excited. With a quick
splash of cold water on her face and a few pins jabbed into her
unruly hair, she stepped into the fray. She immediately heard the
words "thief" and "stolen" through the angry babble and watched
as a red-faced desk clerk tried to reassure his patrons.

"The police have been sent for; we'll get to the bottom of this.
We have an excellent patrolman working for the town," he said.

From behind her, Jane heard a voice with a good public
school accent. "'Pears there have been some thefts from the rooms
overnight."

Jane turned with a smile, pleased to speak with someone from home. He stood several inches shorter than she, his clothes shiny with wear.

"Nothing of mine seems to be disturbed," she said.

He rocked back and forth on patent shoes that were cracked across the instep. "Nor mine. Nor mine."

"Troubling, though," she mused aloud, looking at her own door and the key in her hand.

"Petty thief, I'm sure," the man responded with surprising confidence.

Noticing the folded paper under his arm, she asked, "Is that today's issue?"

He held it before his nose. "This? I suppose it is. I picked it up at breakfast. Pathetic little gossip sheets, these colonial rags, but there's nothing else to read, is there?" Very deliberately, he tucked it back under his arm.

"They may be simple, but the local population reads them thoroughly. At least," she added as an afterthought, "that's my understanding."

"Indeed?"

"I've placed a missing person advertisement in it," Jane said, thinking he wouldn't be interested, but what's the harm? The more people who knew about Billie the better. "I'm searching for a boy."

A look of sly interest settled on his face. "A boy?"

"Yes, about 13 years old. His name is Billie Thomm."

"Thomm, is it? A relative perhaps?"

"Gracious no. He's a Home Child. One of the children sent over here by our mission. To have a better life," she finished lamely.

He laughed with a wet snort. "How sensible of you. Well, I'll make enquiries, if you like. Always happy to help a fellow country-man. Uh, woman," he corrected himself.

By midday, Jane had found a Chinese laundry that promised to have her clothes washed and returned to her first thing in the morning, and a mercantile store, cluttered with everything from fresh eggs to enema syringes, where she purchased a tin of tooth powder and a packet of soap flakes. She had no intention of letting strangers wash the flimsy undergarments her cousin Caroline had talked her into buying; she'd have to do her personal things in her room later.

Down the avenue stood a red-brick post office, one of the few permanent-looking buildings stacked up against the confusion of clapboard and false fronts. She should probably write to Aunt Evelyn and Caroline, but some perverse part of her had refused to keep them in touch with her whereabouts for the last leg of her investigation. She had written a curt note from the Distributing Home in Winnipeg after hearing of Billie's disappearance, which had come on top of Suzette's disgrace in Ontario.

Suzette. A pretty name for a pretty girl. "Too pretty for her own good," the manager of the home had put it. How could anyone possibly be too pretty?

Jane marched past the post office. If their mission society had sent children this great distance to fend for themselves, then she should be able to manage, too. She would find Billie and ensure his well-being before returning east to see what, if anything, could be done for Suzette. At 15, she was half Jane's age.

The town was abuzz with commerce, perfumed with freshly cut timber, alive with promise. The afternoon beckoned like unspent money. Minutes later she stood looking over the North Saskatchewan River and the deep valley that it had gouged into the earth. Above the river on the north side was the town of Edmonton and at her back, the town of South Edmonton, the C & E Railway Station and her last connection to the rest of the world.

She turned east, toward the tent camp she had seen the night before, picking her way around hobbled cattle and their mess of steaming manure. A lad, loafing against the wall of a privy, watched her with open curiosity. Not Billie. Flies stuck to her face and neck.

She felt the hair stand up on her forearms. A prudent decision would be to leave as fast as possible. Two men, lolling in the shade of a lean-to, leered openly. More ominous were the ones who drew back from the light of day and rolled silently into their tents when she passed.

Responding to a tug on her skirt, Jane looked down on a red-faced urchin in a dirty green plaid dress two sizes too big for her. A mop of tangled orange curls framed a jam-smeared face.

"Where ya goin', lady? You comin' to visit my ma?"

Jane tried to pull herself free. Before she could answer she found herself surrounded by a swarm of orange-topped children, each a step shorter or taller than the next.

"My name's Ada Baldwin," said the one attached to her skirt. "What's yers?"

"Ma says, where ya bin, Ada?"

"Ma says, yer gonna git it, Ada."

"I'm jes talkin' to Ma's lady friend. I'm jes takin' the lady to visit Ma." And with that the child jammed her grubby paw into Jane's hand and pulled her deeper into the camp.

Jane tried to shake her off, appalled at the bold-faced lie, but the child stuck like flypaper.

The campsite they stumbled into appeared to centre on what had once been a tent; the walls sprouted growths like dingy fungus reinforced with scraps of lumber, tarpaper and even a faded pink chenille bedspread. In the shade of one of the bulges, a youth lay curled around a black-and-white dog, both sound asleep while a litter of puppies tumbled over them.

In a trampled clearing in front of the tent, a huge woman in a shapeless skirt and a man's grease-splattered shirt stared with lively interest across a kitchen range. A kitchen range out of doors, its chimney sticking up into the air like a flagpole.

Jane snapped her gaping mouth shut and offered her hand. "Mrs. Baldwin, I presume. I'm Jane Priddle. Your Ada seems to think we're acquainted. I'm sorry to intrude into your, uh, home."

The woman wiped her hands, front and back, on her shirt before Jane's hand disappeared into a fist the size of a man's. "Aw, don't pay no mind to Ada. I'm pleased to meetcha, Jane Priddle. My name's Ruth."

"Have you been here long?" Jane blurted out. Years, surely. It takes years to accumulate this much rubbish.

"'Bout a year and a half, give or take a few weeks. Set yourself down. I'll fix some tea. How about you? You and the mister new to town?"

"I'm not married," Jane said, as she swiped at the seat of a backless chair before perching on the edge of it. She hugged her market bag to her stomach and tried to move her legs away from a vile-smelling toddler who pulled at her skirt.

"Not married? Youngsters take to you, though, I see," Ruth commented.

"Yes. I don't know why, but they seem to."

"Well, you know what they say."

"No, what do they say?" The child sat with a thud in the dirt and looked at Jane with accusing eyes.

Ruth sloshed a dipper of water into a white mug, rinsed it about, then threw it on the ground. "Dogs and youngsters. Man likes a woman what takes to dogs and youngsters. You'll find yourself a fella in no time out here."

"I'm not looking for a fella," Jane said. "I am, in fact, looking for a boy. An English boy."

"Are you now?" Ruth asked, handing Jane a mug of tea. "Related in some way, is he?"

"Mercy, no." Jane stared at the oily black liquid in her cup. "My church back home ..."

"Where's home, then?"

"England. London, to be —"

"Thought as much by the way you talk. Real nice. Teacher, I'll wager. Lost a pupil, have you?"

In an exasperated rush to try to finish at least one sentence, Jane said, "No, I'm not a teacher. My church supports a mission that has been sending children to Canada. You may have heard of them? They're usually called Home Children, because they come from a home."

Ruth folded her arms over her ample belly and stared at Jane with bright eyes. "Home Children?" She shook her head.

"An orphanage. That kind of home."

A fracas broke out between Ada and her sisters. Ruth appeared oblivious, her voice booming above the noise. "These kids you're lookin' for. They don't belong to no one?"

Jane took a deep breath, then set her cup on a wooden crate without taking a drink. "Some are orphans, it's true, so you could say they don't belong to anyone. Others have a mother or father, but —"

"Folks let their youngsters come all the way over here by their own selves?" Ruth's long face hung in disbelief.

"Well, yes. In some cases the parents aren't really fit to care for their offspring ..."

Ruth jammed both fists on her hips. "Land sakes alive! If that don't beat all. How old are these kids, didja say?"

Jane looked away for a second before answering slowly, "I was asked to report on four particular children. Billie is the one I'm looking for just now and he's about 13. Some are older." She took a deep breath. "Some are younger."

"How young?" Ruth demanded.

"Ellie is the youngest that I was concerned with," Jane said quietly. "She was four when we put her on the ship that crossed the Atlantic Ocean."

"Four," Ruth repeated in a whisper. "Four years old. Just a baby." She looked from one to another of her own grimy brood, shaking her head, then lowered herself onto another rickety chair and leaned toward Jane expectantly. "Who dreamed up such a notion? Does the government know what you're up to?"

"Of course they know. There are a lot of children back home with no real future. Either their parents have abandoned them or they're too poor to clothe and feed them properly. As for clean air and a chance to go to school, well, that would be a miracle. So various agencies came up with a plan, a policy if you will, that became the British Child Emigration Movement, allowing them to send children to the New World for a better chance in life."

"An' do they? Have a better life?"

Jane squinted into the sun. "That's the question that prompted me to travel here. Our society began to receive a report now and then with news of hurt or lost children, information that all was not as we were led to believe. So I was chosen to come and try to find four of the children and speak to them first-hand." She didn't feel the need to mention the letter, addressed to Jane personally, from Suzette.

"How're they doin'?"

"Two have been lucky. The couple who took little Ellie even want to adopt her." Jane squared her shoulders and looked directly at Ruth. "I was worried most about her. She wasn't even big enough to drag her box along the pier. And now, you see, she has a wonderful life ahead of her."

"Uh huh. And the other lucky one?"

"John?" Jane said quietly. "Well, it took me some time to find him in Ontario. The family he is with discontinued all contact with our Distributing Home. John will be 16 soon. He can, uh, move on soon."

Ruth nodded knowingly. "Had some experience with moving on myself. Why not just send them to the countryside over there? You do have some country left, don't ya?"

Jane was tempted to repeat the sentiment of her aunt, "out of sight, out of mind," but rose instead. "There is a need for farm help in Canada, so the government here supports the movement for that reason."

"Farm help? Little ones? D'ya think the government and the do-gooders know what farm work is?"

Jane refused to be drawn in by this woman. "We heard from other children in the Distributing Home that Billie wanted to reach the west coast. When he, uh, left the farm in Manitoba where he had been placed, some of the neighbours helped him board a westbound train." She didn't see any need to tell a stranger that the kindly neighbours could raise only enough money to get Billie to Portage la Prairie and that Billie probably had found the rest of his fare by less-than-honest means. "In Calgary I learned that a boy meeting Billie's description was thought to be headed north. I hope to find him soon so I can get back to the east coast before winter sets in."

"I'll keep an eye open for him. What's he look like? Maybe

Herbie knows something." She strode over to the sleeping lad and nudged him with her boot. "Herbie, we need to talk to you about a boy."

The lad grunted and rose onto one elbow, staring round-eyed at Jane.

"About your size, I think. He was wearing grey wool shorts and pullover the last time I saw him, but ..." She lifted her shoulders in a shrug.

"Where you staying?" Ruth asked. "I'll send word if we learn anything."

"I'd appreciate that," Jane said. "I'm at the Princess Hotel." She brushed at the fingerprints on her skirt and turned to leave.

"What're you doin' chasin' after other people's kids? You should be married an' have a brood of your own."

Jane ignored her as she stepped around the toddler where he sat on the ground chewing on an old chicken bone.

"Big strapping gal like yourself. Country's full of men lookin' for a woman like you."

Jane's cheeks burned. She turned quickly and took a step toward Ruth. "Well, I'm not looking for them. I just saw some of them back there," she flapped her hand toward the end of the camp, "and they didn't look like much of a bargain to me!"

Ruth Baldwin barked a short laugh before she answered. "Sounds like you'd make short work o' most o' them anyway."

Jane stared back into the homely, open face of the most uncouth woman she'd ever met and her anger melted away as fast as it had come. She grinned in spite of herself. "You're not the first to tell me that, and I'm sure you won't be the last. It's been a real pleasure meeting you, Ruth Baldwin."

"Pleasure's all mine, Miss Jane Priddle. Drop by any time, now we're acquainted. And, if you don't mind my sayin' it, you should try that smile on for size more often. Catch more flies with honey, you know."

∞

So someone else was looking for Billie Thomm. Luc Langevin stuffed the rolled-up newspaper into his back pocket and stomped out of the barbershop without his shave and haircut. He headed for one of the three ferries that would take him across the North Saskatchewan River to South Edmonton. He hoped he could find this J. Priddle and, with luck, get his hands on Thomm. And when he did he was going to skin the little bastard alive and pull his hide over a coyote stretcher.

For someone whose experience had taught him to stay as far away from the English as possible, Luc wondered how the hell he had managed to get tangled up with another one. Let himself feel sorry for the sneaky little brat, that's what did it. Billie seemed to have learned the lingo out here very quickly and Luc had taken an easy interest in him before he realized where he was from. The plank ferry dipped as he stepped aboard.

Matt Edwards was the only other passenger on the suppertime ferry. "Who pissed in your beer?"

"You wouldn't believe me if I told you," Luc said.

"Tell me anyway. Got nothing better to do."

Luc unrolled the paper and smacked the advertisement with the back of his hand. "Take a look at that."

Matt read aloud: "Would anyone knowing the whereabouts of one Billie Thomm please contact J. Priddle at the Princess Hotel. Billie is about 13 years of age, having dark blond hair and light brown eyes. Any information would be greatly appreciated."

Luc snorted. "Light brown eyes! Sneaky yellow eyes like the coyote."

"This the one you were telling me about?"

"Must be. That's the name he gave me, and the description matches the little thief."

"What are you going to do?"

"See what this Priddle knows, I guess."

"Need me to get involved?"

Luc shook his head. "I just want my money back."

"Yup. Well, when you're finished settling that score peaceably, my captain out at Division Headquarters has been looking for you. Has some pemmican needs hauling."

Luc watched the muddy river churn under the ferry, his mind still on Billie Thomm. "Pemmican? No one has seen a buffalo in this country for almost 20 years. Where'd your captain find pemmican?"

"Gabriel Bull's people are making it out at Muskrat Lake, about a day's ride northwest of here."

Luc glanced at Matt. "I know where Muskrat Lake is, but pemmican? Are you sure about that? I'm not one of the greenhorns just come to town."

Matt leaned back and stretched his long legs in front of him, crossing one ankle over the other. "Real pemmican. Or as near to as possible, I guess. They're making it from beef, brought up from Calgary. Gabe has put his little brigade to work slaughtering the cattle and drying the meat, but he'll need help hauling the pemmican farther west to The Crossing on the Athabasca River. We'll throw some scows together and try to get it downstream to our troops at Fort Chipewyan before freeze-up."

"I could do that." Luc forgot the kid for a minute. He liked working for the Mounted Police. They respected his know-how with the people and the country and they usually paid on time. He had hoped to get another week or two of freighting in; might as well be for the police. Then he could leave his horses with his friend Benny to rest until spring and just work his trapline.

They left the ferry, climbing out of the deep valley. "What are you doing in town?" Luc asked Matt. "Thought you were partial to the wide open spaces."

"Aw, it's all these fires. Homesteaders think it's the fastest way to clear the land, then it gets away on them. Whole damn territory's going up in flames, so now we have to fine the fools. Just a bunch more paperwork. I sure hate paperwork."

They parted company in front of the new brick schoolhouse. In the lobby of the Princess Hotel, a young man with bad skin on his face and garters on his sleeves told Luc that J. Priddle was registered in room 22 on the second floor.

The door looked as though it was closed, but when Luc gave it a good rap it flew open and crashed back against the wall. Forgetting he was tired and dirty and mad as a hornet, he wondered if he had walked into one of those expensive bordellos back east.

She'd strung clotheslines around the room and hung more wet, frilly underwear than he had seen in one place in his life. His first thought was that she was too plain for a call girl; still, there was a shortage of all kinds of women in the Territories, so she probably did all right—must, if she could afford the Princess. He wondered if the manager knew what he had up here.

"Really, I wish you'd wait when you knock ..." Jane said with annoyance, looking up from the basin, but it was not the maid she'd sent to get more water. Her first thought was that this must be one of the louts that she'd seen at the camp earlier. His shoulders were too wide for the cheap flannel shirt that he wore and his tight denim trousers were worn clear through on the thigh so that she could actually see bare skin. He had a well-used face, neither young nor old, with a large Gallic nose that wouldn't have fit most men.

Or was he the thief from last night, returned to finish the job? And here she stood, wearing only a light summer wrapper, up to her elbows in soapsuds. A part of Jane's mind wondered if this was one of those situations in which a lady should scream; another part of her realized that he looked just as amazed as she felt. Anyway, she had never screamed in her life and didn't really know how to go about doing it.

As they stood, looking one another over, a voice piped up from the hallway. "Ma says yer lookin' fer Billie Thomm."

For a big man he moved very quickly. He reached into the hallway and grabbed Herbie Baldwin by the shirtfront. Jane rushed to Herbie's rescue, a pair of wet drawers still in her hands. At the last moment, she slipped on the linoleum floor, so he let go of Herbie and steadied her instead.

"He's one of the Baldwins," she said to his unshaven chin. She felt as though she'd run into a tree. Merciful heavens, why did she have to be so clumsy?

He held her at arm's length. "What the hell's a Baldwin?"

She pulled herself free and stepped back. He smelled of horses and hard work. "There's no need for that kind of language."

He waved a hand the size of a shovel at poor Herbie, who had flattened himself against the door frame. "This isn't Thomm. And who are you? I'm looking for a man called Priddle." Only he pronounced it Preedle.

"I'm Jane Priddle," she said.

"Where's your husband?"

"I don't have a h-husband."

"Who put this in here? About Thomm?" He whacked the rolled newspaper against his palm. Herbie flinched and whimpered.

"You're frightening the boy." He was scaring the wits out of her, too, but she tried not to let her feelings show. He'd already seen more of her than was decent in her present state of deshabille. And if there was one person in this village who would know what that word meant, she felt certain it was this one. Not just because of the rough colonial French accent, but because something in the too-wise, tired eyes warned her she was dealing with a man who was much more familiar with the world than Miss Jane Priddle.

"What does he know about Thomm?" he demanded.

Herbie came alive. "Ma says there's a kid come up from Calgary with some cows a while back, might be the one you was lookin' fer. Cows have gone to some breeds what are makin' them into pemmican." He stared hopefully at Jane, but kept flicking glances at Luc.

"Where are these—what did you call them? Breeds?" Jane asked.

But Herbie just shook his head vigorously and inched toward the hall. Jane motioned for him to go.

Luc watched the boy hightail it down the hall, then turned his attention to the woman who had soap bubbles drying on her long nose. It started to sink into his thick skull that maybe he had the wrong impression about her. Floozies didn't worry overmuch about boys who were too young to pay.

"Breeds?" she asked.

"I can find them easy, those people he's talking about. But who are you and what do you want with that thieving li'l' bastard?"

She drew her shoulders back and sucked in a breath that damn near pulled all the air out of the room. He started to think he'd better watch his mouth if he was going to get what he wanted from this woman, when she snapped at him in that superior English accent.

"I told you, I'm Jane Priddle. Priddle. And I have unfinished business with Billie."

Even after all these years, nothing grated on his nerves like that accent, except maybe being corrected in that accent. He didn't give a good goddamn whether she liked what he said or not.

She peeked around the corner of the door and he thought she might be worried about being alone with a common working man like himself, when she surprised him by saying, "Perhaps you should come in and close the door. We don't need to collect an audience."

Luc took one step farther into the room and she took one step back. They repeated this little dance until he could reach behind himself and swing the door closed. When the latch clicked, she flinched like a skittish horse, but her eyes didn't waver from his.

"How do you know Billie?" she asked. "Do you know where he is?"

"*Non*. I was hoping you did. Li'l' bastard owes me some money."

Her ears turned red, but she didn't comment on his language this time. "Money? Why is that?"

Luc snorted. "I felt sorry for him down in Calgary a couple of weeks ago. Bought him breakfast at the Chinese place on First Street, then told him to get his gear and meet me at the livery. I was going to give him work. He said he needed to get to Vancouver, said he had family out there."

"He has no family in Canada." The thing she held in her hand kept dripping so she took it over to the washstand.

"How do you know that?"

She looked back at him from across the room and he noticed for the first time how straight she stood.

"He's a Home Child," she said. "Sent over here by our church to have a better life."

Luc couldn't help laughing out loud at that, but it wasn't funny and they both knew it.

She wiped her hands on a white towel. "We thought they would be welcome here."

"Why? So they could steal from me instead of you?"

She didn't seem surprised. "How much did he steal from you?"

"Twenty-three dollars."

"Is that all?"

He pulled himself up to his full height, anger burning in his chest like homemade whiskey. "Twenty-three dollars is a lot of money to some of us."

"I'm sorry. That's not what I meant. Of course $23 is a lot of money. I meant, is that his only crime? Just theft?"

He raised one eyebrow and managed the first attempt at a grin since they'd met. "What did you expect, *Anglaise*? Murder?"

He saw the answer to that in her clear, honest eyes and still face.

"Jesus Christ Almighty," he said.

three

ane was dressed and sitting on the edge of the bed long before the sun rose the next morning. The flimsy bits of lingerie had dried in a matter of hours and were at the bottom of her trunk, the neat brown parcel from the laundry jammed on top. The desk clerk had taken her trunk down to the lobby 10 minutes ago.

She jumped at a tap on the door, then opened it to the pinch-faced disapproval of the maid. "Your *picnic* lunch, ma'am. Sandwiches and pound cake, as you requested."

"Thank you." Jane took the box and moved to close the door.

Contempt and curiosity warred across the girl's face. "He's just come," she said tightly. "I feel I should mention, ma'am, since you are new to town, that he doesn't have a good reputation with women. Not good at all."

Jane's stomach tightened all the more, but she kept her features as still as possible. "I'm not concerned with local gossip, thank you. That will be all."

"Well!" The maid flounced from the room with a crackle of starched skirts.

Jane wilted against the door. From the open window came the soft jangle of harness. She took a deep breath and headed downstairs.

His name was Luc Langevin, a freighter—what she would call a carter. He knew where to look for Billie, and if Jane wasn't mistaken, she'd better be on hand when the two met.

Matt Edwards propped his backside on the hitching rail out front of the Princess Hotel and watched as Luc checked the harness on his team. "You get too much sun this summer?"

"Nope."

"An Englishwoman? Do you know what you're getting into?" This was touchy territory and Matt knew it.

Luc lifted the heavy leather collar on his big gelding and checked for sores, then looked Matt in the eye. "It's only one day and I'm going there anyway. Might as well let her pay me for my trouble."

"Trouble might be just what you end up with." Matt knew they were both thinking the same thing—another place, another Englishwoman, more trouble than any man deserved.

Luc lifted the front hoof of his chestnut mare and scraped inside the shoe with his pocket knife. "I can take care of myself."

"Can you? Won't need me to hold your head this time?" Now that was pushing his luck. They never referred to the night 15 years ago in Medicine Hat, when, as a green North West Mounted Police recruit, he had been sent out to bring in a drunken Frenchman who was tearing up the town.

"That was a long time ago. This is different."

"Well, we're older, that's a fact." And maybe wiser, Matt had to hope. Back then they had both been homesick and lonely down on the banks of the South Saskatchewan River, Luc puking his guts out and Matt keeping the fire stoked and the coffee hot. Only 18 years old, both of them.

"I'll dump her off with the nuns at the mission. They can put up with her until someone comes back this way."

Matt lowered his lids against the sun as it spilled over the eastern horizon, gilding the tents, making them look almost pretty. That morning in Medicine Hat, they had watched the sun come up and shared their sorrows. Matt, the third son of an Ontario farmer with no chance of a place of his own, had joined the Mounted Police for their promise of a quarter section of land some day, somewhere. And Luc, well, Luc had talked into the morning about his lost love, Felicity, the English rose who had broken his heart in Manitoba. Matt had never heard him mention her name again.

"I'll be along in a few days," Matt said. "Keep you company to The Crossing." One thing Matt had learned that night was that a helping hand went a lot further toward keeping the peace than a heavy hand. He practised that lesson to this day. Prying himself off the hitching rail, he turned to leave as the hotel door opened. He tried to keep his jaw from dropping.

She marched toward Luc with her head high and her shoulders back, a case in each hand and a box tied up with string under her arm. Her light-coloured clothes would be covered with dust in about two miles. Expensive clothes, if Matt was any judge. And, if he remembered the one time he'd seen Luc's lovely little Felicity, that was the only similarity between the two.

"Good morning," she said to the back of Luc's head and then hoisted her cases and dropped them into the wagon bed. The horses spooked.

"Whoa!" Luc grabbed the bridle closest to him and turned to the woman. "What the hell you doing?"

Her chin lifted a trifle more and she stared him down. "Working horses should be quieter than that."

"Oh, boy," Matt said. No one criticized Luc Langevin's horses.

The woman darted a glance in Matt's direction, then back at Luc. False courage. Matt had seen it a hundred times or more. She wasn't nearly as in control of herself as she wanted Luc to believe.

"Like I said yesterday, my fee is three and a half cents a pound. I'll make that a dollar for both bags and—oh, about six dollars for you, I guess."

Matt cringed. She was tall, no doubt about that, but six dollars?

"And what's in the box?" Luc went on relentlessly. "You plan on paying for that, too?"

Confusion clouded her wide eyes as she looked from the box to Luc. "I will if you like. It's the lunch I had the cook make for us. You said we would be on the trail all day."

Luc had the good grace to look sheepish. He swiped his hand through his hair. "*Oui*. All day. Time to get started."

He climbed onto the buckboard, leaving Miss Jane Priddle to find her own way aboard. Matt moved to help her, but without fuss she hiked her skirt up, put one foot onto the hub of the front wheel and, with another stretch of her long legs, sat cautiously beside Luc. She looked down on Matt. "Thank you," she said in that clipped accent she had, even though he hadn't helped her at all. He wondered if she was thanking him for just being there.

He touched his hat. "Sergeant Edwards, Miss Priddle."

She gave him a wan smile.

Luc screwed his brows into a disgusted frown and gave Matt a see-what-I-mean look, then slapped the reins on the backs of the horses. Matt watched them until they turned down the hill to the ferry, wondering which one he should feel sorry for, or if either of them needed his concern.

They crossed the muddy North Saskatchewan River on the first ferry of the day, alone except for the grouchy operator. Sharp autumn air lifted the horses' manes and smudged the smoke from prairie fires into the bare aspen trees. As they pulled out of the north side of the valley, Jane turned to look back at the village of South Edmonton and the end of the railroad. They passed the tumbled remains of the Fort Edmonton fur-trading post that had given the community on this side of the river its name. Before long, both settlements were out of sight.

Sometime between their singular meeting yesterday and this morning, Luc Langevin had found time to clean up. He still wore flannel and denim but now they were clean and mended. His chin had been scraped and the heavy, grey-streaked hair blowing over his forehead was a trifle shorter. He sat leaning forward, feet on the front of the wagon, forearms resting easily on his parted knees.

Jane began to ache from clinging to her side of the seat. "Fools rush in where angels fear to tread." She had never thought of herself as a fool, but this had begun to go beyond an adventure or a stubborn attempt to prove a point. As they bumped past a few scattered homesteads, she tried to imagine what her aunt would say, or the church council. That she had taken her assignment much further than she had been authorized to do, that's what. Further every minute. She should be on the ship now, heading home, listening to seagulls. Instead she watched the dark heads of a flock of Canada geese bob up and down in a stubble field, chattering to one another. There seemed to be real intent to their talk and a few tried their wings. As the wagon drew alongside, the palaver grew until they rose as one, their heavy bellies sagging back down over the grain as though the temptation to feed was more than they could bear.

Jane twisted in her seat as they circled overhead, jockeying for position. She could look into their unblinking eyes and see the primal pull that was greater than greed. The weight that seemed to want to pull them back to earth gave way to the stronger force of their powerful wings and the wild need to be gone.

"Winter."

Jane started. "What?"

"Winter. She's on her way." He had turned his head only, looking past his own upper arm.

Jane found herself staring directly, and at close range, into very blue eyes. "*It's* on the way."

Lids dropped partway over eyes that turned to ice. Winter could not possibly be as chilling as the steady, unwavering look he gave Jane.

She wanted to bite her tongue off. Instead, she said, "I'm sorry."

The lids lowered a little more. She reminded herself that she had no experience with a man like this and it was impossible to know what he might do. He could put her off right here, in the middle of nowhere. With luck, that's all he would do. With luck, she would some day learn to keep her mouth shut when the occasion called for it.

"That wasn't necessary," she said inanely.

Like the geese he didn't blink. As with the geese she had a pretty good notion of what he was thinking, and it was just as primeval. He slowly turned his head, looking once again over the horses' ears. She waited, hoping he would say something, even in anger, but he seemed to have forgotten she was there.

The sun at their backs sent shadows dancing down the trail ahead of them, indicating, Jane deduced, that they were headed west. During the course of the morning, they met two more wagons and three solitary riders. They all seemed to know Luc and stopped for a short visit.

The men looked at Jane with interest, but he made no effort to introduce her and she learned what it was like to feel as if she didn't exist. Wasn't that what sad, quiet John had told her in Ontario? He might as well not be alive for all the concern he received from the farmer he had been sent to. Maybe she would end up sleeping in a stable too, eating scraps of bread and potatoes after everyone else had eaten their fill. She sat, unbending and thirsty, regretting her impulsive rush into territory which, she felt certain, angels had abandoned centuries ago.

Hours later, with the sun high in the southern sky and perspiration pooling in the small of her back, Jane gave up on any pretence of propriety and doffed her jacket. She whacked dust from the shoulders and folded it neatly on her lap, then tensed when the freighter unravelled his considerable length into a full and luxurious stretch, pushing his hands to the sky. His right arm dropped behind her and before she had time to consider her action, she ducked foolishly.

His hand reappeared with an earthenware jug. "Drink?"

"What is it?"

He laughed with a flash of strong, white teeth that were a trifle uneven.

"Pure, sweet water," he taunted. "Take it or leave it."

She took the heavy jug and lifted it to her mouth, hoping she wouldn't break a tooth. She let the cold, refreshing water run down her throat and dribble over her chin and bosom. Lowering the jug, she took a clean hankie out of her skirt pocket and mopped at her shirtfront. As an afterthought she wiped the top of the jug before handing it back. She hoped that was proper frontier etiquette.

He let the water run down his chin, then replaced the cork and put the jug back under the seat. Swiping the back of his hand across his wet chin, he said, "So. This Thomm. You said you have money for him."

"Yes," she answered quickly. "Yes, I do."

"If we put out word that you have money for him, he'll show up, for sure."

"It's wages from farm work in the Manitoba District."

"This farmer in Manitoba, he gave you money to bring to Thomm?" His look clearly said he didn't believe a word of that.

"Well, not really." No need to mention that she had set aside a bit of her own money for Billie.

"Uh huh."

She tried to explain. "But you see, the farmer was supposed to pay him. That's part of the terms of indenture for these children."

He didn't respond. They passed a dry pond where black birds with red insignia on their shoulders swooped and scolded. She began to feel nauseated from the motion of the wagon—it was as bad as the train.

Then he took a deep breath and sat up straight. "I don't know what that means. Indenture."

It took her a few seconds to gather her wits and compose a careful answer. "It's just a fancy word for agreement. Like a contract. In this case, both parties agreed to meet certain requirements ..."

"And Thomm? He went along with this?"

Jane squirmed in her seat, and not just because she had a sore backside. "Billie knew that he had to work for his room and board. In return, we expected the children would have decent clothes and a chance to go to school."

"This farmer in Manitoba? He didn't pay Thomm?"

"N-no. Well, he couldn't, really. Billie sort of—left."

"He ran away."

Jane's shoulders slumped. "It's a long story."

He squinted at the sun and crooned to his horses. The big gelding that he called Lobo flicked his ears. "So," he said. "Tell me this story. It's a long drive to the lake."

Jane steadied herself and her thoughts. The hazy air and endless horizon disappeared as she let her memory take her back to the stagnant streets of London and what she knew of Billie's story.

"He showed up at the Eastwood Mission Home for Waifs and Strays in the middle of the night about a year and a half ago. That's the mission that our church supports. The cook startled him when she came to work. Billie had fallen asleep on the back stoop and she almost stepped on him. He didn't say much and it wasn't until later that we learned he was running from an incident that involved his little brother. And the police. We forgot about him in the next two or three days because one of the children had died of whooping cough, and it was just two weeks before 30 of them were to leave for Canada. The Canadian authorities are very strict about illnesses like that.

"Somehow, Billie managed to disappear into the muddle of little boys in the dormitory over the stables. He came to my attention about a week later when he convinced us he could fit into the clothes of the boy who had died. It seemed a waste—not to use the clothes, I mean. Each child was supplied with a small trunk with a change of clothes, a brush and comb and a Bible. Everything they would need," she finished weakly.

Luc slanted a sardonic look in her direction, and then seemed to lose interest. She was happy to stop talking for a change.

The trail became tougher and they hadn't met anyone for miles. With the noon sun high overhead, Jane felt sore and drained. Her ears rang with the complaints of the wagon, the creak of the harness and the constant moan of the wind.

uc lay flat on the ground with the back of his head pillowed on the palms of his hands. He bent his right knee up and propped his left ankle on it, as comfortable and at home as the deer mouse he heard nearby. He listened to the two voices of the wind: the restless muttering in the trees and the soft sigh that worked its way through the grass. If he let it, the sound would put him to sleep as easily as a mother's song.

Through narrowed eyes, he noted the angle of the sun, then turned his head to look at the woman propped against the wagon wheel with her legs poked out in front of her like sticks, her skirts smoothed over her lap and tucked tight around her calves as if she was afraid something would crawl up there. She was going to be stiff and sore when she got up, for sure. Felicity had never been anything but soft and willing.

Luc heaved himself to his feet and walked to where the horses dozed under some bare poplar, talking to them more loudly than necessary. His family had been right about Felicity after all. She had just been playing around with him, amusing herself while her rich, old husband made more money. He had come to that realization himself years ago, but he was damned if he would admit it to anyone.

Right now he had to get this woman to the nuns. She'd slowed him down enough. She shook the crumbs from their lunch out of his blanket, folded it and stuffed it back under the wagon seat.

As she set one foot on the hub, he asked, "What do you have on your feet?"

Her eyes widened. "Pardon me?"

"Do you have fancy stuff on your feet? It would be best to walk awhile. Break up the day."

He didn't know what he'd expected—something expensive and useless maybe—but she hoisted her skirts up over good stout boots and gave him the first smile he'd ever seen from her. "I wear these, and I love to walk."

In that moment, she became a different woman. If he tried hard enough, he could ignore the flash of stockings she had treated him to, but the lopsided smile with all the dimples? That was a different matter. She loved to walk, did she? He stretched his legs into the long, loose-jointed stride that had carried him thousands of miles back and forth across this country.

"So—Thomm ended up coming here to steal from me because someone died?"

She took her time answering, working hard to keep up. "I guess you could look at it that way."

She bent her head, watching where she put her feet. The sun beat down on the back of her neck and the wind whipped strands of hair around her face. Luc wondered why anyone would wear a silly little hat like that if it didn't do any good.

"It took 14 days for them to cross the Atlantic Ocean—two days longer than usual because of the weather. A young vicar and his wife, who were being sent to a parish in Ontario, escorted them. I met the couple and they told me that many of the children suffered terribly from seasickness. Most were homesick, too. Lonely and frightened.

"Not Billie, though. In fact, he was first in line for food and managed to eat the portions that were intended for the sick children. Other than that, he kept himself apart from the rest of the group. Although," she shot a look at Luc, "by the end of the first week, there were several reports of things gone missing."

"I'll bet there were."

She was too honest to argue with him. He'd looked into the faces of plenty of men and women who were not honest and she wasn't one of them.

"Billie's first home was with a shopkeeper in a small town in Ontario. The stealing started immediately, mostly food from the store. The shopkeeper was willing to overlook that and even cut him extra large slabs from the wheel of cheese. What couldn't be tolerated was Billie's belligerent way with the other children at school. It seems he carried a knife and, well, there was reason to believe he might use it."

They walked beside the horses, quiet for the moment. He could afford to let her take her time telling the story.

"So he was sent back to the Distributing Home in Ontario ..."

"What's a Distributing Home?"

"That's a place, like an orphanage, where the children live until a family selects them. Anyway, by this time, Billie had a reputation as a troublemaker."

"He was a troublemaker long before that, I think."

"He's just a child."

"Thomm was never a child," Luc said.

Her head came up and she looked long and hard at him.

"Hell, I know lots of youngsters who had to grow up real quick, never had a chance to play or go to school."

"You're probably right. From there Billie went to a Distributing Home in Manitoba run by a very strict fellow who told me he was tired of hearing people say that he was importing the scum of the British Isles to come over here and contaminate good, God-fearing Canadian children. In January of this year, Billie went to the farmer I mentioned. He lasted four months."

The wind dropped and dark clouds began to bunch in the west. Flies took advantage of the still air and pestered the horses. The Englishwoman tried to brush them from Lobo's eyes, but he didn't take to strangers.

"Whoa! *Doucement!*" Luc said, and stroked the horse's nose.

"How many languages do you speak, Mr. Langevin?"

"My name's Luc. I speak French, English"—he lifted a brow at her—"not so good, I guess. Then Cree and some other dialects."

She blushed and looked away. "You speak English very well. Where did you go to school?"

Did she think he was one of those kids they were talking about? "I went to school," he said, "in Manitoba. But we are talking about Thomm."

"I travelled to the farm where Billie was supposed to be. The farmer was a huge man with a cruel face, battered and misshapen. One eye was lower than the other from an accident or injury or …"

"Or a fight maybe," he finished for her. He wondered what misshapen meant and why she couldn't talk like normal people.

"I'm sure that's possible," she said and he saw her staring at the scar that cut through his own brow. Maybe she would call him misshapen, too, when she got back to her society friends.

"His wife was as coarse and mean-spirited as he was. Their house was two rooms, just a shack, dark and foul smelling."

"We don't have a lot of, what to call them? *Châteaux*? No fine houses out here."

She stopped and flared up at him. "I didn't expect *châteaux*. I did expect the children to be better off than they were before. That brute was no better than what Billie was running from back home."

Aw, Christ, now she wanted to preach at him. Luc kept walking and the horses followed, leaving her in the dust to jaw all she wanted. Then he thought back to what she had just said.

"What was Thomm running from back home?" he asked quietly.

That took the starch right out of her. She started to walk again, slowly, with her head bent. "The police came a short time after the ship had sailed and told us of a scrape that Billie might have been involved in about the time he showed up at our mission. We visited his mother again to see what we could learn. We'd talked to her of course, before we could let Billie emigrate. We don't just steal children off the streets, you know."

"Who said you did?"

"Quite a few people. Here in Canada. We thought they would be welcome."

"Seems like a waste of time to me, sending youngsters over here and then losing track of them."

She ignored him; just kept on walking and talking as though she needed to sort it out in her own mind.

"His mother lived in one room over a pawnshop."

"A what?"

"A pawnshop? That's where people take things to trade for a bit of money, you know, and then maybe come back later, to buy it back."

"Ah. I understand."

"Yes. Well. Two small children slept on a dirty mat on the floor. It seemed Mrs. Thomm lived and cooked and, uh ..."

"And?" Thunder rumbled off in the distance.

"And conducted her, uh, business, all in this one room."

"Business?" It would be interesting to see if she could tell the whole story.

"Yes. Business. Sh-she *entertained* men in her home for a living." Her toe caught on some tangled grass and she stumbled. She gave him a quick, flustered look and then seemed to realize he was playing with her. She clamped her mouth shut and glared at him. He couldn't help laughing.

"I fail to see the humour, Mr. Langevin, in a life so destitute that a woman has to sell herself to eke out an existence!"

Eke out an existence? Luc's moment of enjoyment vanished. It was that superior way she had that grated on his nerves. "I've met many women who were real happy to *sell themselves* if it got them what they wanted."

"Indeed? And their children, too, Mr. Langevin? Do you find that humorous, too?"

Christ almighty, what had he landed himself with? "*Non*. No, it isn't funny. But that's not what I was laughing at, *Anglaise*. I was laughing at you."

She stood there blinking at him, like a fish out of water, a lace collar-thing billowing along her neck like gills. The wind brought the smell of rain. Luc picked up the pace so he wouldn't be stuck out here in a storm with her.

"The way I understood it, her eldest daughter does, you know, the same kind of work as her mother. Only she worked for one man, a man called Hobson. Hobson was killed one night behind a tavern. Stabbed to death with a knife, the police said."

"Thomm?" Luc wondered how dangerous this little bastard was; maybe he had been lucky to lose only some money down in Calgary.

"That suspicion was raised. Billie had been known to brag that one day he would get even with Hobson. It seems he hung around outside the tavern where Hobson conducted his—affairs." She glanced quickly at Luc.

"Hobson was a pimp?"

She threw her hands out from her sides in a wide gesture. "*That* word you know!"

He shrugged. "You'd be surprised what I know."

"I doubt that very much indeed, Mr. Langevin."

He kept on walking and she hurried to catch up. "We learned that Hobson didn't buy and sell just girls. He had received a sum of money for Billie's little brother, Denny. Billie was probably, uh, used in the same way. Denny was about eight years old at the time and small for his age. He didn't live."

Luc couldn't think of a word to say. He'd heard of things like that—men sat around a bottle and talked of the damnedest things sometimes, things that made him feel sick—but he sure never expected to hear it from a woman. Especially this woman.

She finally shut up, just walking close to the head of his little mare, touching her mane now and then.

"Why do you do this? Chase after these kids?" he asked.

She pushed Rouge's mane under the bridle strap. Then, as though talking to herself, or maybe reciting a piece she had been told to learn, "It's my duty. To be of service to others. Women like myself, of a certain station in life, have a responsibility to help others."

∞

A stream, mostly hidden from view by fallen trees and scrubby undergrowth, cut through the muddy bank and into the river. Billie shucked his clothes and stretched out starkers on his back in the fast, clear water. The cold near took his breath away but he forced himself to stay there, with the icy water trickling past his ears. It must be about three o'clock in the afternoon, he figured, and a storm was coming up over the ugly bare trees.

Grit ground into the crack of his bum. Using his hands as scoops, he heaped some onto his crotch. The water washed it away, so he piled on more, ground it in and let that wash away, too. The rough, dead weight felt good on his privates and the muddy water smelled sweet way back in his nose.

His whole body started to turn numb, but it didn't feel as good as he had hoped it would. His fingertips tingled and his legs ached. A flash of lightning lit the black clouds. What had he heard about being near water when lightning flashed?

"Hey, you! What the hell you doin' in there?"

"You! Boy! Git up outta that creek. You crazy or something?"

Billie scrambled out of the water, grit between his legs. It was just a couple of old prospectors, working the sandbars. A sorry pair, bent over tin pans from morning until night with nothing to show for it but a few sparkles.

"Whatcha doin' naked in broad daylight? Git, or I'll call the police."

"Bugger off," Billie yelled back automatically. He pulled his clothes over his wet body and tried to run at the same time, scraping his foot on some brambles.

"Why ain't you in school?" he heard as he hustled up the bank.

"'Cause I'm smarter'n you already, you gormless ol' mud mucker!" School? Sure didn't need any stupid teacher looking for him. Or the police. Bad enough that mission woman was in town. He couldn't remember which one she was, but he'd seen the advert whether he wanted to or not. And when he had pretended he couldn't read, it was read out to him loud and clear. A woman from home, right there in the hotel, looking for Billie Thomm. Must be about that mess back home with Hobson, or that bloody bully on the farm last winter.

Upstream, Billie wandered into a sawmill where workers were loafing around outside having a cigarette. He wheedled some tobacco and papers from them and kept going. Farther up the bank, he rolled a smoke with the cheap dry stuff and sat down in a crotch formed by gnarled tree roots. He pulled the raw smoke deep into his lungs and kept it there as long as he could. Letting the smoke trail out through his nostrils, he sagged back.

Directly across the river was a place known as The Flats. Some tarpaper shanties, clapboard shacks and a few little hovels built of logs squatted under the willows and scrub brush on low land near the water. Even this early in the day, Billie could see men, bold as brass, wending their way through the trees looking for a tart. It made him think of his ma again. She had always been quick with a cuff on the ears, but she'd share what she had, even if it was just a scrap of bread.

His belly growled. He was always hungry. The money he had stolen in the hotel had been taken from him, and a good-sized wad it had been, too. He fingered an empty cigarette tin where he used to keep his cash and tried to swallow the lump of tears at the back of his throat. A fine pickle he was in now.

The money he'd stolen in Calgary had been spent on real cigarettes, new boots and—what else? Food, he supposed, and clothes, better clothes than what were in that stupid box from the mission. No one wore short pants here, unless they wanted to freeze to death or get eaten by bugs. Some day he would wear nice clothes all the time—clean clothes that fit him proper.

The empty hole in his belly reminded him of a pokey bakeshop back home where he could get a stale meat pie for a ha'penny. The baker had been a fat, sweaty man with a big dirty apron and a pet ferret, a nasty thing with lips peeled back from yellow teeth. It was supposed to be good for keeping rats away. Billie had hated that thing. He was hungry, he had no money and the tender place between his legs stung like fury from the sand. Then there were the police and that woman. Instead of being on his way to Vancouver, here he sat, afraid to go back to the hotel and afraid not to, because another kind of ferret waited for him there.

The locals called this ferret "the Dook," laughing at him behind his back. He liked to gamble, and that would be where the money he took from Billie would go, because he had said in his high and mighty way that he didn't drink or smoke. Didn't *approve* of it. He'd been sitting in the hotel waiting for money from back home so he could follow the gamblers north.

Billie rose, ground out his butt and wandered through town, looking over the bedraggled gardens as he went. Maybe one of the mean and suspicious old women in this town had left something behind, some carrots or something. He took his knife out of his boot and opened the blade, running it lightly over his thumb.

He couldn't go back to the hotel until after dark, and even then he'd have to sneak in so no one saw him. And if he didn't show up at all, well, the ferret had said outright that he would go directly in search of the town patrolman and turn Billie in. Absently, he scraped the blade over a scab on the back of his hand. As he watched the blood well up, dark and sticky, his belly filled up with hate so thick and hot it almost scared him. He tenderly put his tongue to the puddle of blood.

five

**T**hey were well into a tent camp before Jane realized it; there was none of the mess of the settlement in town. Tents, and even conical tipis, were scattered at a reasonable distance from one another under the trees. She was lulled by homely smells and sounds — supper cooking, children playing and men calling greetings to Luc.

The smoke from dozens of fires hung in cloudy clumps about hip deep. The horses fought their traces in spite of a tiring day. At first Jane thought they were worried about the packs of snarling dogs tied under the trees, but as her eyes became accustomed to the darkness, she saw that the camp was littered with pole frames draped with ragged purplish strips that swayed stiffly in the wind like ghoulish laundry left out in the night air. Each time one tattered bit grated against the shrivelled edge of another, a sibilant rasp set the horses' hides aquiver.

She realized Luc had disappeared just as a naked child darted through the circle of light cast by the fire, the little face stretched in a soundless howl of fury, like an imp escaped from the netherworld.

She must have made a noise herself because the horses lunged forward and Luc's hand appeared to grab them.

"What the hell's the matter?" He glared up at her, his eyes merely dark holes in the ridges and planes below his heavy brow.

"The fire," she said. "I was afraid for the child so near the fire." But in truth she was overcome by a sense of being in a most unnatural place.

She found the nerve to wave her hand at the grisly racks. "What *is* that, hanging there?"

"That? Just the meat drying and smoking. For the pemmican. Horses don't like it much."

"They're not the only ones," she muttered as she hobbled from the wagon. Her legs buckled and her stomach lurched.

"We can eat here," he said. "The sisters eat early."

"I don't feel well. I'm not sure I need anything to eat."

"That's from the wagon. You'll feel better when you get some food in you."

Two women stood shyly back from the wagon and some instinct informed Jane that the women, and probably Luc, were waiting for the Englishwoman to make her excuses, to decline their simple meal.

She forced a smile. "It smells wonderful." That part at least was true. She would eat some of what smelled like stew, even if it killed her, and the way she felt, that might be the case.

The women turned to their work, but Luc looked at her for a long moment before saying, "Uh huh. Gaston will take your belongings up to the school and let them know you're coming."

Hearing something in the tone of his voice, Jane wondered if she had done the right thing. Had they really counted on her refusal? It was too late to change her mind; the horses were being led away by a handsome young man who could have stepped from the pages of a book.

Her foggy mind registered what had just been said. "The school?"

"School. Mission. Same thing." Then he nodded his head toward the older of the two women. "This is Gaston's mother, Louise Bull."

"Please sit down," Louise said.

Jane folded her long legs onto a three-legged stool that was placed before a wooden trunk. The younger of the two women, so pretty Jane willed herself not to stare, handed her a steaming mug of tea. Louise brought a blue enamelled plate with stew and placed it in front of Jane.

"This is Rosie, my daughter," Louise said, and Jane noticed for the first time that Rosie was very much in the family way. "And over there—her husband, Guy."

A vague figure in the shadows waved in a friendly way.

The imp reappeared from the bushes and was grabbed by Rosie. "Off to bed now, whether you want to or not," she said.

Luc accepted a plate, then sat on the ground with his back against the trunk of a fir tree. Jane poked at her food, tried a tiny bite, then had to admit that he had been right. Her stomach began to settle. If she kept her eyes on the plate and ignored the racks of drying meat, she might manage.

She blinked eyes dried by sun, wind and smoke and tried to remember enough schoolgirl French to follow the conversation. It seemed Luc had recently made a journey east to see his family and that this was something of a momentous occasion.

He appeared reluctant to talk about himself and, pointing his chin at Jane, said, "She's looking for a boy. An English boy with yellow eyes. See anyone like that around?"

Louise straightened from her work with alarm. "Your boy? You lost your boy?"

"No, not my boy."

"She's a missionary," he said. "Out here looking for a bunch of lost kids."

"A missionary?" Louise's expression turned to one of respect that Jane knew she didn't deserve.

Jane wrapped her hands around her mug. "No," she said directly to Louise. "I'm not a real missionary. I'm just doing a job for our mission society back home."

"There are no white boys here," Louise said.

Lightning sizzled across the lake as what appeared to be a bundle of clothes hobbled out of the shadows and sat near Jane's feet. A voluminous skirt was decorated with leather fringes and clumps of feathers and—was that *teeth*? A striped blanket was draped around bent shoulders and tied across the chest. A face, so aged and brown that it seemed to have collapsed in on itself, stared up at Jane.

"This is our Kokum, our grandmother," Louise said as she knelt by the trunk and mashed stew onto a plate, the way a mother would for a child.

The old woman felt along the trunk until she found a spoon and Jane realized that the eyes that seemed to hold the secrets of a thousand life experiences were really only clouded with cataracts. Jane sipped her strong, sweet tea. No white boys here. She'd put herself through all this for nothing. It would take some explaining when she returned to civilization.

Out of the corner of her eye, Jane thought she saw some movement under the trees, but when she looked, there was no one there. Then a movement on the other side caught her attention; when she turned, it was gone. Were these people trying to hide something from her or had her wild imagination begun to play tricks? Then, considering the threadbare clothes and meagre belongings of her hosts, she had an alarming thought and spoke aloud, "The children. When do the children eat?" Had she accepted a meal, only to deprive some children of theirs?

Startled by her anxiety, the others stopped what they were doing and stared at her. All except the bundle at her feet.

"That's just Julie," the old woman mumbled.

At that, a child crept into the circle of light near the safe haven of the crone's bent back, all the time staring at Jane. She pulled on the strings of beads at the nape of the bowed neck, tugging at them even as the old lady tried to eat.

It was all too much for Jane. Her corset jabbed her under the arms because she was too tired to sit up straight anymore; she could feel the grit on her face and between her fingers and she wondered if she would ever get the smell of smoke out of her hair. She slumped, gazing stupidly into the fire, trying to ignore the unblinking stare of the strange child with large, dark eyes that appeared to have no pupils, set in an elfin face framed with short cropped hair that poked straight out in all directions. The child had a fragile, ethereal air about her as though she might disappear, just drift away with the smoke. As Billie seemed to have done. To make her misery complete, rain started to drizzle down her neck.

Luc watched the rain sputter on the fire. It wasn't going to amount to much, which was too bad for all the grass fires, but would give Gabriel and his people a chance to finish the pemmican. He stood and set his plate on the trunk. "*Merci*, Louise."

He jerked his head at the Englishwoman. "Come, I'll take you up to the school now." She held onto the trunk to get up, and he guessed she'd be good and stiff tomorrow. Probably never done a day's work in her life.

The sisters had their school on higher ground, so he started up the trail that cut through the trees, past the drying meat and the dogs that had been tied up to keep them from eating it. If he remembered what he had heard about making pemmican, he figured it would take another week or 10 days for the job to be finished. Once the meat was well dried, it would be pounded or ground up in some way, then tallow added back in to preserve it.

As the trail got steeper, he remembered the woman and turned to let her catch up. She was straggling along, picking her way through the roots and underbrush. Waiting for her, he tried to figure out if he would need his other team and wagon. Only a couple of the men here had wagons; the rest still used carts. And they had their own families and belongings to take along with the pemmican. On top of that, he'd seen their horses and they were a sorry-looking bunch. Maybe he could get word to Matt to bring his other rig.

She stopped a step or two away and looked at him expectantly. He could hear the rain pattering on the fir branches above them but not much reached the ground. A rich smell of damp, dead poplar leaves rose from underfoot. The air felt cool and pleasant after the hot, dusty day. Her face shone pale in the dark and he knew, tired as she was, that she was also nervous — scared even — not at all sure of where they were going. Or of him.

"Stay close," he said.

"I'm sorry," she said with a little break in her voice.

He shook his head impatiently and started walking a little more slowly. Light glimmered from the kitchen window at the mission. Good, someone was still up. He led the way through a well-kept farmyard, then past the chicken coop and garden to the kitchen door.

Without knocking, he pushed the door open and called, "*Bonsoir?*"

A coal-oil lamp sat in a puddle of yellow light in the middle of a huge, scrubbed pine table.

"Ah, Luc. Luc." A sturdy nun with a big white apron over her habit struggled up from a straight-backed chair and hobbled over to greet him with a kiss on each cheek. She smelled of yeast and camphor.

He gave her a hug that lifted her off her feet. "Sister Marthe. How have you been?"

She swatted his shoulder until he put her down. "Not so well. Not so well."

"Aw, you'll live longer than all the rest of us."

"Humph. What will you eat?"

"We ate already. Louise fed us."

"Ah, *oui*. Us."

They turned together to look at the door. Gaston had set her bags just inside and Miss Jane Priddle stood as close to them as possible, her long fingers stretched toward the handles as though she was reaching down to touch a reliable old dog, trying to reassure herself. Or grab her belongings and run for it.

She stared at Luc and then past him. He heard a familiar and dreaded rustle from his own school days and knew that the other nuns had entered the room, and that they would have their hands tucked into their sleeves, lined up behind him, like crows on a branch. They would be giving a good once-over to this English-woman who travelled around the country late at night with a man like Luc Langevin.

Huge eyes in a face coloured only by dust and dirt took in the whole room. Nervous and tired as she must be—hell, he could use a good night's sleep himself—he saw her delve inside herself and draw on something that put steel in her spine and courage in her eyes. There was another element in her examination of the room and the nuns that he felt pretty sure was plain, old-fashioned curiosity.

att rode into Gabriel Bull's camp like someone who had nowhere to go and all day to get there. Luc knew it was Matt by the easy way he sat his horse—none of the poker-up-the-ass poses of the English recruits—and the good-natured way he was greeted throughout camp.

"About time you got here." Luc ran a rough brush over the rump of the scrawny horse he was working on. Gabe's horses were not in good shape, and his people were not much better. The money they would be paid for this job would help carry them through the winter.

Matt wrapped his right leg around the saddle horn and sat with his arms crossed, watching as Luc turned his attention to the sorry state of the animal's hooves.

"Did you stop for a visit at The Flats?" Luc was determined to get a rise out of his friend.

"Visit? Is that what it's called now?"

Luc grinned and flipped a hank of hair out of his eyes, then, with a tilt of his head, indicated a group of people pouring hot tallow into the pulverized beef and packing it into cowhide bags. "I thought you were supposed to be supervising all this."

"Gabe doesn't need me to tell him how it's done. He's been shooting buffalo and pounding pemmican since before the ark landed."

"Well then, tell me—where's my other team? Did you get my message that we'd need it?"

Matt kicked his left foot free of the stirrup, disconnected his right knee from the saddle horn and slid, facing forward, to the ground.

Watching him saunter over to the wagon tongue and sprawl along its length, Luc thought, as he had many times before, that it was hard to know what this man did for a living. Everything about him seemed to be one colour; his dark blond hair blended with the weathered tan on his face, and the fringed buckskin jacket was pretty much akin to the faded duck trousers. Only the high black boots—police issue—marked him as anything other than just another fellow looking for adventure. And the boots would go in favour of moccasins as soon as the snow flew.

He's finally put on a little weight, Luc realized. But then, they both had—it was part of getting older. As the years went by and he got easier with himself, Matt had given up bits and pieces of his uniform. Nowadays, if he showed up in full uniform, it was a pretty serious situation, for sure.

Interesting also how things had turned out after that night on the river. Matt had talked about staying with the North West Mounted Police for only three years, long enough to qualify for a quarter section of land of his own. Somehow he had never got around to calling it quits and taking up his land. Luc had just wanted to get away from bad memories so he'd wandered west, turning his hand to whatever came along until he could afford a team of horses and go into the hauling business. Now he had two good teams and all the work he needed. Neither of them would change their lives for anything.

"Your other team is about three hours behind me. One of the new recruits is driving it for you."

Luc jerked upright. "A recruit?"

Matt grinned. "Farm boy from Ontario. Like me. Your precious horses are in good hands." And then more seriously, "So, how is the pemmican?"

"Not so good. Gabe says the beef's too fatty." Luc put the hoof trimmers down and picked up a heavy rasp. Working with a gentle rocking motion, he filed the rough edges of the hoof. The horse drowsed in the sun with its bottom lip sagging. "Not much of the pemmican will be fit for the men to eat, but they can feed it to the dogs."

"How soon? Weather's been real generous so far, but ..." Matt shrugged his shoulders.

"Day or two at the most."

"Going to be able to haul it all?"

"Well, I'll have my two outfits. And Gabe's people are all going to their wintering grounds up by The Crossing, so they'll each take as much as they can. A couple of drifters came into camp yesterday. Say they're willing to work their way to The Crossing. Don't look like much use to me but maybe you want to talk to them."

"You want one of them to drive your second team?"

"Hell, no! Young Gaston wants a chance. He's a good boy, under that wild streak. Guy and I will watch over him."

"Speaking of boys," Matt said. "I asked about Thomm. Seems a youngster who suits that description has hooked himself up with a character folks call the Dook."

"The Dook? What the hell does that mean?"

"A Dook? Well, that's an English nobleman, I guess. Kind of like a lord or something. He's not really, though, according to Charlie Taylor at the newspaper. Charlie claims this Dook is just another one of those remittance men. Family got fed up with him so they shipped him over here to loaf around and stay out of their hair. They send him money now and then to make sure he stays here. Good reason to be fed up with this one, I hear. Or ashamed would be more like it." Matt pulled at his ear. "I don't know how Charlie learns all this stuff, but he's pretty reliable."

Luc absent-mindedly stroked the fetlock in his hand as he looked at Matt. "Ashamed?"

Matt grunted. "Has the boy sharing his room, if you get my meaning."

Luc swore under his breath and looked across to where the missionary woman sat. He thought back to the things she had said about Thomm that had made her blush. He put the hoof down and stretched his back, then told his friend what Miss Jane Priddle had told him, including the part about the English police looking for the kid.

Matt listened, his eyes on the woman, before he spoke. "I'll try to keep an eye out for them. And maybe I'd better talk to the captain and see if he thinks we should write back to the Old Country. The remittance man has checked out of the hotel and talk has it he's expecting money from home. There's also rumour he plans on heading to the Klondike."

"Not overland?" Luc asked.

"Yup."

"Damn fool."

"He's not the only one, but it makes more work for us. This time of year, they could freeze to death. Or starve. Then we have to go find them and bury their frozen carcases in an icy hole somewhere. Do you know how much paperwork there is ·for something like that?"

"Do you think they're on their way to The Crossing?"

A couple of late mallards skimmed the lake, denting the surface of the water with their wings before landing.

"Don't know. If he's serious about the Klondike, he should be heading farther north, up around Fort Assiniboine."

Luc wiped the blade slowly on his pants. "I suppose I should go tell her."

"I'm surprised she's still here. She doing missionary stuff, praying over folks, things like that?"

"No, doesn't seem to be. She just wants to find Billie. There haven't been any outfits to send her back to the train with, just riders. Gabe doesn't have any horses to spare, that's for sure. Anyway, she's got all that luggage so we can't put her on a horse."

"Well, do what you gotta do. I need to find something for this nag of mine to eat." And Matt wandered off with his horse following on his heels like a big puppy.

Jane stood to put the last of the vegetables into the pot and groaned from the stiffness in her legs. One way or another, she had managed to spend most of the last two weeks around the campfire, watching Louise's father-in-law, Gabriel Bull, organize his little band of kin with all the diplomacy of a born leader. The harmony of the camp, and the feeling of well-being that Jane found in helping with the chores, let her forget her predicament for a few hours at a time.

Seven people lived in the two patched and smoke-smudged ti-pis that faced one another across Louise's cooking fire, including her son, Gaston, and daughter, Rosie. The youngest was her grandson, the child Jane had mistaken for a demon on first meeting, and the eldest was Kokum, the old lady with the bad eyes, who seemed to be related to everyone.

And of course, Julie. Julie of the wild eyes and wilder spirit, born nine months to the very night her father, Jules Bull, had died of smallpox. Jane could certainly understand why Louise would treasure this lovely little child of her late husband, but in her estimation the whole family went too far in humouring the girl, catering to her flights of fancy and encouraging what Kokum insisted were spirit *connections* with animals. Evidently, Julie's particular animal connection was the squirrel.

Turning from the soup pot, Jane nearly bumped into Luc. She stuffed the carrot she had peeled into her pocket.

"Got your fiddle tuned up, Guy?" he asked.

Guy Delorme, gap-toothed and horribly pockmarked by the smallpox epidemic that had claimed Julie's father, was Rosie's husband. Jane herself had been inoculated as a child and she still found it hard to believe that in this modern day and age, whole communities of people were struck down unnecessarily.

Guy grinned. "I do, for sure."

They were referring to a party for the 30 or so people who made up the whole of Gabriel Bull's family, the ones who had worked hard to get the pemmican ready to take west to the Athabasca River.

"Well, you earned a party. Matt's pleased. In a hurry to get on the trail, but pleased all the same," Luc said, then looked directly at Jane for the first time. "He had some news about Thomm, too." He gave a bit of a motion with his head and walked away.

Jane hurried to catch up, wiping her hands together to clean them.

"Thomm is headed for The Crossing, too. Maybe already there," he said over his shoulder.

He could have told her that in front of Louise, surely. "Why would Billie go there?"

"Matt says he's travelling with another Englishman. He's been — sharing quarters — with him for a while now." They reached the horses and he started cleaning his farrier tools.

Jane formed a knowing "Oh" with her lips. She watched his hands as he wiped a nasty-looking blade, trying to think what this news could mean, considering what she knew of Billie. There was always the chance it was an innocent attachment. "Who is this Englishman?"

He placed his clean tools in a wooden case, just so. "A remittance man. Ever heard of a remittance man?"

Jane heaved a sigh and dared to look him in the eye. "Yes, I'm sorry to say, I have. But why would they go to The Crossing? Billie likes cities."

"Word has it, they're interested in the Klondike." He must have seen the baffled look on her face. "Farther north. People claim to have found gold there. Either these two think they can go there and pick gold up off the ground like some other fool *Angl-*" — he stopped short of finishing the word — "or they'll pick everybody's pockets instead." He gave a shrug that strained the thin stuff of his work shirt.

It seemed that Billie had slipped away from her again. She absently brought the carrot out of her pocket and palmed it for the horse he had been working on, all the time thinking that Louise and the rest would be gone in a day or two and she would be stuck here in the cold misery of the mission until someone chanced by.

Luc moved to the other side of the horse and ran a currycomb over its flank. "'Course you could always come with us to The Crossing. Only be another week or so, three days up — faster coming back, if you can find a ride. I'll be staying there until spring."

Only a week. That would make it well into November before she returned to Halifax. Did she want to cross the North Atlantic in the winter? The real question was, would it be worth another week of hard travel just to be away from the sisters? She looked up to ask where she could stay if she went as far as The Crossing when she saw something in his eyes. He didn't think she would do it. Her first impulse was to accept the challenge, then he said, with a twinkle that could have been amusement or contempt, "You'll have to ask Louise if she has enough room for you. Or you could sleep under the wagon, like I do."

That suggestion brought a cold flood of reason to clear her mind and a hot flush of blood to her cheeks.

"Thank you, I think not," she said tightly.

He gave that careless shrug of his. "Suit yourself."

The next morning was Sunday, and although it warranted no less work for the schoolchildren, it did mean more time spent in the chapel. Jane couldn't bring herself to go and remained in the dreary room upstairs, tidying the clothes in her suitcase and trying to decide what to wear to the party that evening. No one else would have anything special.

She heard a creak on the stairs, then a dark shape blocked the poor light from the doorway. The little girls loved to sneak away and dig through the Englishwoman's cases. So far, nothing was missing, but Jane sat still in the shadows to see who the culprit might be this time. The eldest girl, Emilie, entered and went stealthily to her own narrow cot where she dropped to her knees and, without a sound, dragged a burlap bundle from underneath it. Jane wondered if she should speak, feeling every bit the Peeping Thomas that she was. Emilie opened the bundle with reverence and withdrew a simple red gingham frock, which she held to her young woman's bosom, stroking the cotton with her broad, strong hands. With a muffled curse, she rewrapped the dress and shoved it back under her bed, then combed her fingers through her shaggy hair.

On tour with Mother Alphonse her first morning at the mission, Jane had been amazed to see most of the children, boys and girls alike, with the same wild hair. "Is their haircut a tradition?" she had asked.

"Ah. *Non, non.*" The nun's full lips twisted into a thin line. "It was the lice. All of them." She had waved her arm in a graceful, sweeping motion. "At the end of winter. Lice in the hairs. We cut them off," she said with a dismissive flip of her hand. "Then Sister Hugette, she treat them with — uh, how you call it? Cold oil?"

Jane had stopped in disbelief. "Coal oil?"

"*Oui.* That one. Cold oil."

"Is that your party dress, Emilie?" Jane asked now. "I was looking for something to wear tonight, too."

Emilie took two steps toward the door, as though ignoring Jane, then stopped and said bitterly, "I can't go."

"I thought everyone would be going."

She didn't turn, but her shoulders dropped. "No. Mother Alphonse said I have to stay here with Sister Hélène. You know how she wanders."

"I'm sorry," Jane said honestly. As far as she could tell, Emilie's life was entirely devoid of pleasure, and now they expected the 15-year-old to sit with frail and demented Sister Hélène while everyone else enjoyed the evening. "I'm not fond of dancing myself, but I wanted to say goodbye to Louise and her family. They'll be gone at daybreak tomorrow."

Emilie turned and slowly walked to Jane's cot. "I've never been to a dance. Or a party."

Jane slid over and patted the bed, as she had done with Suzette a month ago. She felt certain that nothing in her experience had prepared her to act as advisor to either girl, but at least she could listen.

Emilie dropped onto the mattress, her hands worrying her apron. "They know I won't leave Sister Hélène alone. She's always been so good to me, teaching me to draw and sew."

In spite of the bitterness in the girl's words, Jane dared to touch her hand. "I wish I could help."

"Maybe—maybe," Emilie said, clutching Jane's hand for a moment. "You see, Gaston," she stood, agitated, and turned away from Jane. "He asked me to dance with him," she said. "Maybe you could help, tell them you would like me to come with you."

"I wouldn't want to do anything that would get you into trouble."

Emilie made an almost animal noise deep in her throat. "I'm in trouble all the time anyway. Nothing I do pleases them, especially that old Hugette."

"Now, Emilie," Jane said, feeling as impotent in dealing with Emilie's anger as she had with Suzette's humiliation.

But Emilie's scant patience had dissipated. She clomped across the hollow room. "Never mind. I'll run away one of these days. I swear I will. Just wait and see."

After the noon meal, Jane escaped once more out of doors, and was headed for Louise's tent when she saw a movement near the small shrine beside the chapel. It was Julie, circling the plaster Madonna, trailing her hand over the chipped blue paint. At that moment, Mother Alphonse stepped from the chapel and, seeing the child, clasped her hands in front of her, twisting and flexing them. Jane lengthened her stride but the stretch of dry grass seemed to grow longer and her legs to move more slowly. Her sense of foreboding increased as Gaston, who set foot on mission property only when ordered to, stepped out of the trees and marched silently on hide-covered feet toward his little sister. Jane grabbed a handful of skirt and broke into a trot.

"So cold," she heard Julie say dreamily, as she ran a small brown finger over the cheek and chin of the lifeless statue.

Why did Kokum and Louise think this child had the special right to speak whatever she felt, do whatever she wanted?

Gaston bore down on the nun but she ignored him, her features twisted in loathing.

"*Ne touchez pas!*" she said.

Julie, whose bright mind had absorbed at least three languages that Jane knew of, said sweetly, "*Je ne comprend pas.*"

Jane came to a breathless stop beside Julie.

Spittle flew from Mother Alphonse's mouth. "You do. You do understand. Do not touch Our Mother!"

"I understand that part. I just don't understand why. Why not touch the Holy Mother?"

"Julie," Jane said quickly. "Run along with Gaston now. Let him help you get home past the dogs."

Gaston came to a halt six feet away and barked something in Cree. Julie ignored him, but Mother Alphonse's face turned red with fury. No one was to speak Cree in her presence.

Julie prattled on. "I can't go home because of the dogs. Will the Holy Mother protect me from the dogs?"

For the life of her, Jane wanted to believe that the child was as innocent as she looked. But this was Julie, who now stepped right onto the base of the statue and ran her hand over the painted brow of the Madonna.

The nun's hand snaked out in one swift movement, grabbed Julie's arm and flung her away from the shrine. Gaston took two deliberate steps closer, bringing with him the strong smells of smoked hide and the decayed eagle's head that he wore tangled in a tuft of hair on his crown. Something truly ugly crossed Mother Alphonse's face and even as she glared at Gaston, she pulled back her hand and struck the watchful Julie with a blow that stunned all four of them.

No one moved. Not a sound was heard, even from the magpies. Then a stream of blood spilled over Julie's bottom lip and down her chin. Gaston lunged at Mother Alphonse, his fist raised, but Jane was closer. Without thinking, she leaped to put herself in front of the young man, grabbing him by the upper arms.

"No! Gaston, don't do it." They were of a height, but Gaston was willowy and strong. She trembled from head to foot, knowing she had no more control over this young man than Louise had over Julie. The knuckles on his raised fist turned grey. He wouldn't really care who he hit. Someone—a white woman—had hurt his precious little sister and someone would pay.

Jane stared into his hate-filled eyes and tried not to blink. "Think of your mother. Get Julie home now. Get her past the dogs."

The muscles bunched in his jaw and his gaze flicked from Jane to the nun.

"She's not worth it, Gaston. Not worth the trouble you will make for your family. Please. Go."

Just when Jane thought she could hold him off no longer, he turned, scooped up his sister as easily as a leaf and stalked toward the woods. A bloody-faced Julie stared over his shoulder with wide, tearless eyes.

Sagging with relief, Jane turned in time to intercept the look of hatred that Mother Alphonse had transferred from the Bulls to Jane. The nun crossed herself and walked back into the chapel.

ane picked her way down the path behind Sister Marthe, being careful not to trip and dump the rolled jelly cake that she carried into the underbrush. Jellyroll was Sister Marthe's specialty — egg-rich sponge cake rolled up with raspberry jam and sprinkled with powdered sugar.

The path opened into a clearing, an uneven circle filled with the light cast by lanterns and fires. Packed earth, 20 feet across, would serve as a dance floor, and boys were being recruited to drag logs around the edge to provide seating. Women congregated around a makeshift table with food; the smoky air vibrated with the squawk of a fiddle.

Guy and another man tried to outdo one another to see who could play the loudest and the fastest. Rosie and Jane tapped their feet and the wet, sloughy smell of earth rose up as dancers pranced and twirled in bright shirts, their headgear decorated with feathers, shiny medallions and chunks of fur.

Jane felt a tug on her hand.

"Dance with me, Jane. Dance with me," Julie begged.

"I don't know ..."

But everyone seemed to be joining in. Women danced with men, with children and with one another. Maybe no one would notice her. Head down, she mimicked the child, shuffling her boots in some sort of rhythm.

Matt Edwards enjoyed his work. So much, in fact, that he often forgot when he was on duty and when he wasn't. So when the bottle passed his way, he had to stop and think a minute before shaking his head. Luc passed, too.

"Not partying tonight?" Matt asked.

"I tried some earlier. It's godawful. I don't know what they made it from." Luc shifted his shoulders against the tree trunk they leaned on.

"Don't tell me anything I don't want to hear." Matt crossed his arms over his chest and watched the dancing.

The young recruit, Gibbs, stood directly across from him, ramrod straight in his bright new uniform. He probably hadn't figured out there was liquor at the party, because no one would have offered it to him. They knew he would feel obliged to pursue the subject of who was a genuine Indian and who was not, and that would lead to an investigation of who was responsible for giving alcohol to an Indian—an illegal act here in the North West Territories. It all got too confusing to bother with because the fact was, these men would all be up before first light, hangover and all, ready to put in an 18-hour workday.

Matt narrowed his eyes to watch the two drifters Luc had told him about. Those two now, were more of a worry, partaking of the local hospitality. What he had seen of them so far hadn't impressed him at all.

Luc turned up the collar of his buckskin jacket against the wind. "Smells like snow."

"Any time now. What day is it anyway?"

"November, I think," Luc answered.

Matt snorted. "November's not a day. How much of that stuff did you say you had?"

"Not much. I never know what day it is. I don't have to do government reports. You're the one should know what day it is."

"Yeah, well, I just want to get to The Crossing as soon as possible, find some barges and get this stuff moving before the river freezes up."

"We'll make good time. The muskeg has stiffened up already and the horses are fresh."

Matt let his shoulders relax. "You hungry? Looks like the food's almost all gone."

"Had some of your pemmican," Luc said.

"Any good?"

"Not as bad as I expected. Louise rolled it in some flour and fried it."

"Well, they won't be too particular up north."

Matt watched the last two nuns pick up their dirty dishes and leave. He saw Guy put his fiddle down and pull Miss Jane Priddle out to dance some kind of jig. Her coat, a flimsy thing that wasn't going to do her much good in this country, flopped open as they bobbed up and down.

"Time for me to turn in, I think," Luc said as he shoved himself away from the tree and wandered off.

Matt watched his friend disappear into the dark shadows of the loaded wagons. Young Gibbs had already gone. Back at the dance, he saw that one of the drifters, the big one who called himself George, had pulled the Englishwoman away from Guy. She put the flat of her hands on his chest and shoved him away. Looked like she could take care of herself. Matt went to find his own bedroll.

The comments the lout had made about her snuggling with breeds chilled Jane to the bone. She flexed her fingers at her side, then squeezed a fold of her wool coat in each hand, trying to wipe every trace of him away. His gaze followed the motion of her hands and his leer turned uglier.

In mere minutes, the evening had changed. The dancing wasn't amusing anymore; it was wild and—yes, savage. Most of the women had disappeared with their tired children and dirty dishes. A flash of red that might be Emilie appeared and disappeared from just beyond the light. The remaining men openly passed bottles from hand to hand.

Despite the light of a wintry moon, Jane floundered through the undergrowth, searching for the trail. A biting wind pierced the bare trees and penetrated her thin coat and organdie shirtwaist. Where were those infernal dogs?

Searching the side of the trail for a stout stick she thought she saw another movement, the red gingham dress, perhaps. She stood, wondering what, if anything, she should do if Emilie had defied the nuns and sneaked out to be with Gaston. A twig snapped behind her.

"You waitin' for somebody special, lady, or will anybody do?"

The man she had danced with, the one called George, stood not three feet from her.

"I'm going back to the mission. I don't need an escort." She wished she felt as sure as she tried to sound.

"Still pretty high and mighty, ain't ya? The nuns know what you do down here at night? All these breeds pawin' atcha?" He stepped close enough to bring his personal stench into her face. "Maybe the nuns have a little fun with their pet Injuns, too, do they? I've heard stories about them *Catliks*. Ain't you heard them stories, Jake?"

"Ya." Jake sniggered. "I heard 'em, too."

Jane felt a moment of righteous anger on behalf of the sisters, then concentrated on her own predicament. Naive though she was, she knew that she was in serious trouble. She also knew that, as with the other mongrels that lurked in these woods, she couldn't let Jake and George know she was frightened. She simply turned and walked away.

"Don't you turn your back on me, you uppity bitch!"

A hand grabbed her collar; ragged fingernails tore the skin on the back of her neck. Her open coat slid down over her arms, making them useless. She cried out once — not loud enough — and tried again. A hand slapped over her face, smashing her teeth against the soft fleshy part of her mouth. She tasted blood and unwashed skin and experienced a moment of cold, pure terror.

Then time stood still. From somewhere else, Jane watched, caught in a nightmarish bubble, as the men wrestled her into the bushes. All motion became slow and precise, every detail as crystal clear as the sparkles of hoar frost on the twigs that scratched her face. Some part of her looked on as though she had shaken a snow-filled paperweight and held it in the palm of her hand to see where the flakes would fall on the little artificial world inside.

Thick hands grabbed at her chest, pulled at her clothes. George grunted with satisfaction as the dainty pearl buttons from her shirtwaist arced slowly away from her, twinkling in the cold, indifferent moonlight, falling without a sound on the spongy forest floor.

"You gonna need to scrub more'n your hands when I'm finished, bitch."

Like schoolyard bullies, they had to team up to trip her to the ground. She fell with an animal-like grunt, a sharp stick tearing at the back of her thigh. The pain pierced her dull mind. She dragged herself into a sitting position. When she tried to tug at her tangled clothes, George drove his knee into her stomach, down low where the soft part of her groin joined her hipbone.

She wheezed, unable to breathe. Dear God, she was going to die. Her body contorted, trying to ease her bursting lungs.

With his knees and hands, George pried her body flat, then sprawled on top of her. "You smell better'n most of the sluts I bin with."

"Hurry up. Hurry up." Jake pranced around her, opening his trousers, kicking leaves into her face. When he stepped on her loose hair, Jane thought that fear and lack of breath must have pushed her to some kind of madness, because she heard, as clearly as she saw the stars in the wintry heaven, Suzette sobbing: "They said it was my fault, miss. That I encouraged him. They said I should have said no, and I did, miss. But he was so much bigger than me."

The dead weight rolled off her. She lay stunned, unable to grasp what had happened.

"What the hell?" George snarled beside her. "Jake, what the hell you doin'? Wait yer turn."

"Weren't me, George. Were that damn kid."

Gaston.

Jane gulped a mouthful of clean air, saw the fear on Gaston's face and shook her head. "Don't," she whispered, then pointed a shaking hand at the camp, willing him to go for help.

George caught Gaston by the shoulder and spun him off balance. He landed at her feet.

"Get up, Jane. Get up."

She couldn't lie here and let him risk life and limb without fighting back herself.

Jake looked nervously around. "Maybe the kid's not alone."

"You scared of a goddam Injun?"

Jane hauled herself up on her elbow as Gaston scrambled away. George leaned across her to grab at the boy. She kicked out, connecting solidly with his ribs, then lunged to her knees, feeling her stockings pop and tear. George responded with a backhand blow to her face that sent her reeling, her ears ringing.

Still, Gaston was there. Like a sparrow hawk tormenting a crow, he swooped in and out, striking, then ducking away. But he was only one and they were two. George caught him long enough for Jake to pound a closed fist into his face. Her warrior went down.

George straddled her, panting. She swallowed hard to keep from vomiting.

Then, amazingly, Jake sidled off into the trees and broke into a run. Jane saw why—Guy Delorme and Luc Langevin running hard toward them, their faces strained with shock.

Emilie was there too, bent over her hero, wringing her hands. "I couldn't find them right away, Gaston. They'd all gone from the party."

Nothing made much sense to Jane except that red dress; she never thought she'd be so happy to see Emilie and that dress.

Luc saw the Englishwoman crawling on her hands and knees through dead leaves to Gaston, who was shaking his head and holding his jaw.

The scrawny little drifter thundered through the trees like a buffalo. The hefty one looked as if he might want to argue a bit, then to Luc's disappointment, he lumbered off after his partner.

Guy started after them, but Luc called him back. "Go tell Matt. They don't have any horses so they can't go far unless they steal some." And then, to Emilie, who couldn't stop blubbering, he said, "Go with him. Get Louise. Bring some rags or something."

Christ! What a bloody sight. Gaston and the woman knelt,

facing one another, swaying like two saplings in a strong wind, both jabbering at once.

"I'm sorry, Jane," Gaston said.

"Oh, no, Gaston." She shook her head, then groaned and touched her forehead.

"I tried to help …"

"You did help. I'm fine, truly I am. *Je suis très bien,*" she said in terrible French. "I have only bumps and bruises."

Luc knelt beside them. "Can you get up?" He tried to tug the coat back over the woman's bare shoulders. "It's freezing out here."

But at his touch she cringed and hitched herself away on her backside, her skirts bunched up so he could see her bleeding knees through torn stockings.

"Whoa!" He pulled his hands back and held them high. Her eyes were wild and round, her face a sick-looking white under the smears of blood. "It's just me, Luc," he said in a reasonable tone.

She blinked a couple of times. "I can get up by myself."

And by some miracle, she did. She pulled herself up the nearest tree and stood there, weaving back and forth. Luc grabbed Gaston under the arms and hauled him to his feet. Even with just the light of the moon, he could tell the kid was going to have a black eye.

"I should go back to the mission now," Jane said with an eerie kind of calm.

"Louise is coming," Luc said, but she didn't seem to hear him.

He had once seen a doe, mortally wounded by wolves, wade into a clearing of deep snow. She'd held her head high on her graceful neck, gulping for air, eyes wild and roving but not seeming to see anything. Luc felt he was watching the same thing now. Like the deer, *l'Anglaise* walked cautiously, lifting her feet high, concentrating hard on staying upright. But, like the deer, she was too hurt to pull it off. Her legs buckled very slowly and she collapsed with all her weight onto her battered knees.

"Shit," Luc muttered. That had to hurt real bad.

She wiped the back of her hand across her face, then held it out to look at the dark streaks of blood. "Such a mess," she said with a sigh.

"Ah, Jesus." He crouched down and put his arm around her shoulder whether she liked it or not.

"Do you have to swear about everything, Mr. Langevin?"

He chuckled with relief. "Louise is coming to help you. Let me get you up. I won't hurt you."

Once she was up, he kept his arm around her shoulder. "Put your arm around me, like this. Hold onto my belt." But that made her coat hang open and she seemed to realize her clothes were torn. Her long fingers shook as she tried to drag the edges of her coat together.

Luc propped her against a tree. "Here, let me." He started to fasten the buttons. She sucked in her breath and froze, staring at him with huge eyes. His hands stilled. "I won't hurt you," he repeated. Without taking his eyes from hers, he slowly buttoned her coat. The skin felt clammy under his knuckles. This woman needed a good, stiff drink.

Louise came with towels and her usual calm way of taking care of things, Matt close on her heels. "Come back to my place. We need water. We'll clean you up and get you home." Louise looked Emilie up and down. "Both of you."

Matt couldn't seem to find the words he needed. "Is she—that is, was she ...?"

"No, she's just roughed up real bad," Luc said. "Help me get her down the trail. Did you find them?"

"Not yet. I put some men to watch over the horses." Matt gingerly tried to take Jane's arm but she winced and pulled away. Luc kept her moving. She was too cold and weak to stand around very long.

Matt followed close on their heels. "Why are you taking her back to the camp? Shouldn't we take her to the mission?"

Luc couldn't answer that. Something had told him to send for Louise instead of the sisters, but at the mention of the mission the arm under his hand trembled all the more.

She spoke quietly. "May I come with you?"

He studied her bent head, knowing what she asked, and why. He remembered the cold reception from the nuns the day they had arrived, and he'd heard about her keeping Gaston out of a mess of trouble with Mother Alphonse yesterday. What she'd said to the Mother Superior, "She's not worth it," had been repeated a hundred times around the fires all night, always with a grin and a chuckle. Now this.

"I don't know if that's such a good idea," Luc said. Over her shoulder, he saw Matt shake his head vigorously.

"I can't stay here," she whispered.

Matt stepped closer. "We'll get them. I sent Constable Gibbs out with some men, so you don't have to worry. You'll be safe at the mission."

She finally stopped and looked directly at Luc and he saw the bruise darkening on her cheekbone and the blood drying on her swollen mouth. "Please?"

He noticed the sheen in her eyes and knew that he wouldn't know what to do with a woman like this if she started to cry. He had a feeling she was not the whining type, even though she had good reason.

Matt grunted something in disgust, but Luc nodded his head even as he said, "It'll be a real hard trip. And you'll have to find your own way back."

"Thank you," she said in a slightly stronger voice. "I'll try not to be a bother."

Matt shoved past them and marched down the trail.

They made it to the camp where Louise pulled back the flap of her tipi. "Kokum. We have need of your medicine."

A lantern flared and the women disappeared inside. The men shuffled their feet and stared at the shadows stretching up the inside of the walls.

"Party over?" Luc asked.

Matt exploded. "It sure as hell is! Do you know what you're doing?"

"Well, as far as I've thought it out, I'll get her to Benny and Tina's. You know the sisters are going to make her life miserable here." That was the best Luc could come up with on short notice because the truth was, he *didn't* know what he was doing.

"Benny and Tina are three days from here. We're supposed to be moving fast."

"I'll get you where you're going like always."

"Uh huh. I'm going to see if Gibbs found anything."

Guy kept his silence, leaving Luc alone with his own thoughts, which weren't so different from Matt's. He pulled his buckskin collar up around his bare ears.

The flap opened on the tipi and Louise came out with Emilie. "If Jane is coming with us, she needs her cases," Louise said placidly. "Guy, would you take Emilie up and help her get them? She says she knows where they are."

Guy looked relieved to have something to do. Emilie looked as though going into the mission in her party dress was the last thing she wanted to do. Luc figured she wasn't supposed to be running around the bushes at night with young Gaston.

"Try to get in and out without waking anyone," Louise said.

"If they catch you, Emilie, and make a fuss, you'll have to come with us, too. They'll never give you any peace."

Luc saw Emilie's back straighten, her dark eyes flash in the moonlight. Was Louise joking? If she didn't know what was going on between this girl and her own Gaston, she was blind.

But that wasn't the whole story. Little Julie had a swollen face from where that nun had hit her. Louise had a score to settle, and taking young Emilie who, from all accounts, did the work of three men, was as good a way to do it as any.

Jesus. Women. He headed back to his bedroll to get an hour or two of sleep.

eight

ven when Jane huddled down in the wagon box, surrounding herself with lumpy bags of pemmican, the wind pierced her to the bones. Grim clouds whipped out of the northwest, so low and laden that they threatened to snag on the tops of the fir trees. The wind exploded now and then in gusts that pelted her face with kernels of dry snow that was nothing like the wet, fluffy stuff back home. And when the clouds broke for a few minutes, she could see high above them, like a loose thread lost in the firmament, a tardy flock of geese floundering southward.

Yesterday, as Jane watched Louise and her family break camp and pack their goods into their wagon, Luc had come to get her. He'd studied her bruised face, then looked her directly in the eye. "You think you should come?"

"I can't stay here," she'd said, knowing he wanted nothing more than for her to stay behind. "I only have a headache. I'll be fine."

"A lot of people have headaches this morning," he'd said with a trace of a grin that didn't reach his eyes.

So, for the past two days Jane had alternately scrunched down in the wagon or limped beside the team. Few words had been spoken, or at least nothing that could be heard over the din. All the gaiety of the party had dissolved into the serious business of delivering the pemmican, receiving the desperately needed payment and then settling into their winter camp before too much snow piled up.

Since first light today, snow had sifted into low spots, outlining hollows and ruts on the colourless landscape. Jane attached a pathetic hope to the evidence of a well-used trail, holding onto the belief that she could get back to the train at South Edmonton whenever she chose.

As well as wagons, there were a few carts, with high wooden wheels and not a trace of grease to ease the din of wood grinding on wood, that were pulled by one horse, or, in two instances, oxen. They fanned out, weaving and screeching their way through scruffy bushes and around straggling firs. A small, loose herd of five spare horses travelled freely, making a nuisance of themselves with the working teams.

Daylight faded early. Gabriel Bull rode by to tell them he had found a campsite by a stream some two miles distant where they would spend the night. Jane turned her bruised face away from the wind and saw that, directly behind them, Gaston was struggling with his team. She reached up to the wagon seat and tapped Luc on the back of his hide coat.

"Gaston may need your help," she said.

He turned to watch for a minute, then looked down at Jane. "Can you handle a team?"

"Well, I have driven before." She compared the dainty steppers at home with the shaggy brutes out here and didn't feel in the least confident. But somehow, she had to do her part, be more than just a burden on everyone.

"They won't give you any trouble. They're too tired." His blue knit stocking cap was pulled low over his ears and forehead, a long, brightly coloured woven scarf wrapped around his waist. Other than rosy cheeks, he looked quite warm and comfortable sitting up there in the elements.

Jane clambered onto the buckboard and took his place while he made his way to the back. She felt him jump off as they continued to move. The horses also felt the change and broke rhythm, tossing their heads. She held her breath, but Luc had been right; they were too tired to act up. The grey lethargy that had haunted her for two days lifted slightly and she looked around for Sergeant Edwards, wishing he could see her contribution. A few minutes later, she felt a dip at the back of the wagon and Luc climbed into the seat beside her. Jane handed him the reins and flexed her stiff fingers.

He looked at her kid gloves. "Is that all you have to wear on your hands?"

She shoved her hands into her pockets. "I didn't expect to be here this long, and I didn't expect it to be so cold." She couldn't steady her shaky voice. She felt as though tears lurked in her chest and throat but couldn't spill over.

"She's—it's—not so cold yet." He handed the reins back to her and dug under the seat, coming up with a pair of thick grey mittens.

Without hesitation, she pulled off her gloves and stuck her hands into the rough wool. "Thank you." She tried to smile but the scab on her lip cracked. She ran her tongue over it, tasting blood.

His expression was serious but distant, like everyone else these past two days. Some avoided looking at her, others treated her with measured politeness, none mentioned her embarrassing incident. She'd felt like an outsider since she'd put foot in this country, but never as much of a pariah as she did now.

"Rub your hands together," he said. "They'll warm up faster."

"I must get some mittens of my own. Where did you buy these?"

He looked surprised, then some of the mocking returned. "You don't buy mitts, *Anglaise*. You make them, knit them."

The trace of banter felt good, more normal somehow. "Indeed," she said. "And did you make these?" She tried another small, painful smile.

His burst of laughter was cloudy in the cold air. "*Non. Ma mère* — mother — made them. And this toque. But you will have to make your own."

Jane braced herself for more teasing. "I don't know how to knit."

"Your mother didn't teach you?"

"My mother died when I was six."

He assessed her slowly, then turned back to the horses, their conversation finished.

Gabriel Bull directed them into a circle of wagons and, with the efficiency of generations of practice, the camp was assembled for the night. The horses were watered, then hobbled so they could forage for grass under the snow. Campfires flared, kettles boiled for tea. Everyone had a job to do. Jane wandered off with Julie in search of dry firewood.

Feeling no hunger, she ate a bit of bannock and cold meat. Experiencing no thirst, she forced herself to drink a cup of sweet tea. The clouds had been torn apart and now their tattered scraps flapped like dirty rags over the moon. Tobacco smoke circled the campfire but even that smelled distant and foreign to her.

Then the hair stood up on the back of her neck. An unholy

howl rose from just beyond the wagons, a series of high-pitched yips, ending in a long keening wail. The mongrels cowered close to the fire.

"They like to see the moon, too," Louise said calmly.

"They? What is it?" Jane whispered.

"Song dogs," Kokum said.

"Coyotes," Julie said, snuggling into her mother's side.

"So close?"

More coyotes joined in, harmonizing with the rest.

"I saw them alongside the train as I crossed the country," Jane said to no one in particular.

"They're very bold," Louise said. "They'll eat anything, live anywhere."

"I want to go in," Julie whined. Dogs, which included coyotes, seemed to be the only creatures that Julie wasn't on familiar terms with.

Jane stayed out to listen, turning in the direction of each new chorus until she had made a complete circle. When the last yap died away, Guy and Gaston set their empty cups on the trunk and left without a word.

Jane waited, wanting the coyotes to begin again.

"They're finished for the night." Luc remained, motionless in the shadows.

"Oh," Jane said. "I thought I was alone."

"You're not afraid, like Julie?"

"No. Should I be?" She couldn't see his face. Maybe he was laughing at her again.

"*Non.*"

"I think they're splendid," she said.

After a time, he repeated, "Splendid," then left without another word, heading, she assumed, for his bedroll under his wagon.

With reluctant steps, she entered Louise's tipi and picked her way through the bodies already wrapped in their blankets on the moulting old buffalo hide that comprised the floor. Without removing any of her clothes, she pulled her blanket to her chin and lay staring at the cone over her head. Louise cupped her hand around the lone candle. Darkness was instant and deep.

"You don't come inside with us?" Kokum asked.

"I was listening to the coyotes," Jane answered.

"You like those coyotes? They follow you on the train?"

"Uh, well ..."

"Maybe they are your totem, your special animal."

"I'd hate if those song dogs were my totem," Julie said.

"That's enough talk now," Louise said. "We have to be up early. Go to sleep."

"Old womans don't sleep much," Kokum said.

Nor do I, Jane thought as she stared into the endless blackness over her head. She couldn't tell how many hours passed. Sometimes her eyelids drooped, so she busied her mind counting the days it would take to return to the coast. Around her the steady breathing of the other women reminded her that she, too, had another long, hard day tomorrow, but as soon as she closed her eyes, she felt rough hands on her breasts and thighs, smelled the stink of men, sweaty with arousal. She tried sitting up, but finally slumped sideways, her head on Kokum's hip. She felt a gnarled hand on her head and drifted into a troubled sleep full of grinning coyotes.

The next day dawned bright and clear and terribly cold. Jane's dreams stuck around the edges of her mind like the ice rimming the water bucket. Then she considered her circumstances, jammed between piles of hide bags full of half-frozen meat and suet, headed to an outpost in the middle of nowhere with a man who probably prompted decent mothers to lock their daughters in the house. No wonder she had bad dreams.

They stopped about 11:00 to rest the horses and cook a hot meal. Some of the wayward horses were caught and exchanged for animals that were tired or had developed sores from their harness. Later in the day, Jane walked beside the wagon to stay warm, watching a black cloud of smoke develop on the horizon.

Sergeant Edwards rode by. "I'm going on ahead to take a look."

"Is there much danger from fire this time of year?" Jane asked Luc.

"Still pretty dry. Not much snow."

Before long the horses had to step nervously onto burned grass. Ahead of them, flames licked as high as the bare aspen.

"Damn fool," Luc said. "Could have pastured a couple head of horses on this burned-out patch all winter."

Little tendrils of smoke came from clumps of smouldering grass, and trees blazed in the distance. Slowly, the clatter of carts and wagons ceased as everyone, even the straggling horses, stopped to eye the fire.

A squat shelter huddled to the south of the burning trees; it was the same colour as the blackened ground around it and Jane could see that it was made of blocks of earth stacked one atop the other. The only other signs of habitation were a small pole pen for a horse and cow and, halfway between the house and the animals, a water pump. As Jane watched, a woman and two small children crept out the door, the mother swollen with another child.

Matt dismounted and stalked over to the homesteader who seemed to actually be throwing logs onto the fire.

"He's not even trying to stop it," Jane said.

"*Non*," Luc agreed. "They try to get everything to burn so they can put the plough to it. Trees, grass—everything. Damn waste."

One by one, the men hopped down from their rigs with shovels and blankets and hurried to help Matt.

"I'd better go, too." Luc dug into the wagon for a shovel. "Hold the horses for me."

"I don't know ..."

"Just stand and talk to them. You can do it."

"But ..."

"I'll be right back." And he was gone.

Merciful heavens, Jane thought. He's left me alone with his precious horses.

The women waited, watching their men smack at the flames. Someone worked the pump handle while others soaked their blankets. The tallest trees were doomed, their upper branches crackling like tinder. There would be nothing left to protect the little dirt house from the winter elements.

The horses snorted hot breath into Jane's face. The muscles quivered up their legs.

"Whoa, Lobo." Jane stroked the gelding's creamy muzzle, but he didn't want to be wooed. She tugged at the ear of the roan mare called Rouge, then danced out of the way of their prancing hooves and tried to keep up a steady patter. Talk to them indeed!

Just as she began to feel they had settled down, Gaston's team lurched into the back of their rig. Lobo tried to rear but only backed himself into the traces, taking Rouge with him. Jane gave thanks for her height and long arms, which she wrapped tightly around Lobo's neck.

Then, like something out of her nightmares, she saw a rabbit bound out of the burning bush and streak partway across the scorched grass. Befuddled, he flopped this way and that, his winter pelage smeared with ash. Jane stared, mesmerized, willing him to go back—back to the other side of the bush where there was still some vegetation that hadn't been destroyed. But of course he was beyond sense and hunkered down in the middle of his own hell.

Jane wasn't the only one to see him. As she watched in horror, the mongrels rampaged across the short distance and within seconds, amid snarls and howls, tore the animal limb from limb, even as it lived and breathed. She thought she heard a high-pitched scream just before steaming entrails splattered across the grey ash.

The horses were on top of her. It was one insult too many for their frayed nerves. Part of the wooden rigging hit her in the ribs as she was dragged under the wagon tongue but she dug in her heels, thinking only that she couldn't let them bolt. If she didn't do anything else right, she had to keep these horses from running away. She struggled upright, catching her heel in her hem. Steadying herself, she pulled hard on Lobo's bridle, forcing him toward Rouge so that he couldn't lunge forward. But Rouge didn't want any part of that and reared, jerking Jane's arm up and backward at a crazy angle. She nearly fainted with the pain.

hen they turned back to the wagons, Luc saw the Englishwoman wrestling with his horses. He started to hurry, but she appeared to get them under control. She was good with horses and didn't seem to know it.

"Someone should shoot those dogs," Matt said as they passed the bloody mess that had been a rabbit.

"I won't stop you, for sure." Although Matt was still in a touchy mood about Jane Priddle, Luc had to agree with him about the pack of mongrels.

As they approached the team, he thought he might tease the woman a little; she'd been so sad and hurt looking. Then she turned and he saw her face.

"What?" Luc asked.

She hung onto Lobo's bridle, keeping herself upright. Then he saw the unnatural angle of her shoulder, her arm hanging uselessly, the hand turned too far backward.

"Could you take them, please? I seem to have hurt myself."

Matt came by with his horse. "Ready to roll?"

"No," Luc said.

Matt looked at Jane, then hard at Luc. "Now what?"

"Nothing. I just twisted my arm a bit." She lied badly.

"It's not twisted," Luc said. "I've seen this before. It's—how you say? Displaced? Out of the joint?"

Matt spoke through tight lips. "Dislocated."

"Dislocated," Luc agreed. "And it hurts real bad."

She stood there shivering. "It's cold. We should go."

Gabe rode by to see what was holding them up and Luc made a quick decision. "Go on. We'll catch up down the trail."

Matt threw the reins over his horse's head. "What are you going to do, for God's sake?"

This wasn't the way to win back Matt's good humour. "This shoulder is going to hurt like hell until it's fixed."

"And who's going to do that, tell me? You going to fix it?"

"Well, I saw it done, a while ago. It was a man, but ..."

"All right," Matt said. "Tell me what to do."

"We have to get her coat off. More than that maybe."

Jane held her arm and watched their faces, making no sound.

Matt flung his arms into the air. "What are you saying? We undress her out here?"

"No, you're right. It's too cold." Luc looked around. "We'll have to go over to that homestead."

Matt exploded. "I just gave that fool a summons and now you want me to ask for his hospitality?"

"I'll ask him," Luc said. "If you would just stay with the horses?" He finally spoke to Jane. "Do you think you can walk over there?"

"Of course. I'm sorry to be so much trouble."

"You'll be more trouble if we don't fix it." He saw what looked like more pain in her eyes and wished he'd found a better way of saying that. They made their way across the puffy ashes to where the farmer was stomping around, still fuming because they had stopped him from burning down the whole damn country.

"The lady's hurt," Luc said. "We need to go inside."

"No stay here!"

"We don't want to *stay* here." Who the hell would want to stay in a pigpen like this? "We just need to get out of the cold for a few minutes."

Without waiting for the homesteader to refuse, Luc ducked his head and pushed Jane through the low doorway. He had to use sign language to get a lantern lit. The place was as dark as sin and smelled like a cellar full of rotten potatoes. The wife cowered against the wall, her little ones hanging onto her skirts. All three had bare feet. If he lived to be a hundred, Luc would never get used to the sight of little ones in the winter without anything on their feet.

"We have to get your coat off." He started to undo the buttons he had done up a couple of nights ago. Looking into her drawn face, he shrugged and grinned. It earned him a wan smile.

There was only one chair in the place. He set her on it carefully. "We should take more clothes off."

She stiffened.

"It would work best, I think."

She stared at Luc, then looked helplessly at the burly homesteader, who watched them as though they were going to steal his chair.

Luc used sign language again. "My wife—clothes off—you out." He managed to back the man out the door.

With one shaky hand, she unbuttoned a blue sweater and under that, a shirt in a softer shade of blue. He turned his back and let her do it by herself, hoping it wouldn't take too long.

"I had to say that—that wife business," Luc said. "I didn't know how else to get rid of him."

When she didn't answer, he turned slowly. She sat in a frilly lace thing with her sweater clutched over her chest. Luc knelt and put his right hand on her bare shoulder. His hands were colder than her skin, so he rubbed them together, hard.

"It doesn't look so bad," he said, hoping his voice wouldn't give him away and reveal that he was thinking hard about what he needed to do. The old sawbones he had watched years ago had used his fist. Luc balled his hand as tightly as possible and lifted Jane's arm slowly. She held her breath.

"You have to breathe." He didn't need her fainting on him.

He put his closed fist in her armpit, then cupping his right hand over her shoulder, quickly pulled and rolled it over. That is, he tried. She cried out and the woman against the wall squealed. It didn't work.

"I think I'm going to be sick," Jane said quietly.

"Breathe deep. Again." He looked around the soddy. "My hand is too big. What can I ..." Then he saw the wild-eyed woman against the wall. Her hands were smaller than his. With some difficulty, he made her understand what he wanted her to do. She kept her eyes on his face the whole time.

"Ready?" he asked.

Both women nodded, staring at him with a look that said they wanted to believe he knew what he was doing, but they weren't too sure.

He steadied himself and even offered a little prayer, for the first time in many years. "Mary, Mother of God ..."

She must have been listening. He felt the shoulder slide back into place as the Englishwoman groaned and slumped against the back of the chair.

She didn't object when Luc gently pried the clothes from her hand. He used the sash from around his middle to bind her arm to her body, then got her back into her clothes the best he could. The red-and-blue sash looked bright against her white skin—white except for the bruises on her collarbone and some ugly scratches lower down on her chest.

When her coat was buttoned over her bundled arm and her shawl wrapped around her head, he helped her to her feet and waited until she was steady before heading to the door. She stopped for a moment to thank the little woman, who looked so startled at being treated with good manners that she could barely nod her head.

It took both men to get Jane into the wagon. Luc wrapped her up in a blanket and set off, Matt riding alongside. The first good-sized bump they came to, she groaned. Luc pulled up.

"You help her," Matt said. "I'll drive." He tied his horse to the back and took the driver's seat.

Luc crawled into the back and braced himself with his shoulders and feet, then pulled her across his lap. He tucked the blanket around both of them.

"How long to the Stopping House?" he asked.

"'Bout three hours," Matt answered.

Luc spoke to the shawl-covered head under his chin. "Tina and Benny Lindstrom are friends. They'll take care of you."

"Whatever you think best," she said.

"It will be best," he said, but couldn't help wondering how a proper English society woman was going to get along with Tina. Probably be good for both of them.

Three hours, they said. It was going to be the longest three hours of Jane's life. Her shoulder throbbed, her neck ached and she dearly wanted to stretch her cramped legs, but Luc had gone to so much trouble to try to make her comfortable that she didn't want to squirm. He seemed to know how the wagon would move so that he could cushion the worst of the bumps. She tried to hold her head up for a while, then gave up and let it sag.

"I'm sorry to be such a bother," she said.

"Would have been more of a bother if the horses had run away."

The sky dulled from an icy blue to the colour of steel as the short day disappeared into dusk. Without light or shadow, the world flattened into a dreary monochrome. The harness on the horses jangled in rhythm with their determined footsteps. Matt hunched forward on the buckboard, his elbows on his knees, now and then stomping his feet on the floor or whacking his hands together in their leather mitts. The persistence of the two men, the doggedness of the team and her own agony were the only things that held reality for Jane.

A lifetime later, long after the snow had begun to fall in earnest, they left the trail and turned into a farmyard. Matt brought the team to a stop and hopped to the snowy ground in front of a building of squared logs with low windows, the bottom ledges barely coming to his knees. Jane had an impression of tidy outbuildings and a good-sized barn.

A thickset man of medium height came out of the house, shrugging into a sheepskin coat.

Matt pulled one mitt off to shake hands. "Hello, Benny. Do you have a spare bed for a few nights?"

"Ya, we do."

As they helped Jane from the wagon and dug out her cases, a youthful figure in grey tweed trousers, blue sweater and matching knit cap ran down the path to greet them.

"Luc, Matt. You will stay for supper?"

"Hello, Tina," Sergeant Edwards said. "We can't. This is Miss Priddle. She's the one staying with you."

Benny grabbed the handles of Jane's bags in one broad hand and headed toward the house as Tina tried to persuade the men to stay, but the sergeant was already mounted on his horse.

At the last moment Jane remembered the mitts and sash. Pulling the mitts off, she handed them to Luc.

"Keep them. I have more," he said.

"Thank you. And the sash?" It would take some time to get the sash off.

"I'll be back this way in a couple of days. Go now, get warm." Then they were gone in a blur of blowing snow, the horses' shoulders furry with frost.

The first room Jane entered appeared to be a simple storage room. There were bags of flour and sugar, tins of coffee and tea and some canned goods on raw plank shelves. Carpentry tools hung on wooden pegs on the wall. A pot-bellied heater glowed from the middle of the back wall.

She was quickly steered through a door to the right of the heater, into a pleasant room that ran the length of the building. It served a threefold purpose, kitchen as well as dining and living room. Colourful wall hangings had been nailed to the log walls; bright rag rugs were scattered on the bare wooden floor. The long pine table could easily seat six or eight people.

Tina hurried Jane past a black-and-chrome stove and into a bedroom not much bigger than her corner at the mission. Here, however, the narrow metal bed had a brilliant patchwork quilt, and a wooden chest the colour of honey standing at the end like a footlocker.

"How did you hurt your arm?" Tina set a coal-oil lamp on a narrow dresser under the single window. With the knit cap gone, curly hair, so fair as to be almost white, sprang loose from a coil on the top of her head. Her slender back stretched over the bed where she folded back the sheet and quilt with chapped hands.

"While I held the horses. The men went to fight a fire, so I had to hold the horses. Then they bolted." Jane propped herself against the closed door, not sure how much longer she could stand.

Tina straightened and looked her over. "Do you need help undressing? Where is your shift?"

Jane fumbled with the buttons on her coat. "My what?"

"Shift. Nightdress. You know, to sleep in."

"Of course. In the biggest case."

Tina hefted the trunk onto the bed with ease and dug through it, finally holding Jane's flimsy gown up for inspection. "This little thing?"

"I didn't expect to be here in the winter." How many more times would she have to say that?

"Well, it will have to do for now. Here, let me help."

Together they managed to undress her down to her chemise and drawers.

"What's this?" Tina surveyed the bright sash with an amazed grin, walking right around Jane to get a better look.

Wearily, Jane said, "Mr. Langevin did it."

"Luc? You mean Luc did this?"

"Luc. Yes." Jane felt her cheeks turn pink and she sank onto the edge of the bed, all hope of modesty gone.

"Well, well, well." Tina stood with her legs spread, hands on hips. "And how does that feel?"

"How does *what* feel?" Merciful heavens, did she expect a description of the whole dreadful thing?

A burst of girlish laughter. "The bandage, of course."

"It holds the shoulder secure. That's what Lu — Mr. Langevin said it needed." She fought back tears of exhaustion, pain and humiliation. Would this forward little hussy just go—leave her to her misery?

"Good," she said. "We'll just leave it, then. Benny is fixing you a hot drink."

They slipped her nightdress over her underclothes and the sash. Jane swung her legs into bed. Tina left and returned almost immediately with a white crockery mug and a hot rock wrapped in a piece of old carpet.

Jane sipped her drink, then took a generous swallow. "I don't normally care for hot milk, but this is good," she said. "What's in it?"

"Honey." Tina tucked the hot rock between the sheets at the foot of the bed. "And brandy."

"Oh, but I don't drink spirits."

Tina took the empty cup in one hand and the lamp in the other. "You just did."

he purring finally woke Jane. She opened her eyes to the glare of white light flooding the room, illuminating the chinks of plaster that had loosened between the logs, highlighting the childlike rendering of a blue fjord nailed directly onto the wall over the bed. The entire world was silent, except for Siggy, the fat, lazy cat at the foot of the bed.

Jane snuggled in bed a while longer, then mustered the courage to toss back the quilt and step carefully onto the blue-and-grey rag rug, avoiding the icy floor. The four days she had been at the Stopping House had mostly been spent sleeping, waking now and then to the fear that her body would never work properly again. And during those four days it had snowed, great silent mounds layered one atop the other just like the snow globe. Only this time she was inside it. There had been no visitors. Luc had not come back.

Slowly, stiffly, she struggled into her clothes. With one hand, she tried to control the stringy strands of her hair, longing for the wherewithal to give her scalp a thorough scrub. She stepped into the tidy main room to be greeted by two more cats and the smell of coffee. The porridge pot had been cleaned and hung back on a hook over the stove, but the coffee just stayed there all day, stewing to the consistency of molasses.

She'd slept through breakfast again. She dipped some warm water from the reservoir on the stove, poured it into a basin on the washstand and, with only a bit of a mess, she managed to finish washing her face and hands just as Tina stomped in, coming from the storage room with a burst of crisp air, and with her pockets full of eggs.

"The snow has stopped. The sun shines." So did the round blue eyes under the blue knit cap. She put the eggs into a wooden bowl and doffed her sheepskin coat, looking for all the world like someone's little brother.

"Bjarne left early for The Crossing to deliver potatoes and eggs. We have a good market there now, with so many heading north." She hung her coat and cap on wooden pegs behind the door and shook her head until loose strands of hair flew into a feathery fringe. She regarded Jane with a half-smile, but her eyes were guarded.

The time they had spent together had been strained and distant. Jane felt as though Tina had been assessing her and found her lacking. For her part, Jane had no notion of how to associate with such an odd little creature.

"The eggs are in, the cows milked and the animals cared for. Bjarne won't be back until after supper, so we have the whole day to ourselves."

Jane knew by now that the animals included chickens, pigs, horses and two milk cows, not to mention a host of cats, both indoors and out. She had also learned that a stopping house was a rudimentary type of roadhouse. Besides Benny—or Bjarne, as

Tina preferred to call him—and Tina's room, it had the small room that Jane used, plus a loft that evidently held four single beds. This could be reached by a ladder that dropped from the ceiling in the front storage room when a rope was pulled. For 50 cents a man could get a warm place to sleep and a hot breakfast before heading out in the morning. Besides the income from the Stopping House and the sale of goods at The Crossing, Benny earned money from the pine furniture that he crafted—cupboards, tables, chairs and even the bowls they used.

"First we will have something to eat—something simple, I think. I will scramble the eggs and you will make toast." Tina rattled a wire toaster onto the stove and sliced thick chunks of bread.

Jane stood at the stove, determined not to let the toast burn. With quick, efficient movements, Tina cracked eggs into a striped bowl and whipped them into a froth then poured them into a sizzling pan. She sprinkled the eggs with salt and pepper before glancing at Jane with the saucy grin that seemed to lurk at the corners of her mouth much of the time. "How are you feeling today?"

"I feel quite rested now, thank you," she said.

They sat politely across from one another in a spill of sunlight, eating eggs and toast with fresh butter and wild cherry jam, drinking coffee so strong it made Jane's head hurt.

"The eggs were wonderful," Jane said finally. "I'm embarrassed by how much I ate."

"It's the weather. And the hard trip you've had. There are always good reasons to eat, and I like to have people to cook for."

"That's just as well," Jane said. "If I had to cook for myself, I'd starve to death. I'm not very good at domestic chores, I'm afraid."

"I thought missionaries had to learn how to take care of themselves. Especially when they are sent to the untamed wilderness." She flashed that grin again and to Jane's mind it looked downright sarcastic.

Jane placed her cutlery neatly on her plate and dared stare back into the round bold eyes—eyes that could turn hard and cold at a moment's notice. "I'm not a missionary."

Pale brows lifted in surprise. "This work with orphans that you told me about isn't your religious—what? Calling?"

"Indeed, it is not," Jane said, then realized that her comment and tone sounded very much like a rigid old missionary. She relaxed against the back of the chair and decided on the truth, told straight and plain. "I fell into this assignment with the very simple qualification of having the most time of anyone in our church. And, I'll admit," she held her gaze firm, "money of my own to help pay the way."

"How long will you be in Canada? Do you have a lot of orphans to account for?"

"No, we chose four to investigate. Two, Billie and Suzette, we knew were in trouble and needed our attention. Then there was John, who just seemed to have disappeared. We've sent more, of course, over the years ..."

"Years? You've been sending them for years?"

"Not just us," Jane said defensively. "Various organizations have helped with the effort. I think the first group came about 30 years ago."

"Hundreds of them, then?"

"More like thousands."

"Thousands!" Tina whistled through her teeth, a sharp taunting sound, then asked, "What about number four?"

"Four?"

She counted them off on her fingers. "Two in trouble, one lost—that's only three."

"Ellie is the fourth and she is in a very good situation."

"But you needed to help her do well?" She tilted onto the back two legs of her chair, her hands behind her head.

I did decide on the truth, Jane thought. "No, I visited Ellie so that I can stand before a meeting of our mission's wealthiest contributors and tell them how successful the placement was, and what a fine cause this is."

For some reason, that took the smirk off Tina's face. She nodded her head. "Ah, yes. Tell people what they want to hear."

"In the end, it would seem that I'm not much better at finding lost children than I am at anything else."

Tina didn't even blink. "Why do you say that?"

"One child, Billie Thomm, seems to have eluded me."

"Ee-loo-dead?" Tina repeated, bringing her chair onto all four legs with a thump.

Jane sighed and looked away. What was the point? She fingered a loose strand of greasy hair, thinking she might be better off sleeping on the floor of Louise's tipi; at least no one had watched her every move.

Jane rose to clear the table, and Tina jumped up to help her. "Let's do the dishes and then have a bath," she said.

"A bath?"

"Yes. And wash our hair." She waved her hand at the vast sea of snow beyond the window. "Snow makes wonderful water for washing hair."

"You have a tub?"

This time the sardonic look was accompanied by a trill of laughter. "Certainly I have a tub. Did you think we're not civilized enough to have a tub?"

Jane's cheeks burned. "I didn't think at all, I'm sorry. I just haven't seen many tubs lately and the thought of one is a pure delight."

Tina nodded. "I'll bring in the snow and your job will be to keep both stoves, this one and the one in the front storage room there, burning hot. Can you do that?"

"I think so."

Before long, both stoves were covered with pots and pails of snow that sizzled and popped as it melted. The tub, a marvellous bronze hipbath, warmed before the open oven door. Jane found scented soap and talc in her toiletry bag and Tina supplied a pile of striped towels.

"I believe it is getting colder and colder out there," Tina said as she dumped a last armful of wood into the box beside the stove. "It will be very cold by morning."

But it was a golden afternoon. Wintry sun soaked into the pine furniture and reflected from the slick log walls. Wood crackled in the stove, cats purred and steam rose from pots, then collected on the windows, where it froze in sparkling streamers. The smells of coffee and scented soap permeated the very rafters.

Tina went into her bedroom for her nightclothes and returned with a man's blue-and-white striped flannelette nightshirt, which she offered to Jane almost defensively. "Someone left this here last year," she said. "I washed it, but he never returned. It will be warmer than your little shift."

Jane took it with her good hand and pressed it to her cheek. "I love flannelette," was all she said.

Tina's shoulders seemed to soften. "Do you need help undressing?"

"Perhaps—the sling."

She stepped close to Jane, bringing with her the smells of hay and milk and the outdoors, reaching right around her to unravel the sash. Standing face to face, Jane had no choice but to look at Tina and then to follow her gaze down to the scrapes that had begun to fade on her chest.

"Did the horses make those marks?"

"The horses?"

"The horses, when they hurt your shoulder," Tina said.

"No. That happened before we left the lake."

Tina turned her back, making a great show of gathering her knitting. "One of the students at the mission?"

Jane quickly shed her last bits of clothing and sank into the tub. "Ahhh. This water feels like warm velvet."

"Snow makes that kind of water. Try to get your shoulder down into the water and move it around." The rocker squeaked. "You should be using it as much as possible so it doesn't stay stiff forever."

"Would that happen?" Jane peered through the steam at Tina.

Tina shrugged. "Why take the chance? Exercise is always good to get your strength back. Something gentle at first. Like knitting."

Jane slid deeper into the tub. "That's something else I don't know how to do. I only had a couple of lessons from my governess, years ago."

"You could learn now."

"Could I make myself some mittens?"

"Well—maybe you could start with a scarf. Now then, you didn't say. Was it a student at the school?"

"No." In her warm and misty cocoon in the tub, Jane experienced a return to that odd distance she had felt at the time, as though she stood outside a window and watched a stranger live her life for her. Should she tell it all? What did it matter, with this forward little woman? Someone would come by soon and Jane would be gone anyway.

In a cool and antiseptic voice, she recounted the filthy hands, the foul breath, the fear so encompassing that she couldn't bear it, had to remove herself from it. When she had finished, she realized that Tina had stopped knitting and rocking. Common sense returned.

"I'm sorry," Jane said. "I didn't explain that very well. I didn't mean to offend or—disgust you."

"You explained it very well. Better than I could have. Let me help you with your hair." Tina rose and stepped to the tub, bringing the enamel hand basin with her.

Alarmed at the woman's proximity, Jane sat up and slopped the washcloth over her bare chest.

"Bend forward." Tina pushed Jane's head between her knees.

"Merciful heavens!" Before Jane could catch her breath, a deluge of warm water cascaded over her head. Spluttering, she saw Tina's very competent hand dip the basin into the tub and slosh more water over her head, into her eyes, ears and even her mouth. Then strong fingers massaged soap onto her scalp, once, twice, before more water rinsed the suds away. In no time, Tina wrapped a large, soft towel around Jane's head, then returned to her rocker.

Jane stood, fumbling a towel around her wet body, clambering out of the tub so quickly that she barked her shin. Turning to find her nightclothes, she came face to face with Tina, stark naked, blithely pouring a bucket of hot water into the tub. She twisted away quickly.

She heard Tina slide into the tub with a contented sigh. With care, Jane eased her shoulder into the flannelette nightshirt. It hung loose and wide and too short by at least three inches, but seemed more comfortable than anything she had ever worn.

From the depths of the tub, Tina said, "I have some men's socks that will cover all that bare skin."

This is how it starts, Jane thought, the slide from ladylike apparel into men's clothing.

Jane's light wrapper fit snugly over the heavy nightshirt. She curled up on a gaudy, gold velvet lounge with knitting needles and dark blue wool, pulling a brown afghan over her lap.

"Do you know how to begin? How to cast on?" Tina watched her over the rim of the tub.

"Yes, that much I think I can remember. I'll try, anyway."

"That's a good place to start."

A comfortable quiet settled on the room. Jane concentrated on her knitting and Tina tilted her head onto the back of the tub and hummed along with the kettle.

A silver kitten finished her nap and stretched as only a cat can stretch before she saw Jane's ball of wool and pounced, turning herself inside out. Jane's stitches were gone. Tina laughed and stood straight up, water shimmering on her pale, child's body. Jane ducked her head and started to cast on stitches again.

By the time they had bundled their coats over their night-clothes and hauled out their bath water, the day had faded into evening. Coal-oil lamps were cleaned and lit, spreading a liquid yellow light across their shoulders as they bent close to the stove, drying their hair in front of the open oven door. They made a supper of bread and butter and tinned herring in tomato sauce, which tasted much better than it looked. For dessert they had leftover rice pudding with heavy cream, and in deference to Jane, a pot of tea.

"How long have you been here?" Jane asked.

"Going on three years."

"Are you ever homesick? Do you miss Sweden?"

"We're not from Sweden. Everyone just calls us the Swedes. Like Luc. They call him the Frenchman, but he was born and raised in this country and so were his parents and grandparents before him. Probably back a couple of hundred years."

Jane picked up her knitting. "And has your family been here for a couple of hundred years, too?"

"No. We came from Minnesota." Tina rose abruptly. "Popcorn would be good, yes?"

As she rattled corn kernels into the wire popper, Tina went on, "Louise and Rosie and the rest of them, their people have been here for hundreds of years. Their winter camp is only about an hour away. We could visit them when you're better."

"Oh, I'd like that," Jane said, and put her mess of wool aside to enjoy the popcorn.

They drank cooling tea as the timbered walls complained with the cold, and in the firebox pieces of wood dropped with a splutter. Jane felt lulled by the warmth until Tina took a leather bag down from a shelf and removed a corncob pipe. With what looked like years of practice, she filled the pipe with tobacco from the bag, pressed it into the bowl and lit up.

Jane was reminded again that she was a long, long way from home.

Finally. A small yellow light flickered in the distance and Luc knew they were near the Stopping House.

The snow had stopped and the temperature had been dropping all day. They should have stayed at The Crossing until morning and tackled the trail in the light of day. He could see the outline of Benny's rig ahead, could hear the squeaking complaint of the sled runners on the snow. The sharp bark of a coyote drifted over the snow once and then fell quiet. Even the coyotes stayed home tonight.

It wouldn't have hurt anything to spend the night at The Crossing. But that was Benny. Wouldn't leave Tina alone for one night even though she had that Englishwoman with her this time. Not that she would be anyone to rely on.

"I'll be back in a couple of days," he'd told her. Then they had all got work loading the scows that would take the pemmican down the Athabasca River to Fort Chipewyan. By the time Matt got on his way, the snow had settled in for good. It wasn't as if he'd promised to get the woman back to South Edmonton. Hell, he'd clearly told her she would have to find her own way back. He had other things to worry about, like opening his cabin for the winter and getting some venison hung in the shed so he would have something to eat.

Benny's team picked up their pace when they realized how close they were to a warm stall and a bucket of oats. His own four horses followed suit. This year he could afford to leave them with the Swedes until spring, not have to worry about finding feed for them near the cabin.

He recognized the smell of flowery soap as soon as he walked in the door, but there was something else in the air that took him some time to recall. Popcorn. It must be nearly 20 years since he'd had popcorn. Luc and Benny toed their moccasins onto the mat at the door and went into the main part of the house.

"Hello, you two. I'll get you something to eat," Tina said.

Luc sat at the end of the table and stretched his legs, feeling the stiffness in his shoulders wash away with the rich smell of coffee and the easy talk between Benny and Tina. Maybe Benny had the right idea after all—coming home to this was worth a cold ride. He looked down the length of the table at the English-woman. "How's your shoulder?"

She pulled a brown blanket closer around herself, then pushed the loose hair back from her pink face. It occurred to him she wasn't as old as she wanted people to think.

"It's a bit stiff, so I'm trying to use it more. Maybe even make some mittens." She showed him some uneven-looking knitting and a hint of dimples. The last bit of tightness went right out of his neck.

Tina put a plate of salmon sandwiches on the middle of the table. "Her arm is too sore to travel."

"Weather's too cold, anyway," Benny added.

Luc raised his eyebrows at the missionary woman to ask, Do you agree? She responded with a shrug and a small nod that seemed to say, They probably know more than I do. Relieved, he sat forward and reached for a sandwich. Now he wouldn't have to make excuses about not being able to take her back. He told himself that someone would come through with a wagon before too long and she could catch a ride to the train.

The sandwiches were good and the coffee strong and hot, the way he liked it. Tina brought him and Benny each a bowl of canned peaches and some kind of sweet bread with raisins. You could always count on a good feed from Tina.

With a warm fire and a full belly, Luc pushed his chair back from the table and crossed one ankle over the other. Between them, he and Benny managed to make entertaining news out of the few happenings at the settlement they had just left.

"There are more tents along the river this year than last. A few people are looking at land, but most of them are hoping to go north for gold," Benny said.

"And Billie? Did you see or hear anything of Billie?"

They turned to look at the woman on the lounge. She had been quiet all night, listening and watching. It seemed as though she found a lot of pleasure in life from observing everyone else.

"No," Benny said. "The kid you described — I asked around and no one's seen him."

"There are only about a hundred people at The Crossing," Luc said. "And most of the men and boys turned out to help with the scows. Good money for all of us. Thomm wasn't one of them."

Benny poured more coffee. "Matt will keep an eye out for him when he comes back in a week or two."

"Youngsters are tough," Tina said. "He'll show up sooner or later."

They sat on into the evening, drinking coffee and talking. Luc had to admit it was a lot more comfortable than anything he could have found at The Crossing. But he had to get up early in the morning. He stretched and stood to go upstairs.

"Oh, wait, please," Jane said. She rose from the lounge in one motion, all hair and eyes and big grey socks, then went into her room and returned with his sash and mitts. "Thank you."

He took the sash but handed the mitts back. "You'd better keep these for a while."

Her cheeks turned pinker. "Perhaps you're right. Thank you."

eleven

 he old Ulster overcoat dragged on the ground behind Billie, gathering up the powdery snow and spilling it into the backs of his boots. He'd had to put up with a preachy old woman at the Presbyterian Church in order to get the tatty garment, but it had proved to be worth it. The burned hole down the side, with stringy bits of frayed thread, stank of scorched wool but it kept most of him warm as he picked his way to the lean-to. He stayed close to the rear of shacks and sheds, out of sight as much as possible. This part of town didn't have real streets or alleys for a fellow to hide in.

He nearly stumbled over three Indians, huddled against a wall out of the wind, their feet wrapped in old newspapers tied up with hide strips. They didn't pay much attention to him and he couldn't tell if they were drunk or nearly frozen to death. If *they* couldn't stay alive in this sodden outhouse of a country, who could?

Billie worried his broken tooth with his tongue, trying to protect it from the cold. It pained him like nothing he had known before, worse even than the wrist he'd broken during his short stint as a chimney sweep. He had fallen three floors, bouncing and heaving off the sharp corners of brick and stone all the way down. The master had threatened to break his other arm, he'd made such a din and a mess. Ah, well, that was long ago and almost seemed like good times, looking at it from where he was now. He felt weak and shaky, slogging through the snow. It was pain that did that, he remembered. Pain and hunger.

Not much to show for his tramp through the cold today. He braced himself for the abuse he would get when he came in with only a bit of firewood and a packet of rolled oats. He really shouldn't care about a tongue-lashing. Who could curse with more flair and fury than his own ma? That had never killed him. But there was something downright evil about the quiet stream of filth that spewed from the Dook, especially now he was brought so low.

The lean-to had been patched many times with cardboard and tarpaper and now it had snow piled up the side of it. Some old-timers had told him to do that, said it would make it warmer. He thought at first they were greenhorning him, but they were right. It didn't make any sense, something as cold as snow making a place warmer, but it did.

No light greeted him through the suppertime dark. Billie hoped that someone had left water so he could cook the oats. He would have liked something more for his hollow belly, but folks around here were on to him now. No one had caught him red-handed, but they watched him closely. And when he couldn't pilfer as much anymore, they'd had to move out of the Princess and onto the fringes of the camp, where even the railroaders didn't tarry after dark.

Billie went in and closed the door. Cold as it was, the place reeked of dirty bodies and rotten food. He fumbled in his pocket for matches and lit a stub of a candle. In the corner, right where they had been dropped weeks ago, were the two fine suitcases.

The Dook had ranted in that low, deadly way of his, spittle flying from his rotted teeth, slathering blame like rat poison. "This is what you've brought us to? With your sloth and slovenly ways, your insolence among your betters?"

The shack he stood in now was about 12 feet square, made of poles and old packing crates—rubbish, mostly. Belonging to many, it was owned by no one, and if the smell of it meant anything, it had sheltered hundreds who were down on their luck. The bright blankets that Billie had stolen from a clothesline lay tangled about, so dirty it was hard to tell what colour they had once been. Cigarette stubs were ground into the dirt floor near an empty sealer jar from last night's card game.

Moonshine. Billie could still smell a whiff of the pure alcohol and remembered how quickly the men who drank it lost what little sense they had. All but the Dook. He just sat there with that smirk, drinking tea, pretending to be friendly and ending up with a few coins at the end of it all.

With an old shingle, Billie scooped the ashes out of the make-shift stove, a cranky contraption that had started life as a copper boiler and now sat atop an overturned galvanized washtub. He dumped the ashes on the ground outside the door on his way to the well for water. He hoped it wasn't frozen up again.

The hut heated quickly, being so small. Billie put a tin of water and the oats on to cook, then ate more than his share while they were still half raw. The Dook wouldn't know how much he'd had, and would just call him down anyway. Billie's tooth throbbed so much there was little pleasure in having something to eat or even in knowing that he had taken most of the porridge. He felt only a sad and angry knot sitting with the oats in his belly. And then, because he had learned in the past that being sad never helped anything, he turned himself over to the anger until it festered inside him.

He kicked the blankets into a heap near the stove, wrapped his overcoat around his shoulders and settled himself, grateful that this frozen hell was too cold to grow bugs, because they would have a nest full of them. The food and the fire warmed him, but the most comforting thing of all was thinking about his special tobacco tin, buried under a tree in the river valley so no one could take it from him again. The thought of his own money, skimmed here and there from the take he was supposed to give the Dook, warmed him in a way that the smoky stove and heavy porridge could not. It was a sore temptation to go there, but he daren't. His tracks would show in the snow. Wouldn't this lot like to get their hands on his money? To gamble and drink and the rest of it? No, he would leave it alone until he had enough, and then go and pluck it out just before the train left. He would never take a chance on someone fleecing him again.

Billie considered getting some more water to wash himself. He was itchy with grime and his hair hung in oily strings down his neck. Maybe Bessy had some scissors. Maybe she would even help him cut his hair.

Coal Chute Bessy. The only person he knew hereabouts who was worse off than he was. She worked right here in shanty town, plying her trade in musty bedrolls and filthy quilts for as little as an onion or a rabbit, skin and all. Two of the Dook's cronies, Jake and George, liked to get drunk and threaten to take Billie to her for an *education*, and that would get the Dook to ranting in his high-falutin' language until foam gathered on his lips and turned solid and crusty like old custard. The Dook hated women, even poor Bessy, who wasn't a woman, really, just a feeble-minded girl whose brain would never catch up with her body.

Footsteps squeaked in the snow outside. Thinking about the Dook must have brought him. That was Ma's way of reasoning, anyway. The farther someone was from your mind, the farther they were in earnest. The Dook dragged more than the cold in with him; he brought a new kind of tension as well.

"There's oats on the stove," Billie said quickly, before the ranting could start.

"Porridge is it, Billie, m'lad?"

"'Twas all I could get."

"Well, I'm pleased you had a good feed. You'll need your strength in the next while. We've much to do." In a feigned afterthought, he added, "I had a nice bit of roast beef myself, over at the Princess."

The uneasiness that had entered the shack with the Dook swelled. Billie felt a moment of panic: had the ferret found his stash? He took a deep breath and tried to be casual, sarcastic, even. "They let you back in there?"

The Dook picked up one of his suitcases and smacked it onto its side. "I had the price of my meal, didn't I?"

"I'll finish the oats then," Billie said.

"You do that, son. You do that." The Dook rooted through his shirts. "Must have my laundry done soon." He snuffed at the wrinkled wad of a shirt and must have determined that it was the least dirty of the lot. "Jake and George will be stopping by this evening." He spoke with such importance that it was downright silly.

Billie dipped his spoon into the coagulated lump of oats and let him babble. Worried as he was about his tobacco tin, he wouldn't give the ferret the pleasure of asking where he had found some money.

The ferret's real name was Frederick James Smythe. Smythe,

not Smith. Billie knew this because he had found ways of going through everything in the suitcases, and had read some letters. Smythe's kin lived back home in England, and they wrote to "Dear Freddy" when they sent money—and told him over and over not to come back yet. Until "things" settled down. It seemed his family knew about his association with young boys and didn't want him getting caught near home, where their neighbours might find out about it.

"Do we have coffee or tea to offer our business associates when they come?" Frederick James Smythe asked amicably.

Business associates now, were they? Billie didn't bother to lift his head. "An' where would I get coffee or tea?"

"Well, buy it, m'lad! Look here," he said to get Billie's attention. He pulled a wad of bills from his vest pocket and peeled a few back. "How much do you need?"

Billie nearly choked on his oats, no longer able to pretend that something momentous hadn't happened. "Have a good day at the cards?"

The little man giggled and squirmed, thrilled to get a rise after all. "No, no. But a good day at the post office!"

It took a few seconds for Billie to get the full import of that. The Dook had finally got some money from home. He tried to keep his face straight and not look impressed; he just eyed the roll of money, new vistas opening up in his mind.

Out loud he said what the ferret already knew, "The shops are closed by now."

"Right you are." Smythe jammed the wad deep into his pocket so fast Billie wondered if he had really seen it. "You always were my best source of information in these matters. A good ally. Good allies are hard to find, what say, boy?"

"I say, don't flash that lot around here or you'll have your throat cut by morning." Billie wasn't sure what an ally was, but he didn't like to miss an opportunity to remind the Dook that when it came to surviving on the rough edges of town, he needed Billie a lot more than the other way around.

"You're awfully smart-mouthed for a boy that the law, and a few other people, might like to talk to. Maybe it's time I found that missionary woman and turned you in. Find myself a new travelling companion, a true aide-de-camp."

Billie let that pass. It was a common enough threat this last while, especially since the Dook had witnessed Billie's handiness with the knives he carried. It was all this talk about going north, where gold was lying around on the ground for people to pick up, that kept Billie from bolting, or at least that's what he told himself. Anyway, where else could he go?

Gold now, that had his interest. Billie longed for a chunk of gold to cover the raw stub where his front tooth used to be. How the gold might get from the ground and into his mouth was a mystery to him, but he knew it could be done; he'd seen lots of gold teeth. With gold, he could do anything he wanted.

"Never mind old grievances, shall we, lad?" Smythe said. "Let's get tidied up here. We've plans to make, things to organize. That's where our good friends Jake and George come into the picture."

At Billie's look of scorn, the Dook gestured widely. "Don't you see, boy? They can get us to the Klondike. Good help, cheap help, is hard to find at the best of times, and we know these two—their habits and, uh, indiscretions, if you get my meaning. Something like you," he finished with a smirk.

And you as well, Billie thought to himself. He would keep what he knew about Frederick James Smythe in his head until he needed it. He would also keep to himself the fact that he could read and write. In fact, Billie had learned that keeping his mouth shut protected not only his broken tooth, but the rest of him as well.

So he lounged on his blanket without a word as the Dook went on and on with his grand plans of heading to some frozen wasteland with George, who even Billie could see was downright evil, and Jake, who wasn't much brighter than poor Bessy. A passel of nincompoops the devil himself would turn his back on. Only, from the accounts he'd heard, the devil liked things a lot warmer. Billie had listened in when the cranky old newspaperman said it had been 29 below last night. Below what, Billie wasn't sure, but he did know you could die out there if you weren't careful.

Then, over his worry and through the cold, cold air, he heard the distant cry of the train whistle as it ploughed its way into the station, wailing long and loud and full of hope. Billie dug deeper into his blankets and let himself dream of better things to come.

Matt wondered if he'd ever get used to the cold, learn to revel in the danger of it the way some did. The men liked to sit around the barracks on a cold night and compare frostbite stories. They'd all seen black, rotted toes and fingers, and someone had even seen a whiskey trader from Montana with no nose. It made good telling in front of a hot stove, with a coffee in one hand and a full pipe in the other.

Not nearly so romantic from where he sat now, looking down at the crust of frost on his horse's neck. He glanced back at Gibbs, but the young trooper seemed to be keeping up just fine, a scarf wound round his face so that only his eyes and lambskin hat were exposed. They followed a trail made by a couple of wagons—a week or 10 days ago by the look of the snow that had sifted into the runner tracks. The first set could have been anyone; the second looked like they might be Luc with his two rigs hitched together.

The thing that made the cold bearable was a grey band of cloud low on the southwestern horizon. Could be nothing; could be a mild spell moving in. They were about three miles out of The Crossing, headed back to the detachment in Edmonton with mixed news about the pemmican. They'd met the troops and their Indian guides at Fort Assiniboine, but the cold snap threatened to freeze the Athabasca River before they could get back to Fort Chipewyan. The last leg of the trip might have to be made by dog sled. A lot of work for a bunch of hungry dogs and their even hungrier owners, but it would be worth it.

In 1882—or was it '83?—when their troop had ridden out on patrol to meet up with a band of renegade Indians, he had carried some wild notions in his head about the painted faces of savages who would want to relieve him of his nice curly hair. He had looked instead into the faces of starvation and a sorrow so big he had to avert his eyes. He hoped he had done a little something this week to offset that kind of thing.

By now he knew where the tracks were headed. Straight to Benny and Tina's. Matt checked on Gibbs one more time and waited for him to catch up. "Ready for a cup of coffee?"

Gibbs pulled the scarf down so he could speak. "Sir?"

"Just over the next rise is the Stopping House. Tina makes a fine cup of coffee."

The corporal managed a stiff grin and sat a little taller in the saddle.

Coming down the knoll and across the creek to the Stopping House, they could see three people in the farmyard. So Miss Priddle was still here. Matt raised his arm in salute and got a cheery wave from the smallest of the three.

The place had been well laid out with the solid log barn to the north, blocking the worst of the winter wind. Spreading to the east of the barn was a fenced paddock of 8 or 10 acres where Luc's four horses foraged beside Benny's team in the snow with their heavy front feet, looking up at the newcomers and snorting the snow from their nostrils. About midway between the house and the barn Benny had built a henhouse, close enough to discourage coyotes, but not so close as to fill the Stopping House with flies during the summer.

Gibbs dismounted first, landing stiff-legged in front of Benny. "Good morning, sir."

"Name's Benny, son. Got time for coffee?"

Gibbs's face lit up like a kid on Christmas morning.

Beside the well, Tina hoisted a bucket of water in each hand. "Come in, come in. You must have had an early start."

"Yup." Matt met Jane Priddle's hazel gaze. "Good morning, Miss Priddle. How're you feeling?"

She looked back at him steadily. He felt he had become pretty good at determining what people were thinking, but she appeared easier to read than most. What he read was that she knew he had hoped she would be gone by now.

"Tina feels I need a few more days before I'm ready to travel. And no one has been through to South Edmonton since the snow. Except you," she added, with something like a glimmer of a challenge.

He lifted his brows, but couldn't find it in himself to muster a smile. The last thing he needed or wanted was to have to drag her back to South Edmonton. Her dark blue skirt hung wet and stained around her calves and she'd wrapped what appeared to be a knitted brown blanket over her thin grey coat. She cozied half a dozen eggs inside Luc's big mitts. Looked like one of those street urchins she was chasing after.

Well, he certainly hasn't changed his opinion of me, Jane thought, as she entered the house behind Benny. I'm one more foolish newcomer for him to keep track of this winter. The two men were hanging their coats in the storage room as she unlaced her soaked boots and placed them near the outer stove to dry. She looked up to see the policeman studying her bedraggled skirts and stained boots.

He waited for Benny to go into the main room before he spoke. "Not meant for this weather, were they?"

"Somewhat like me. Is that what you're saying, Sergeant?"

One shaggy brow shot up at her sharp tone. "You're very quick, Miss Priddle."

"Yes, I am. I didn't intend to be here in this weather. And I don't intend to stay any longer than necessary, so you needn't worry about me."

He stood back and motioned for her to precede him into the welcoming smell of coffee, as the younger officer came in from the cold. She had to pad ahead of him in her squishy wet stockings, her head as high as possible.

"I have no intention of worrying," he said in a dismissive tone.

"What are you not worrying about, Matt?" Tina asked gaily.

"Poorly dressed Englishwomen stranded three or four days from the train," he answered bluntly.

Jane cringed and escaped toward her room as quickly as possible.

"Oh, we've talked about that. She just needs some moccasins and a decent coat." Then, with a glance at Jane's wet skirt, Tina added, "And maybe some pants."

I knew it, Jane thought. I knew it would come to this. She passed through the long room with hot cheeks and her hair hanging down her neck while three men and that impish little woman looked her over, found her wanting and grinned at one another.

She closed the door to her room with more energy than necessary and started to peel the freezing wet stockings from her legs. She snuffled and swallowed a lump in her throat, feeling more hurt and lonely than she had in days.

ach new day came reluctantly, but when it did, as though to make up for its shyness, it burst through the grey dawn with a furious blush of rose that hung for long minutes in the east, then paled to mauve and finally a clear blue. Jane watched the mauve slip away with apprehension.

"This will be a new kind of shopping trip for you, I guess," Tina said. "But at least we'll come back with some decent footwear."

"You should get started." Benny shoved a piece of wood into the stove. "You have a good day for a walk. Only six or seven degrees of frost."

Jane donned her stiff boots and an old green mackinaw of Benny's as Tina wrapped a loaf of bread in a tea towel and put it in a canvas bag along with a jar of jam. "I left some lunch for you," she told Benny. "Under the crock."

"Away with you. I can feed myself."

"Are you sure you won't come with us?" Tina asked.

He took her by the shoulders and directed her gently toward the door. "You will be very safe, the two of you. Nothing to worry about."

Tina's concern did nothing to put Jane's mind at rest. Thinking they must be worried about her, she mustered her courage and tried a light tone. "I can walk three miles," she said. "I've done it many times. If it seems like I don't have the strength, we'll turn back." Hefting the canvas bag, Jane stepped valiantly into the brilliant day. Tina followed.

The slice of moon from last night lingered overhead. Aware of the short allowance of sunlight at this time of year, Jane was keen to be on the trail. "Sooner gone, sooner returned," she said, and turned with a smile. She froze, her mouth open, as Benny placed a gun in Tina's hands.

Tina tucked the smooth wooden butt under her right arm with practised ease. "Just in case."

"In case of what?" Before Jane could recover from the shock of seeing the gun, Tina ran back to Benny, threw her left arm around his neck and kissed him, long and wet on the lips.

Jane sucked in a chestful of cold air, whirled away in mortification and stumbled to her knees in a snow bank. They had no sense of propriety whatsoever! And at night—the sounds and giggles that filtered through the thin wall. Really, the two of them!

By the time Jane had scrambled to her feet and kicked the snow out of her petticoats, Tina had glided past her, striding toward the ridge above the creek, chin up, small pointed nose sniffing the air like a pedigreed pup.

They walked single file, staying on high ground where the wind had kept the snow shallow and hard packed, heading in a south-southeasterly direction as far as Jane was able to determine, keeping the frozen creek to their right. Snow flowed away from them, levelling the low places, sculpting small bushes and clumps of grass into elfin mounds. They trekked on for 30 minutes through a landscape with no trace of human habitation; the only footprints were their own and the faerie scratches of bird's feet on a snow slate. Feeling more confident of her footing, Jane lifted her head and straightened her shoulders.

Puffing to the top of a particularly steep hill, Tina stopped beside an exposed rock. Centuries of weather had gouged it into the rough shape of an old man's head. Deep crevices were partially lined with clumps of silver moss, like scraps of beard from a bad morning shave.

Tina perched on the rock, leaning the rifle beside her. "Rest a bit," she said. "Are you tired? Do you need to turn back?"

"No, I'm fine so far." Jane slid her bottom onto the rock so they were shoulder to shoulder. "It's all so vast. If I turned around twice, I think I would lose my direction."

"Well, don't turn around twice," Tina responded. Then, softening her tone, she dropped to one knee before a clean patch of snow. "It's easy." She dropped a mitt on the snow. "This mitt is the Stopping House, north of where we are now, and," she dropped another mitt, "this is south, where Louise lives. The creek that we're following," she pointed to the frozen stream, "is west of us." She drew a wavy line.

"What is the creek called?"

"It doesn't have a name yet. If we stay long enough, maybe they'll name it after us," Tina said, in her offhand way.

Jane couldn't help smiling. "I would love to think there is a stream somewhere in the world that has been named after someone I know."

Tina turned from her drawing to stare at Jane, but didn't seem to have one of her usual retorts. Returning to her map, she drew a deep trench to the west of the creek. "This is the Athabasca River, and here," she jabbed a hole in the snow beside the river, "is The Crossing. It makes a triangle, see? Our home, Gabe's camp and

The Crossing—all about three miles from one another. Oh, and here, across the creek and closer to the river, is Luc's place. All are an easy walk for us."

The rifle began to slide on the rock, so Jane carefully pulled it back up. "Do you know how to use this thing?" she blurted.

"Of course I do," Tina returned to her perch on the rock.

"What would we need it for? Are there bears around here?"

"Ya. But they should be asleep by now. At least I hope so, because this little thing wouldn't be of much help to us." She patted the butt of the gun.

Jane turned her head sharply and stared at Tina.

"It's only a .22," Tina apologized.

"What does that mean? Twenty-two what?" Jane demanded.

"Twenty-two calibre. It's a very small rifle." Tina unfastened her coat and let it hang from her shoulders.

"Well, if it's too small for bears, what did you bring it for?"

"Nothing, I hope."

"Nothing?"

"It would scare off a coyote. Or a wolf, if one should happen to come out in the light of day."

"Wolves?" Jane whispered, searching the bushes.

And then, so quiet Jane wasn't sure she heard properly, Tina said, "It could kill a man if he came close enough."

Jane stared at Tina again, but when nothing else was forthcoming, she asked, "Who taught you to shoot a gun?"

"Bjarne, of course. Who else?" Tina rose and put her coat on, tucking the rifle under her arm.

"I thought it might be your father or a brother."

"I don't have a father or a brother," Tina curtly. "Let's move on."

Jane hurried to follow.

They came eventually to a trail of sorts, with wagon ruts cutting back and forth atop one another. Jane needed to watch more carefully so she didn't turn an ankle.

"Almost there." Tina cut down from the hill and onto the creek bed, striding forward like a Norse goddess.

Wisps of chimney smoke drifted over the treetops on both sides of them. Jane noticed cabins, some no taller than herself, and tents and tipis of various sizes sheltered throughout the bushes on either side of the creek. She thought it might be a lovely situation in the summer. Then the dogs started to yap and she wondered how she could have forgotten those wretched creatures. Two of them attempted a snarling approach and were rewarded for their boldness with a clout on their snouts from the cold blue muzzle of Tina's gun.

"Well done," Jane said, as she watched them slink away.

"Kristina Holte."

Distracted by the dogs, Jane walked right into Tina's back.

"Uncle," Tina responded in the same formal manner.

Standing directly in their path was a man so tall and thin and old he could have been one of the aged birch trees that surrounded them. His clothes flapped out from his body like the peeling bark of the trees, only more colourful. Combination underwear, frayed and faded to a pale pink, showed from under a blue striped sweater unravelling at the cuffs and waist, worn with denim trousers that stopped three or four inches short of his moccasins. That gap on his shins was filled in with the pink combinations. Over all this he wore a red tartan waistcoat and, on his head, a battered black sombrero weighted down with silver coins. A real live scarecrow, Jane thought.

"This is Jane Priddle," Tina said.

"Jane Priddle," he repeated in the same velvety monotone.

"How do you do?" Should she call him Uncle as well? Then, realizing what he had said, "Who's Kristina Holte?"

"Jane needs some moccasins," Tina said. "We are going to see Louise, to see if she can help us."

The man called Uncle looked at Jane's sorry boots and nodded his head several times. He touched the brim of his sombrero by way of saying farewell, then stepped off the path so they could proceed.

Jane turned to have another look, but he had blended back into the birches. "How *old* is he?"

"Who knows? Ancient. Older than Kokum, I've been told. He stays here all year round now—wanders the hills and creek, lives off the land."

"Who's Kristina Holte?" Jane asked again.

But they had arrived at the door of a small cabin much like the others. A washtub leaned against the log walls, and deadly-looking metal traps hung on wooden pegs. Snow melted on the roof and dribbled down onto a haphazard woodpile, where it froze.

Tina stomped the snow from her feet, knocked, then walked in without waiting for an answer. They stepped out of the glare and were swallowed up by the smoky gloom inside.

Jane stood with all eyes on her sodden skirts. She pulled them up to mid-calf to admire a pair of soft suede moccasins, beaded with rose patterns in red, blue and green. Her brown lisle stockings hung steaming beside a squat black stove. She let her bare toes explore the silken leather of the interior of the moccasins.

"They're magnificent, Emilie," she said.

"They really are." Tina straddled a kitchen chair backwards, her chin resting on her hands. "I feel a bit jealous."

"I'm still learning," Emilie said. "I was never allowed to do beadwork at the mission."

Jane dug into her skirt pocket and handed the girl one dollar in coins, the remuneration Tina had suggested. Emilie's brown face lit up where she sat on the floor, wrapped in a striped blanket and looking for all the world like a younger version of Kokum. Whatever the nuns had tried to turn her into, they had failed.

Around the room were gathered the women of Jane's adventure—or misadventure. Julie bounced from one person to another, chattering all the while, and Rosie sat quietly at the table nursing her new baby. Kokum and Tina shared a pipe of pungent tobacco.

Jane didn't realize how hungry she was until Louise handed her a slab of bread slathered with jam. Conversation swirled around her like the cold draft on the floor. Her upper body felt hot from the stove that belched heat and smoke. She felt only a touch of guilt at enjoying herself so much when she should be worried about the Home Children and how she would get back to South Edmonton.

"How that arm?" Kokum spoke around a mouthful of bread and jam.

All eyes turned to Jane.

"Better, thank you, but still stiff."

"Need to soak it."

"Yes," Jane agreed. "Tina advised the same treatment. I've soaked it a few times."

"Where?" the old woman asked suspiciously. "Where you soak it?"

With surprise, Jane answered. "Why, at home—at Tina's home. In the tub."

"Tub. Bah!" Kokum said, as she groped along the table, then

dug with two fingers directly into the jam jar. Louise smacked her hand but not before the old woman had a generous scoop of jam to suck from her fingers.

"Needs to soak in the waters up in the mountains." Kokum pointed her sticky finger in Jane's general direction. "Best thing. Spirit waters."

"She's talking about hot mineral springs," Tina said. "You know, the ones that come up out of the mountain smelling of sulphur. Bjarne and I went there once and it was heavenly."

"I'd love to go," Jane said. "How far from here?"

"Four, five days," Louise said.

"Oh. That far."

"Maybe in the spring," Tina said. "When it's easier to travel."

Talk went on to a New Year's party called Reveillon that everyone was invited to. But Jane felt she really must be gone by Christmas, never mind making a trip to the mountains in the spring.

Finally Tina leaped to her feet. "Look how low the sun is!" she said. "We must leave now."

Jane scrambled to pull her damp stockings on as Louise hunted out a pair of Gaston's socks to add some thickness inside the moccasins. "I'll return them soon," Jane promised.

"Yes, yes," Tina said impatiently, taking her gun down from the hooks over the door. "Up and away."

Dusk kept pace with them as they hurried home. Jane's feet felt exposed and vulnerable with only a thin layer of hide and two pairs of socks between her and the elements. But the wool of Gaston's socks seemed to soak up the dampness of her own stockings so she didn't feel the cold too badly.

"You'll get used to them," Tina said, watching Jane pick her way around hard clumps of snow. "Still, we're taking the shortest route home, straight across country. We shouldn't have left it so late."

The temperature plummeted with the sun and Jane felt the bite of cold on her nose and cheeks. She bunched her skirts in her left hand and hoisted them to her knees in order to keep up with Tina. Her wet boots hung over her shoulder in the canvas bag.

Twenty minutes later, Tina stopped and waited for her to catch up. "How are you managing?"

"I'm doing well." In truth, she had a stitch in her side and her shoulder ached.

"Bjarne will be worried," Tina said sharply and set off again.

Jane thought she heard an eerie sound off in the distance, but chided herself for having an overactive imagination. She concentrated on Tina's footprints and her disappearing back.

But it came again. Jane stopped, trying to quiet her rasping breath. She heard it clearly, drifting over the frozen hills, a long, forlorn lament—a hundred times more chilling than the weather.

The hair stood up on her arms. "Tina," she called.

On the trail ahead, Tina stopped and turned. "What is it?"

"That sound. What am I hearing?" Jane asked in a trembling voice.

Tina stood still, poised to listen. "A lone wolf."

Jane caught up with her. "A wolf? Is your gun of any use against a wolf?"

"He doesn't care about us. He's just letting other hunters know he's out tonight."

"Other hunters?"

But Tina was already on the move, covering a great distance before Jane could catch up. They came out into the open, crossing a large meadow perhaps a half-mile in length, rimmed on the west with scrub brush and naked poplar. Jane's legs trembled as she struggled to stay close to Tina.

She reached to pull her collar higher around her face, and as she did so, thought she saw shadows moving under the bare trees. Really, she had to be more sensible. She had an idea that they were nearing home and making good time. But there. She saw it again. She stopped and stared until her eyes blurred. There were two shapes, one lurking under the trees, the other braver, coming more into the open.

"Tina?" She didn't recognize her own voice.

Tina came back. "Now what? Are you hurting?"

"I saw something. Under the trees over there."

Tina dropped her mitt to reach into her pocket. "Where?" she demanded.

"Near the trees. When we stopped, they stopped too."

"They?" Tina took a cartridge from her pocket and opened the chamber on the gun.

"Like dogs," Jane whispered. "Would those awful dogs have followed us?"

"Oh, I see them now," Tina said. "Coyotes." She tucked the loaded rifle under her arm, picked up her mitt and set off again. "They're just curious. If they come too close, I'll fire off a shot and they'll disappear."

"How many are there?"

"Two. Probably a pair. They usually mate for life and hunt as a pair. When they have pups, they take care of their family and each other. Good parents, coyotes. Even the males take care of the pups."

Somehow, that didn't make Jane feel any better. She trudged on with weak knees and, heaven forbid, a running nose. Everything ached, especially her feet in the shapeless moccasins. What had she been thinking, "going native," as they said?

Tina started up another hill. "Not far now," she called. "Looks like we lost our friends. They didn't want to come out in the open."

Jane focussed on each footstep, her eyes on Tina's back. She couldn't imagine getting separated. What would become of her? Then, miraculously, a light flickered ahead of them. Someone with a lantern.

Tina stopped dead still. "Bjarne?" she called with trepidation.

"Ya. Hallo," the familiar voice called back.

Tina stated the obvious, more to herself than anyone else, Jane felt. "It's Bjarne. We're home."

Jane stumbled the last few yards, thinking Tina had seemed much more frightened by the appearance of a man than she had by wild predators.

 **H**e'd run out of reading material and it was too early to trap. With a yearling moose hanging in the shed to freeze, time weighed heavy on Luc's hands. He thought he might as well walk to The Crossing and catch up on the news.

The Crossing wasn't much different from many of the other new outposts he'd been in over the years. He picked his way down the centre of town through filthy snow and steaming horse manure. Next to the livery stable the lumberyard had a drunken-looking fence that was supposed to protect the property. He stopped to read a hand-printed sign asking interested parents to meet at the Gallaghers' place to talk about forming a school board. That was Vera Gallagher for you—fussing about a school even though she never had any offspring of her own. But churches and schools and settled families were good for business, and good businesses were something Vera Gallagher did know about.

And if the presence of a school wasn't enough of a sign of the press of settlement, a couple of surveyors strutted around in their leather jackets, making a big show of looking through their fancy equipment. He scratched his half-grown beard and heaved a sigh. He was a squatter, just like Gabe and the rest of them. His friends would be packed off to one of those reserves, or just have to shove on—to any place left in the country the settlers didn't want.

Luc turned his back on the surveyors and stared at the falling-down shack that housed the Imperial Bank and the Dominion Land Office. Things could be different for him if he wanted them to be. Over the last few generations, his Indian blood had been watered down enough to turn his eyes as blue as the sky and his opportunities as endless. All he had to do was walk into the land office with $10 and fill out some papers, and his cabin would be legally his own.

He didn't want to make that decision; he wanted a drink. But there was no tavern here yet. If old lady Gallagher wanted to do something useful, she could build a tavern. He'd been in similar situations, where towns and people started pressing in, and it usually meant that it was time to move on. It didn't feel the same this time. Must be getting old. He went in search of Father Benoît. Maybe he had something to read and a little advice. Or news of Joseph—a man could always spend time with his big brother.

Tina and Jane bumped into The Crossing snuggled into layers of hay in the bottom of the sleigh, cuddling crates of eggs so they wouldn't freeze or break. Benny brought the team to a stop in front of a general store.

To Jane's curious eye, The Crossing looked like nothing more than a sloppy stage set propped up against the horizon. A badly devised stage set at that, erected by children who had tired of their play and wandered off to find something else to do.

They carried the eggs into the store and placed them on the counter before going in search of something for Jane to wear.

They looked over some woollen skirts, but Tina would not be satisfied until she held a pair of men's brown corduroy trousers to Jane's waist.

"They'd fit fine," she said. "And if not, I'll alter them."

"I don't know," Jane began. But she did know—had known for some time—that she envied Tina's freedom in trousers. When would she ever have another chance in life to wear pants?

"Is that you, Mrs. Lindstrom? I said to Mr. Gallagher, 'I think that's the Lindstroms and they might have fresh eggs and butter. Just what I need to do a little Christmas baking,' I said to Mr. Gallagher."

A solid woman charged to a halt in front of Jane.

"We did bring eggs and butter," Tina said. "And potatoes."

"Good, good," Mrs. Gallagher said, but her eyes were on Jane. "I don't believe we've met."

"This is Miss Jane Priddle," Tina said. "A missionary from England."

A pair of sharp, unblinking eyes widened under a strong brow in an otherwise ordinary face. "You don't say?"

Tina grinned. "Looking for orphan children."

Mrs. Gallagher was short but sturdy; some might even say plump. She looked Jane up and down. Her overpowering presence did not have as much to do with her size as with the no-nonsense attitude that she carried before her the way most women carry a handbag. Her black Persian lambskin coat was bald and shiny over her belly; the matching fez-like hat had been jammed over her greying hair. For the first time in months, Jane knew exactly whom she was dealing with. Her mission was full of Mrs. Gallaghers, and that included her own Aunt Evelyn.

"Just one in particular. His name is Billie Thomm. Would you know of such a youngster?"

The woman finally blinked. "Don't concern myself with any one youngster in particular, now you mention it."

"Of course not," Jane responded. "And why would you?"

Tina grinned.

"You just a missionary, or a teacher, too?"

"Neither," Jane said brusquely.

"Neither one? But I thought ..." Mrs. Gallagher turned the force of her attention on the store owner, Carl, as he arranged the eggs on the counter. "Two dozen of those for me, Carl. And mind none of them are cracked." Turning back to Tina, she said, "They didn't freeze on the way here, did they?"

Tina shook her head, but before she could say anything, Mrs. Gallagher spoke again. "You'll come and have lunch with Mr. Gallagher and me."

"Oh, no," said Tina. "We've brought our own, there's no need ..."

"Bring it along. We'll put it all together and have a nice picnic."

While Tina tried to splutter her excuses, Jane eased over to the counter to pay for the trousers she had scrunched under her arm.

By the time she turned with her parcel, Mrs. Gallagher was pushing a defeated Tina out the door in front of her. They picked their way toward a dozen tents huddled under a few bare poplar and wolf willow. Across the river, a thick green forest reached a finger down from the north, but here the prairie made a last stand, and good windbreak was hard to find.

The Gallaghers' tent had a real door on real hinges, and when it opened the whole tent shook. "Tina and her friend have come for lunch," their hostess bellowed to someone in the depths of the tent.

Jane ducked her head to follow Tina. The tent was about

12 feet by 16, and so heaped with cartons, furniture and odd bits of clothing that it was hard to see the floor.

"This is Mr. Gallagher," his wife said, without looking in the direction of the startled man who stood quickly.

"Good day, ladies," he said, pulling his waistcoat over his belly.

Mrs. Gallagher pointed to a clear patch on an overstuffed sofa. "Sit," she said.

Jane sat. Mr. Gallagher sat opposite her on the edge of a rumpled, narrow bed, as though he had just crawled out of it. The centre pole out of the tent was about eight feet high and the pitch dropped to three feet at the walls, walls covered all around with varnished tongue-and-groove boards. Gilt-framed pictures hung askew over the dressers and chairs that were jammed against the walls.

To Tina's generous lunch of headcheese sandwiches and oatmeal cookies, Mrs. Gallagher added tea, a tin of peas, barely warmed, and a few scraps of cold, greyish roast venison.

"Time to eat, Mr. Gallagher," she said, and handed him a fine china plate loaded with sandwiches and cookies. He balanced the bounty on his knee and proceeded to eat as though he hadn't had a decent meal in years.

"Come to the table, Miss Priddle," Mrs. Gallagher said. "There—at the end."

Jane did as she was told, not daring to look Tina in the eye. It was beyond doubt one of the most bizarre luncheons she had ever been to.

"So, you say you're not a teacher?" Mrs. Gallagher asked.

"No, most certainly not ..." Jane began.

Mrs. Gallagher propped her elbows on the table and slurped her tea with relish. "Still, you've had your schooling. At least you speak well enough."

"Yes, I've had my schooling." Jane rescued one of Tina's sandwiches before they all disappeared.

Mrs. Gallagher flapped her hand. "No offence, I'm sure. Out here we're just happy to have someone who can keep order in the classroom. The serious business of reading and writing, well, that would be a real bonus."

"But I'm not ..."

"Well, give it some thought. We'd sooner have a man, of course, but we can't be too fussy. At least you're a good-sized gal."

Tina nearly choked on her cookie.

Jane sat taller and looked down her long nose with a steady stare and a steadier voice. "The *serious business* of investigating the whereabouts of our mission's children is why I am here, and if I could interrupt long enough to describe Billie to you, perhaps you will find your memory improved. No offence, I'm sure."

Tina's eyes widened with something that might have been respect.

Mrs. Gallagher put her cup down with a resounding chink. "My memory is perfectly sound, thank you very much. And as far as lost children, why ..."

"Not lost children. Home Children. Children who have been sent to Canada by organizations like our mission, or Barnardo Homes or, oh, Bessy Macpherson's Home of Industry."

Mr. Gallagher piped up. "Macpherson? That would be like the one your sister had that time, remember? Back in Nova Scotia, that was."

A look of pained embarrassment crossed his wife's face. "I don't suppose it's the same thing at all."

"'Course it is. They sent away for a girl to help your sister in the house." He turned his attention to Jane. "Awful stout, Mrs. Gallagher's sister. Hard time getting her house cleaned up."

A yelp of laughter escaped from Tina. "Sent away for a child? Like ordering drawers from the Eaton's catalogue?"

"Oh, that stunted little thing," Mrs. Gallagher said with a flap of her hand. "What use was she, I ask you?"

Tina tilted back in her chair with a wide grin. "You mean you can't return these kids, like you can return your drawers if they're too small?"

"Don't be coarse, Mrs. Lindstrom. I mean, look at you." Mrs. Gallagher ran a scathing look over Tina's masculine garb.

But her husband was not to be deterred from his opportunity to speak. "Sad little thing. Scared of her own shadow."

"Yes, well," Mrs. Gallagher began collecting dishes. "Enough of that."

"What became of her?" Jane asked, not sure she wanted to hear the answer.

Mr. Gallagher leaned toward Jane as though to impart a secret and said, very quietly, "Took her own life."

The grin disappeared from Tina's face. Jane closed her eyes briefly.

"Nobody knows that for sure," Mrs. Gallagher declared. "I mean, she had such a sullen disposition, always moaning and weeping and making everyone so uncomfortable. She only needed to get busy and ..."

"How old was she?" Tina asked quietly.

"Nine or 10, I believe," Mr. Gallagher said. "Afraid to leave the house for months. Scared of wild animals, scared of the dark, scared of men—frightened of everything. Then one day she up and walks as pretty as you please, down along the lake and right into it, clothes and all. Her body washed up a week later."

"Merciful heavens," Jane breathed.

"See? Mentally defective, like most of those street Arabs they send over here," Mrs. Gallagher said as she rose, signalling the end of lunch. "I'm sure you have other business in town."

A sober Tina gathered the scraps of her lunch and followed Jane into the fresh air. She laid a hand on Jane's sleeve. "That won't happen to your Billie. He sounds a lot tougher than that."

"Billie is. But what of Suzette?"

∞

Jane sat at the pine table, her writing case in front of her. Everything felt wrong. Or nothing felt right. Christmas had arrived and she was still here. Her shoulder had healed, save an occasional pang, and the bruises and wounds from her encounter with the drifters had long faded.

It was Christmas Eve. She should be walking to church with the family, her father and brother leading the way, followed by Caroline and Aunt Evelyn, with Jane tagging behind. They would sit in their own pew, not at the front, but near enough to proclaim some measure of status in the congregation.

Jane stretched her legs before her and reached her arms toward the ceiling. She stood and went to the box on the wall beside the stove, where she found a match and scratched it down the small piece of sandpaper tacked to the wall for that purpose. With the lamp lit, she returned to her chair and took a page of fine stationery from her writing case.

"Dear Father, I don't know if this letter will arrive at your door before I do, but I feel obliged to try to communicate my whereabouts and present circumstances."

She twiddled with a strand of hair at her neck. She wasn't convinced that her father would be unduly concerned for her, but by writing to him, she could avoid writing to Aunt Evelyn.

"First, let me assure you I am well. I have extended my search for one of our wards, a youngster by the name of Billie Thomm, which has brought me to a settlement some distance from the postal service. This evening I will celebrate Christmas Eve at the local church and, with luck, find a rider who will be headed in the direction of the railroad soon and who can carry this letter for me."

The little silver clock on the shelf ticked its way toward supper. Tina and Benny would be in soon from doing the evening chores. They would have a simple meal of cured pork and cabbage, left over from noon. The Lindstroms did not celebrate Christmas, it seemed, and any attempt Jane had made to learn why had been dismissed brusquely. Tina had, however, presented Jane with a beautifully knit green sweater that went well with the brown trousers she wore.

"This part of the New World has severe winters, the like of which we could not imagine at home. In fact, the temperature this afternoon is 22 degrees below zero! It is just such weather that has caught up with me, and has forced me to seek refuge with the Lindstroms, a husband and wife who run a type of roadhouse called a stopping house. These stopping houses differ from our roadhouses in that there are no drinking establishments attached, so you can put Aunt Evelyn's mind at ease. I am not falling into the hands of purveyors of strong spirits."

Jane rose and poked a chunk of wood into the stove. She paced the kitchen once, twice, then sat again, straightening her back like a schoolgirl. How much need she mention? Her injury handling the horses? Not necessary. Her encounter with a pair of thugs? Never.

"Sergeant Edwards, a member of the North West Mounted Police, has offered to look out for Billie, as have prominent local business people."

There. That sounded impressive. Mrs. Gallagher would recognize herself as a prominent business person, and Sergeant Edwards would hold true to his promise to "keep an eye out for the kid," if only to see Jane on her way back to England.

"I have resigned myself to the possibility of not finding Billie at all, and with that in mind, will return to the East at my earliest opportunity. There I will try to set to rights the wrong that has been done to poor Suzette."

She knew, even as she wrote, that her father wouldn't know, or care, who Suzette was. But she also knew he would nonchalantly pass this letter on to Aunt Evelyn, and thus the mission society. Would they see Suzette's situation as being anything more than her own foolish fault? Jane was pleased to realize that she didn't care. She only knew that she would use what little influence and resources she might have to free Suzette from the Home for Wayward Girls where she had been sent.

"I would like to take time to describe to you the amazing geography and wildlife I have encountered during my adventure, as well as the native people who have been very kind to me. However, friends will soon collect me to go to church, which is some three miles distant, so I must ready myself. I will have many colourful stories to share when I am once again under your roof."

She absolutely would not mention that the only church in the vicinity was Roman Catholic. She wasn't even sure herself why she felt the need to go, especially since Benny and Tina were staying snugly at home. She seemed to have developed a yearning to have something—one thing—in her life that felt normal. And church seemed the logical choice.

By the time she reached The Crossing, Jane had only two things on her mind and neither of them was normal: she had to get out from under the foul old buffalo robe that covered her to her chin, and she needed to get into the church to warm up. She'd never encountered anything as vile as the buffalo hide. It was hard and crusty on the underside and mottled on the outer with clumps of mangy hair. It shed bits that stuck to her lips and fluttered up her nose, but when she shoved it away she nearly froze to death, in spite of wearing all her petticoats and two gabardine skirts, one atop the other.

Guy's sled slid to a halt in frozen ruts in front of the church but the inviting yellow light from the windows proved to be a cruel illusion; it was no warmer inside the church than it had been outdoors. Jane looked around for a stove that didn't exist.

Women and children filled the simple plank benches; men and boys stood at the back and along the sides. Jane followed Louise and Julie to the only vacant seats, right at the front. Father Benoît, brown of face and hair and eyes, entered from the back of the church, and the ripe smell of his unwashed body and cassock reached them even in the cold air. His small, round, blinking eyes made him look like a badger coming up into the daylight after a long sleep. Sharp and wary, set in a round, unlined face, the eyes missed nothing. Jane realized that by the time he arrived at the altar, he knew exactly who was in his congregation. And who wasn't.

For two bone-numbing hours the humble congregation in the wilderness listened to the ebb and flow of the ancient Latin text. Father Benoît's voice contradicted his appearance and Jane began to enjoy his rich baritone as he slid from French to Latin, pacing the front of the church and down the aisle, reeling his people in. She understood hardly a word of it, but it was musical in its own way. It was easy to imagine that this little group, in their freezing wooden box of a church, existed all alone in the middle of this vast land, brought together by the cold, the spiritual ceremony and the compelling voice of their shepherd. Jane's mind drifted on the chants she didn't understand. Where was Billie tonight? Not in church, she was certain of that, but it would be nice to think he was somewhere warm and safe.

Luc leaned against the back wall and let the familiar words wash over him. They had been ingrained in his soul since he was a little tyke in skirts, so the responses came automatically. He let his mind wander, thinking of his family back home, probably listening to the same service, and his brother Joseph, standing before his own congregation somewhere in the territory, saying these words himself. He felt a little melancholy, maybe even lonely, if he let himself dwell on it.

He'd had to smile when he saw the Englishwoman pull back from Father Benoît. Paul Benoît's smell took some getting used to, for sure. Still, he had a way with words and the local people seemed to accept him. And Father Benoît returned their acceptance 10 times over, loving every single one of them as though they were his own children.

Luc ran a hand over his winter beard and stretched. He could tell from the cadence that the service was coming to a close. It must be past two o'clock in the morning, the coldest time of the night. The candles had burned themselves down to nubbins. People moved stiffly, trying to limber their frozen joints.

Outside, a couple of lanterns flared to life, drawing people like moths. Some of the congregation tried to sort out who was going where for the traditional tourtière. Others hurried into the dark, heading off to stoke the stoves in their cold tents or shacks. He saw Vera Gallagher tug at Jane Priddle's arm and heard her say, "You should stay the night with us."

"Oh, no thank you," *l'Anglaise* said. "I came with Guy and Rosie Delorme and they will take me back."

Vera pulled her aside, muttering in a low voice so that the taller woman had to bend over to hear. Luc could make out only a few words but he heard enough to know that the newcomer was getting an earful of all the reasons not to travel around with a bunch of breeds in the middle of the night. Luc saw the polite innocence slide from Jane's face as she straightened to her full height.

"Thank you for your concern," she said, in that accent that usually grated on his nerves, but sounded just right this time. "The Delormes are waiting for me."

As she turned away from Vera's pinched face, Jane's gaze met Luc's, and in that moment she pulled the corners of her lips down and rolled her eyes toward the sky. It was a natural, honest kind of thing to do and he couldn't help grinning back.

n Christmas morning, Matt polished the brass buttons on his uniform with a piece of old flannel underwear. When he finished with the buttons, he used the rag on his boots. Now and then it was necessary to wear his full dress uniform; on other occasions, like now, it was downright practical.

He checked himself in the mirror in the hallway, rubbed his hands over his freshly shaven chin and shrugged into his heavy buffalo coat. Sheepskin mitts and a beaver hat and he was ready. Nothing like a smart uniform on Christmas Day to guarantee a home-cooked meal. Outside, the tail end of last night's snowstorm whistled across the river, polishing the exposed ice as he crossed to South Edmonton.

It was nearly two o'clock before the congregation straggled back into the cold. By the time he got down the steps, Matt had received three invitations and decided in favour of the Kendals. Their lumber business had flourished during the last couple of years, so one more at the table wouldn't be a hardship. He plunked down on the open end of their wagon to hitch a ride.

"Make room there, Edwards." Charlie Taylor huffed his boozy breath in Matt's face as he shoved his bottom onto the wagon box.

Too late, Matt remembered that Mrs. Kendal had a soft spot for all bachelors on holidays, not just the ones in uniform.

They doffed their coats in the front hall and Kendal took the two men straight into the parlour, asking, "What's your pleasure, gentlemen?"

Taylor's eyes lit up. "Is that a good Scotch whisky I see there?"

"It sure is. Can I pour you one of the same, Matt?"

"That would be just fine. Just fine, thanks." The smell of roasted turkey saturated the house as Matt sank into an overstuffed chair and propped his feet on a matching stool. The clatter of pots drifted in from the kitchen. He congratulated himself on not having eaten breakfast.

"So," Taylor boomed. "What's the last word on that damned bridge? We ever going to get that *dad gum* train across the river?"

"Well," Kendal lowered his voice and glanced into the dining room, where his youngsters were setting the table. "You know what it's like with politicians."

As Matt swirled the drink around in his glass he sympathized with what Kendal tried to hint at. "Charlie," Matt said. "We're a couple of lucky old bachelors to have the company of young ladies today. Maybe we should talk like respectable gentlemen for a change."

For his efforts he got a dirty scowl from Taylor, a sigh of gratitude from Kendal and a twinkling smile from the oldest daughter as she poked her head around the door to the dining room. He winked at her and she ducked away, blushing.

In spite of Taylor's monotonous complaints, the afternoon

slipped into evening. They were stuffed with turkey and ham, potatoes and fluffy white buns. Mrs. Kendal passed around mincemeat tarts and shortbread cookies. Coffee came with brandy and a bowl of striped candy. The middle daughter pulled pages of music from the piano bench and plunked at some Christmas songs. Even Taylor shut up and pretended to listen.

The soft snap of the fireplace held Matt longer than he usually would have stayed, but finally he had to say, "Well, it was a fine meal, Mrs. Kendal. I thank you very much for your generosity, but I'd better head home now."

"Don't go without a plate." Mrs. Kendal did what he hoped she would—pressed a pie plate wrapped in brown paper into his hands. "In case you're hungry later."

"Bless you," Matt said, and then heated up under the collar, because it wasn't the kind of thing he normally said.

"And I have one for you, too, Mr. Taylor," she said.

Poor Taylor was left with the decision of whether to stay with the bottle of brandy, or insult the cook and miss out on a nice plate of leftovers.

"C'mon, Charlie," Matt said. "I'll see you home."

While he waited for Charlie to find his overshoes, the oldest daughter, the one he had winked at, handed him an orange. "If you put it in your pocket, it won't freeze on the way home." She blushed and disappeared up the stairs.

He and Charlie walked down a deserted Whyte Avenue, the squeak of the snow under their boots echoing through the night. Frigid air pressed the smoke from the chimneys back down around the houses. They cut through an opening between the newspaper office and the mercantile store, then Matt waited while Taylor climbed up the creaky outdoor stairs to his quarters above his office. He heard the door close and waited to see a light come on.

As he turned to leave, he caught a movement by the garbage dump behind the store next door and heard a snuffling kind of sound as something flitted across the street and disappeared into the shadows of the train station. They shouldn't be allowed to throw stuff out in the alley, he thought. It just encouraged stray dogs, or even coyotes. He stepped over a snowdrift to get a better look. Just some rotten fruit, frozen solid.

Heedless of the cold and the thought of his own warm room waiting for him, Matt walked across the empty street to the train station. Despite the brandy in his belly, all his instincts and training sharpened his senses and softened his tread.

Matt almost missed him. Then he spied a dark form huddled in the corner behind a baggage cart. One lone bulb under a tin shield over the station door struggled to light a few feet of the platform. It didn't reach Matt and only made it to where the boy crouched. And it was a boy. Not a dog or coyote after all. He was eating something from the garbage, flinching with each bite.

Matt felt his own supper sit heavy within him. He had seen hunger before, had seen people die of hunger. Didn't make it any easier to look at now. Who was this boy and why was he here alone on Christmas night? Matt stepped onto the platform and heard the hollow echo of his boots announce his presence. The boy pulled back tighter into the shadow, still as the cold night air.

Matt kept his voice even and friendly. "Out late tonight?"

No answer. When he was about six feet away from the cart, Matt saw a bare head with dirty blond hair. "Pretty cold out here. Shouldn't you be at home?"

"I like the trains." The ordinary words were loaded with anger, in a deeper voice than Matt was prepared for.

"There's no train tonight."

"I know that. I just like it here. Bugger off."

"You hurt or something?" Matt had a hunch the kid had been crying, and this wasn't the type to cry easily.

The boy didn't answer for a long time, then, as though he was too weary to bother being angry, "I got a bad tooth. What's it to you?"

In the back of Matt's mind, behind the turkey and the brandy, he tried to put something together. He stood longer than was sensible in the cold, talking to a foul-mouthed brat who deserved to freeze his ass off. Still, no one should be hungry at Christmas.

"Look, I got a plate here. Lady who fed me supper gave me extra to take home."

The hostility lessened in the waiting silence. Then the kid pushed himself on his backside, closer to Matt and farther into the light. "I like the sound of the whistle," he said, trying to seem indifferent to a plate of food. "From the trains."

"So do I, but we won't be hearing it tonight."

The boy stood up, weaving a little in the fuzzy light, a youth in a man's ragged topcoat, no hat or mitts. Outside their circle of light, the world disappeared. Just the two of them in the cold and the quiet.

Matt reached across the few feet separating them, offering the pie plate, his mind still churning. There was something here ... "My name's Edwards," he said.

It was one of those split-second moments when several things fall into place at once. Matt reached farther across the distance, which pulled the sleeve of his greatcoat back. The cuff of his red serge uniform, with the knot of gold braid, shone despite the feeble light.

"Bloody 'ell!" The kid jerked his frozen hand back as though he had been shot. But more telling than his reaction to a police uniform was his automatic slide into a street accent that didn't come from anywhere in this country. He started to bolt.

"Billie! Wait! Billie!" It worked every time. There was something about a person hearing his own name that stopped him for those few seconds that Matt needed. He shucked his mitt in his armpit and reached into his pocket. "Here." He tossed the orange that the Kendal girl had given him. Billie caught it in one hand, already on the run, disappearing into the black void.

But now Matt had a face to put to a name.

Billie crouched low, running hard through the scrubby bare trees toward the lean-to. He dreaded going back there, but what else could he do? A copper! Of all the luck.

A bad day was turning even worse. He'd slept late, cold and hungry in the shack, thinking the Dook might part with some of his hoard of money for a decent meal. But all he got from that direction was some panting and pawing.

Smythe hadn't tried that for some time and Billie was as surprised as he was sickened by his advances. He'd had enough — enough waiting for all that money from back home to turn into something besides hot air about the goldfields. Smythe took himself off to a restaurant every day for a good feed, leaving Billie to fend for himself, then he'd return to the shack and talk big about all the supplies and food he'd bought to head north. Talking and talking about food, and Billie's belly growling so loud it could be heard across town. Probably all lies, he thought. Mean ol' bugger.

Billie hadn't even known it was Christmas until he woke up with the ferret's hands pawing at him, muttering something about a special Christmas treat. Billie had reacted out of instinct, slashing out with his fists and feet. He was more surprised than the Dook when he landed a couple of good ones. By the time he got to his feet, Smythe had a bloody nose and held onto his privates, screaming and hollering until Billie thought he must be going to croak.

He got out of there fast. He'd wandered the streets since, watching families coming home from church, looking through frosted windows at tables loaded with all kinds of food. By the end of the day, he had ended up in the rubbish behind the shop where they sometimes tossed goods that hadn't sold.

Now, weaving through the tent town, Billie heard voices and laughter coming through thin walls. Even drifters had someplace to go. Nervously, he approached the shack, wondering if the ferret was there, and if he had really been hurt in the scuffle. What if he lay dead on the floor? But, as he neared the shack, Billie heard voices—lots of voices—loud and raucous. He stilled and listened. Jake and George, of course. Then there was the Dook's shrill giggle. So he hadn't done him in after all.

Billie stopped, ignoring the cold, and peeled the orange the copper had given him, sucking the sweet juice from his frozen hands despite his bad tooth. He gobbled the fruit and stuffed the peel into his pocket—he'd eaten peelings before, and he wasn't going to share one bit of his orange with this lot. He took a deep breath and opened the flimsy door, hoping the ferret wouldn't want to own up to his dirty behaviour earlier, nor the thrashing Billie had given him at the same time. Not in front of the others at least.

It stank worse than the pigsty on that farm where he had been beaten. They all looked up at him from where they sat on the floor. Jake and George, already on their way to being drunk, Coal Chute Bessy with her empty grin and someone new—a boy a bit younger than Billie. He remembered seeing this lad around town during the past few weeks and took a closer look. Skinny, sickly looking, but worst of all, he had the same dull look in his eyes as Bessy. And Denny.

"Well, well," Smythe said, flopping his arm around the new boy and fondling his ear. "Look who's come snivelling home."

Billie waited for the Dook to tell the rest about all of his failings, including the reason for the bruise that shone on the bridge of the man's nose, but it didn't happen. Then Billie noticed that they were all eating—empty bean tins lay about even as they dug into cans of sardines. Jake lifted his backside enough to break wind, the reek of beans and moonshine nearly taking everyone's breath away. Jake and George roared with laughter and Bessy grinned foolishly, but the Dook was furious.

"You uncouth blighters! Is that how you behave when I supply you with such a bountiful holiday meal?"

Billie took the opportunity to slide to the floor near the door, cracking it a bit so he could breathe. Bessy handed him a can of sardines and he quickly used the key to open the oily fish. With his bare hands, he stuffed most of the contents into his mouth before someone could take it away from him.

Smythe turned his full attention to Billie. "I dipped into our northern supplies so we could have a nice Christmas, and you run off as usual. I don't know why I put up with you, I truly don't." Then he ran his hand over the thigh of the kid beside him. The kid grinned up at the Dook as though he were Father Christmas. "This is Vlasek," the Dook said in a sugary voice. "My new companion."

The greasy fish landed on top of the acid fruit in Billie's stomach. He felt the whole mess rise up and threaten to spill all over the filthy floor. He opened his mouth and gulped his lungs full of cold air, once, twice, feeling saliva fill his mouth. He swallowed hard, determined not to puke, not to waste the only scraps of food he'd had all day.

"Close the door, you imbecile!" The ferret had finally realized the door was open a crack. "Letting the heat out as though you bought the coal yourself!"

"Yeah," said George. "You need a kick in the ass to smarten you up. Mr. Smythe don't really need you anymore, him havin' a new *friend* now."

Jake laughed and snorted, slobbering fish oil down his chin. He lifted his butt again and filled the shack with another putrid fart.

Billie thought the Dook's eyes were going to bug out of his head.

"Stop it, I say! Stop that right this minute!" the Dook screamed.

The men laughed louder; George leaned over and grunted until he managed to add to the stench. They rolled on their backs laughing, their feet kicking in the air.

Billie took a deep breath and scooted to the stove, which bellowed more heat than usual. He took some of the peel out of his pocket and broke it into tiny pieces, then scattered it on the hot stove. He'd seen his ma do that, when the midden out back got really ripe. Soon the clean smell of orange filled the shack.

"Well done, lad," Smythe said grudgingly, his eyes cold and calculating. "You always manage to find a way to make yourself useful, just when I'm ready to toss you out, don't you?"

"What'd you do there?" George asked suspiciously.

"Just threw some orange peel on the stove," Billie answered. "'Twon't hurt nothing."

Smythe's eyes narrowed. "And where did you come by an orange? The shops are closed today."

Billie took his time answering, breaking more peel into bits, swallowing hard to keep the fish and orange down in his belly, knowing he didn't have a place with this bunch any longer and wondering if he cared. Then he glanced at Smythe snuggling Vlasek up next to him, and knew he would hang around as long as he could, just to make the man's life miserable. And maybe protect the boy at the same time—better than he'd protected Denny.

"Got it from Edwards, over by the station," he said nonchalantly.

"And who, may I ask, is Edwards?" Smythe demanded.

"You know. Edwards—the copper," Billie answered, acting a lot more cocky than he felt.

Dead silence followed his comment. His hope was that if Smythe thought he was on speaking terms with a policeman, there would be no use in threatening to turn him in. And he'd heard the mission lady was long gone. He waited, casually tossing bits of peel onto the stove.

The two fools rolling around on the floor sat up slowly. "Edwards?" George said, low and threatening.

"Who be Edwards?" Jake asked his partner.

"'Member, at that camp full of breeds? The Mountie ..."

"Oh, shit," Jake whispered, staring at Billie.

"Who? What breeds? What are you talking about?" the Dook asked in a high squeal.

Billie sat tight, hoping he wouldn't get a good hiding, or worse.

"Nasty son of a bitch," George said, glaring at Billie. "Always snoopin' around, lookin' for trouble."

"You know a Mounted Policeman?" Smythe asked. His arm slid from Vlasek's shoulder.

Billie shrugged.

"Well, you're a deep one, aren't you? Still, maybe we could use an acquaintance like that," Smythe said with a sly grin, taking in the two drifters.

Jake and George glanced at one another, sobering up quickly.

"Yes. Yes, indeed." The Dook nodded his head, his beady eyes on Billie.

Billie leaned back against the wall, wondering if he would ever dare fall asleep again.

fifteen

ew Year's Eve had always been a quiet night for Jane. A glass of sherry with her relations perhaps, but most often she was in bed before midnight and welcomed the New Year at breakfast the next morning. On the last day of 1897, however, she and Tina washed their hair early in order for it to be dry by dusk. They pressed their best costumes, in Jane's case a garnet-coloured cashmere frock with gored skirt and mutton-chop sleeves, and debated whether to wear shoes or moccasins. They helped Benny finish the chores early, then packed their baked treats in the sled and set off for Reveillon.

The Bulls' camp was alive with lights from every cabin, and children and dogs ran willy-nilly from house to house. The party was well under way in Gabe's cabin, and they had to push through a cluster of men who hung around outside in the cold, smoking and drinking from sealer jars.

Then they were inside, where the few bits of furniture had been shoved against the walls. Two lanterns jiggled from hooks at either end, illuminating the centre of the room but leaving the corners murky. They dumped their wraps on a bed already piled high with clothes and babies, and turned to watch the dancing. Emilie came in, tossed her wrapper onto the bed and stood beside Tina. Jane's eyes widened. Emilie's red gingham dress was scrunched up at the front over a round belly. Dear God, the girl was in the family way. Jane looked quickly at Louise, but Gaston's mother was visiting calmly with the other women.

The serious business of dancing was in progress; the log walls began to sweat along with the dancers. The music was as wild as it had been at the lake, the dancers as frenzied. Unease crept up on Jane along with the cold draft around her silk-clad ankles. She searched for a corner to disappear into, then spied Louise at the food table.

"Now, you two," Louise was saying to a pair of rowdy boys. "You take one cookie each and make sure you eat it. If you can't eat it all, leave it for someone else."

"May I help with something?" Jane asked.

"No, no. You look so pretty. You should dance, like the other young people." Louise pointed with her chin, her hands busy with plates.

"I don't think so. It's too crowded for more."

"Never too crowded," Louise said, as Gabe came by and grabbed Jane, pulling her onto the floor.

Jane found herself being passed from one partner to another, bumping and jostling with other dancers. After several minutes, she stumbled and stopped by the table, begging off. "I can't," she panted. "My shoulder—still quite stiff." That was barely true, but she felt so self-conscious out there, bobbing around like a stiff old puppet, that she just wanted to blend into the wall.

Rosie came to stand beside Jane, her fussy baby on her hip.

"I see that Emilie, that is," Jane said quietly, "Emilie appears to be expecting a child."

"Yes," Rosie said. "In the spring."

Like Suzette, in the spring. Jane performed some simple arithmetic. "She was—uh—in the family way before we left the mission?"

Rosie nodded. "It was good she got away. They would beat her—take the baby away."

"Good heavens," Jane murmured. Would they take Suzette's baby away? Of course they would. She was only 15; someone would decide that a 15-year-old mother could not possibly manage to raise a child. They would be right. "What will happen to Emilie now?"

Rosie shrugged. "She will be a mother like the rest of us. Maybe, when Gaston can make his own cabin ..." She shrugged again. "She will be fine."

A blast of gunshots came through the open door along with war whoops and the howling of dogs.

She clasped a hand to her chest. "What on earth?"

"Just celebrating," Louise said.

At midnight, the dancing stopped to welcome the New Year. Jane filled her hands with plates of food and moved through the groups of people, relieved to have something to do.

Later, when Luc came back from a trip outdoors, he saw Jane propped with one hip on the edge of the table, her left foot swinging in time to the music. The Scotch whisky Uncle had been sharing gave Luc the courage to speak to the fiddlers.

He made his way through the crowd as the slow music started, took the Englishwoman's hand from her lap and stepped back so she had to follow. Her mouth fell open and her eyes grew huge.

"It's a waltz," he said. "It won't hurt your shoulder."

She hesitated, glancing around at the empty floor. Was she going to refuse him right here in front of everyone?

"They're playing it just for you." He counted on her not wanting to hurt the fiddlers' feelings. Especially Guy. He took one more step backwards, pulling her with him.

She looked suspiciously over at the fiddlers and Guy gave her a big wink. Luc cautiously slid a hand around her waist.

There was some good-natured complaining about the music. "For old men, this waltzing business."

A couple of boys, about 10 years old, mimicked them, falling all over themselves. Luc watched his partner's face, feeling as though he was watching a skittish colt, saw her glance at the brats, her cheeks bright pink. He grinned at her and started to shrug, then saw a flash of anger deep in her eyes. So she *could* get mad. "It's me they're laughing at," he said.

He could see she didn't believe him.

"It is," he insisted. "You're much better at this than me."

And she was. Head high, back straight, she followed his unpractised step without faltering.

"You have been to many dances, no?"

"No." She looked over his shoulder as other dancers came onto the floor.

"No? How did you get to be such a good dancer, then?" If he asked her questions, she had to answer. It was the polite thing to do.

"We learned at school." Then, apparently realizing what he had said, finished with, "Thank you."

"You learned to dance at school?" He held her away a bit, trying to get her to look at him. "What kind of school was that?"

She looked at him and he felt her relax a bit. "A girls' school. I was always the tallest, so I had to lead." A little smile. One dimple on her left cheek.

He bent closer and whispered, "Are you leading now?"

A bigger smile. Two dimples. "No."

He felt something warm trickle through him. Probably the whisky. He pulled her close. "Good."

The floor had filled up. Everyone loved to dance, even if it was a waltz. Luc manoeuvred them into a corner by themselves and let the whisky, or whatever it was, take over. He knew how controlled she usually was, but he had just seen her get a little mad, and now he knew she could smile without breaking her face. Maybe he could get her off balance a little more. It would be good for her.

In the corner, he suddenly twirled them in a complete circle and tried an exaggerated dip. Something trapped his legs and they started to fall. He heard her suck in her breath as he grabbed her to his chest and put his hand out to the wall to stop their fall. He didn't want to hurt her.

They stood up straight and looked down. She wore a dress the colour of good wine and the soft skirt had swirled around his lower legs and stuck to the suede of his high moccasins like poplar fuzz to a birch tree. They watched the skirt gently let go of the moccasins and drift back down. The music scratched to a stop.

He let his arms fall to his sides and she did the same. He grinned and shrugged. She smiled and shrugged.

The next jig started. Could he talk the fiddlers into another waltz? Never. She stood there, looking up at him expectantly. He was blocking her way. He moved aside. She looked at the other side of the room, then back at him. He was supposed to take her back over to where the women were sitting. They couldn't walk together, so he took her hand and led her, both walking sideways, facing the dancers.

"Thank you," she said, all serious again.

He'd never been more serious in his life. "My pleasure."

The spirit of the holidays emptied into the new year, drained away by long dark nights and short days. Snow and cold kept most folks bound to wherever they had ended the old year, making them cranky and hard to get along with. But for Matt Edwards, it could be a blessing. The fewer people moving on the barren landscape, the fewer he had to worry about.

It was mid-January, and Matt and Gibbs were headed back to Edmonton after burying some fool who had been heading north for gold. He had died of scurvy in a snow dugout near Fort Assiniboine.

Now, coming up on the Stopping House, Gibbs asked, "D'ya think they have the coffee pot on?"

"Always do," Matt answered.

In short order they were at the scrubbed pine table, eating bacon and eggs and drinking strong coffee.

Tina fussed at the cupboard, cutting them some fruitcake. "What brings you out our way?" she asked.

Matt glanced at Jane Priddle who sat at the end of the table with wide, cautious eyes. He related the finer details of the death by scurvy, although not for Tina's benefit; she had seen stuff like that before. "He still had three of his molars clutched in his frozen fist. Always lose their teeth."

Jane watched and listened without flinching, elbows in a green sweater on either side of her cup. When he finished his story and went back to his eggs, she got up to help Tina wash the dishes. He had a good look at long, long legs in brown corduroy pants.

"Saw your boy, Billie," Matt said.

"Where? Was he well?"

"Well?" Matt shook his head. "I won't try to fool you, he

wasn't in great shape. Cold and hungry and looked like he'd been in a scrap—a little banged-up."

She pressed a towel to her chest. "What happened?"

Matt shrugged. "Don't know. I tried to talk to him, but he ran off. Doesn't much like uniforms, your friend Billie."

"No, I'm sure he doesn't." She looked hard into Matt's eyes. "Where was he?"

Matt shifted in his chair. "He was eating from the garbage out back ..."

She closed her eyes for a second, then looked back at Matt.

"... out back of a mercantile store in South Edmonton."

"Merciful heavens," she said to no one in particular. "Does he have no place to live? What is he doing to get beaten up?"

"Well, you heard about the remittance man he was hooked up with. Not exactly a secure place for a boy."

"What's his name, this remittance man? Do you think he's the one who hurt Billie?"

Tina and Benny kept their silence, looking from Matt to Jane and back again. Gibbs just kept eating everything that Tina brought him.

"Name's Frederick Smythe. I hear he showed up around town with a few bumps himself, so I'm guessing, when all is said and done, Billie can take care of himself. He's just finding all the hard ways of doing it."

"That sounds like Billie. And we haven't done such a good job of taking care of him ourselves, have we?"

Matt bristled. "We?"

"Our mission, of course. Billie could have got into this much trouble at home, and at least been in familiar territory."

Matt nodded. "And familiar weather. He was pretty cold when I saw him."

"God help him. I don't suppose you've heard of anyone headed back to South Edmonton?" she asked.

Tina and Benny exchanged looks.

"No, but I can put out word," Matt said. "What do you hope to do?"

"Help him get to Vancouver, if that's what he wants. Or back home. I owe him that much, at least."

Matt sat back in his chair, holding her gaze, thinking he might have been wrong about this woman. She stood in the middle of the warm kitchen, a taller, quieter version of Tina with the same red knuckles from outdoor work and a lean, healthy look about her. He could see her mind turning over, thinking what to do next.

"If you're not in a hurry, I'd like to send some letters with you," she said.

"Sure," Matt said. "If Tina has more coffee."

She went quickly into her bedroom and returned with a fancy writing case. "The first letter," she explained, even as she wrote, "is to the Imperial Bank on Whyte Avenue. They have some money in my name and I'd like them to release a draft in this amount," she underlined something on the page "to Miss Suzette Merriman, at this address in Ontario."

Gibbs stopped chewing and stared at her. Could be the first woman the young trooper had ever known who had a bank account in her own name.

"And *this* letter," she went on in a businesslike way, starting a fresh page, "is to Suzette herself." She paused and twiddled her pot of ink. "I suppose, while I'm at it, I'd better tell that awful home that Suzette and her baby are in my custody as of now." In short order, she slid three envelopes and a 10-cent piece across the table. "Can you see to that for me, Sergeant? Is that enough for postage?"

"Yeah, sure. Suzette? Who's Suzette? I thought we were talking about Billie Thomm."

"We were. But I have to agree with you, Sergeant—Billie will look out for Billie. My first priority is to get a girl called Suzette out of a home for wayward women before they take her baby away."

Matt smacked his cup down. "What are you talking about?"

Jane closed her writing case with a snap. "I *am* here for a purpose, Sergeant, whether you want to believe it or not. And that purpose is to right the wrongs that have been done to our children. Suzette is a young girl who was wronged in the worst possible way, and has been incarcerated in a home for wayward women, where, I am told, she will be badly treated, and quite possibly have her baby taken from her."

"Baby taken?" Matt sputtered.

"Taken," she repeated flatly.

Matt had to acknowledge that, in spite of her male garb, he was dealing with one of those women of a certain class who knew how to get what they wanted.

Jane seemed to be the only thing moving. She often wandered by herself now, exploring the snow-choked valleys and standing for long minutes on the tops of hills, feeling more a part of the blue bowl of the sky than an inhabitant of the earth.

Now, she found herself well into the meadow before she realized that she was being followed. As had happened when she crossed this meadow with Tina, one animal hung back in the long shadows of the bushes while the other, smaller one wandered zigzag fashion into the meadow, coming closer with each passing. It could not be interpreted as anything but deliberate.

Her first surprised thought was that she really could feel her heart pounding. Her second thought was that she should run, but she discarded that as being dangerously foolish since the coyotes moved through life at a trot and she hadn't run since she was 12 years old. Instead, she looked for some kind of weapon, a stick perhaps. But of course, everything was buried under the snow.

It occurred to Jane that, while both coyotes had been keeping pace with her, they could have been much closer by now. In fact, they could have "been upon her" as the fairy tales put it. She slowed her shaking legs.

The smaller one, which she assumed to be the female, slowed as well; the male stopped and sat back on his haunches. Jane stopped and faced the animals, regaining her breath. The female retreated a few steps, then stood quivering as though poised for flight and her mate rose back onto all fours.

What to do now? Jane stared, unblinking, into the dying light, unsure of her next move. Tina was right—they were just curious. Still watching them, Jane took a few cautious steps backward, toward home. They didn't move. She turned and hurried on, glancing now and then over her shoulder until she saw them trot off into the brush as though bored with their game.

At the Stopping House, Tina and Benny were reassuring as she pulled off her moccasins and babbled out her story, although Benny conceded that their behaviour was brash, even for coyotes.

"Maybe we need a dog," he said. "You could take a dog with you."

Both women pulled a face at the mention of a dog.

Tina loved her cats. "Where would we get a decent dog out here?"

Jane hung Benny's old green mackinaw on a peg. "And what good would it do? We listened to coyotes howl one night on the trail when we were coming here and the dogs were more frightened than we were. The meanest mongrels I've ever seen in my life and they just whimpered by the fire."

"Well," Benny said, "a dog would make a noise, if nothing else."

"Just annoy the coyotes more," Tina said.

"Doesn't sound like they were annoyed, just curious," Benny said. "The winter has been mild enough so they shouldn't be hungry, and I haven't seen any sign of disease."

"Disease?" Jane asked. "What kind of disease?"

Tina's face lit up with inspiration. "We could teach Jane to use the gun. She could take it with her when she goes out alone."

Jane was more horrified at the thought of using a gun than she was at the notion of diseased coyotes. "I couldn't use a gun!"

"Why not?" Tina demanded.

"I couldn't bring myself to kill anything."

"You don't have to kill anything. Just scare them off."

"Scare myself to death into the bargain," Jane muttered.

Benny perched on the end of the wood box to put his slippers on. "It's a good idea to be familiar with a gun, Jane. Even if you never have to use it."

"See?" Tina turned to Jane triumphantly. "It'll give us something to do. We'll practise every day until we are the best shots in the whole territory."

"I don't need to be the best shot anywhere," Jane said.

"You don't know that for sure," Tina said. "What if something awful happens, just because you wouldn't learn to use a gun?"

"Well, we'll see." Jane knew she was being manipulated, knew also that she was doing what they had all been doing for weeks, and that was compromising, giving in here and there in order to keep the peace and make it through until spring.

sixteen

 ll eyes were on the boots. Outside, the sun shone and the wind howled, but in the shack, with its powerful odour of pee, everyone stared at five pairs of new boots lined up like soldiers.

Billie was proud of the bargain he'd found. They smelled wonderful, like fresh paint and new rubber. They were high canvas boots with three metal buckles and thick rubber soles. The canvas had been waterproofed, and he supposed that was what made the paint-like smell. And if all that wasn't enough, there were new felt liners to fit into each pair.

Vlasek touched a boot with one finger. "I have?"

"Of course, dear boy," the Dook answered as he ran the back of his hand down the boy's smooth cheek.

Jake snickered, but something deep inside Billie's belly went tight and hard. Billie had managed to keep the boy safe so far, but the ferret never missed an opportunity to make it clear what he would be up to if Billie didn't keep watch.

"So—you've made yourself useful again, haven't you, lad?" Smythe regarded Billie with a narrow-eyed stare.

"I don't trust him," George said. "How do we know he didn't steal them, keep your money for hisself?"

Billie dug into his pocket and produced a flimsy piece of paper. "'Cause I had them do me up a receipt."

"How do you know what it says? You tryin' to tell me you can read them numbers?" George made a swipe to grab it, but Billie passed it quickly to Smythe.

Billie could read them, but he didn't feel any need to say so. "Mr. Smythe paid the money, he gets the paper," Billie said, ducking the back of George's hand. "Anyway, the shop had what they called a *surplus* of these boots, 'cause of the streaks in the colour, see?" He held a boot up to the poor light where they could all see the way the green on the canvas went from dark to light and back again. "That's why I got a good price."

George sat with his head hanging, shoulders hunched, watching everything with his mean, greedy eyes. "Gittin' pretty cocky, ain't ya?" he said to Billie.

As a rule, George and Jake kept out of sight during the light of day, but the new boots had brought them out and here they sat, slack-jawed and grouchy, blinking like bats. The Dook basked in the appreciation of his men. Billie felt pretty sure he'd like to call them servants, but some people over here had funny notions about that, especially George and Jake. They came from The States, which meant America, and it seemed to be an insult to an American to be called a servant.

"These look to fit me." Billie pulled a pair toward himself, making sure they were big enough for extra socks and even his knife, if need be.

"We should let our new friend pick first," Smythe said.

Vlasek pulled his old boots from his bare feet, exposing

oozing sores on his heels and toes from wearing shoes that were too small. They smelled like death.

"Ah, shit!" Jake said. "Ya gonna make me puke."

The Dook recoiled as though he'd seen a snake, and even Billie, who'd seen worse on an old rag-and-bone man back home, pulled away. Vlasek tried to hide the sickening mess, tears filling his dull grey eyes.

"I found some Epsom salts when I was out today," Billie said gruffly. "Get some of that boiling water and soak them good. They'll heal up." Even as he said it, Billie wasn't so sure. He'd known that Vlasek had sores, but didn't realize until now how bad they were. He turned away from the worship he saw in the boy's eyes. Didn't want some little brat depending on him again.

"Where'd you get the money to buy salts?" Jake asked suspiciously. Since the Dook had started supplying the bunch to go north, everyone seemed to feel they had the right to question each penny spent.

Feeling secure in his role of scrounger of all things cheap and necessary, Billie grinned and said, "Who said I bought them?"

"Smartassed little punk!" George leaned forward to cuff him, but Billie was too quick.

He knew which side his bread was buttered on, at least for the next day or two. "They're real fine boots, Mr. Smythe, and we're going to need them. Ta—I mean, thank you."

The Dook puffed out his chest and regained some of his hoity-toity air, even trying a pair of boots for himself. "Well, I feel it's my obligation, of course, to see we're all properly geared out for our expedition. Wouldn't feel right about it otherwise," he said as though he were the one who had found the bargain boots.

"C'mon, Vlasek," Billie said. "Let's set your feet to cookin', just in case whatever that is takes a notion to spread to the rest of us." Then he grinned as the three grown men pulled back, staring at the mucky feet.

Jake and George each grabbed a pair of boots and slunk out the door. The Dook dusted the worst of the grime off the front of his greasy vest and went out to "dine." Which meant he was going to the Chinese restaurant to have the daily special.

Knowing they would have the shack to themselves for at least two hours, Billie set Vlasek to soaking his feet in an old enamel basin, then filled a bucket with warm water. He stripped himself naked and, starting at the top, scrubbed and rinsed himself right down to the bottoms of his feet. Then he pulled a pair of pilfered socks out of the lining of his great coat, determined never to set his bare feet on this outhouse of a floor again.

Next he heated enough water to wash his hair, scrubbing the scrap of strong yellow soap right onto his scalp. His hair needed cutting in the worst way, so he took his big knife to it, hacking and sawing around the edges, then combing it behind his ears with his fingers. He wished he had more clean things than just the socks to put on, but even his old, too-small clothes couldn't dampen his mood. It had come into his mind in the last few hours that he was the smartest and most important member of this so-called expedition. Oh, the Dook was wily, but Billie had figured ways of outsmarting him. And the others didn't have an ounce of brains between the pair of them.

"I'm going to get some medicine for those feet of yours," Billie told Vlasek. "Dry them off and wait until I get back to put your new boots on, else you'll spread that mess around." He waited until the kid nodded that he understood. Billie wasn't sure if Vlasek was just stupid, or if he didn't understand proper English. Maybe both.

Today was the second of February, 1898. Billie knew that because it was written on the top of the receipt he had given the

Dook. That meant it was Billie's 16th birthday and he already had two presents. The boots, which added at least an inch to his height, and a clean body. Now what else did the day have in store?

He wandered down Whyte Avenue, stopping long enough to admire his reflection in the window of a photographer's shop. He had a fleeting memory of the scrawny lad who had lied his way onto a steamer to Canada, and grinned at his image in the window. Couldn't lie about his age anymore. He was taller than Smythe and getting heavier every day, now they had some food around the place. He turned his collar up against the wind, stuffed his hands in his pockets and sauntered on. He even tried a whistle, but the cold air hurt his tooth. A pretty shopgirl caught his eye through the window of a general store. He pushed the door open, tossing his hair back from his face.

Matt Edwards lounged in the old rattan rocker near the stove, hidden by feed sacks, and pulled on his pipe. Gregson, the store owner, was out back, leaving his girl Betsy to mind the till. Matt had been enjoying the quiet—his favourite kind of day—when the bell over the door rang.

It took him a few seconds to remember the boy. Matt didn't move a muscle. Billie seemed to have grown in the month or so since Matt had seen him, but maybe it was the swagger. His dirty blond hair was a bit shorter, but still ragged and rough and hard to tame. Somewhat like the kid. He had a few straggly whiskers that he seemed to think were too impressive to scrape off. He was supposed to be 14 or so, if Matt's information was correct. He was pretty sure it wasn't. This was a cocky, smartassed half-man and he was going to be too much for Betsy to handle. Matt decided to let her try though, just to see what Billie was up to.

Matt watched Billie as he strolled up and down the aisles, picking things up and setting them down again. There was a choirboy look to him, if you caught him in the right light, with a shy smile that didn't quite make it to his eyes.

It worked on Betsy. She helped him try on peaked caps. They shook their heads, then tried a Stetson and said no to that, too. In the end, they both decided in favour of the usual toque. Betsy said the colour was perfect for him. Billie said it was the nicest he'd seen, and the best price, too. Said he'd be back for it as soon as he had the money.

"What I'm really needing though, miss, is some iodine." Only he pronounced it "eye-o-deen."

Matt had to stop himself from chuckling out loud. Cagey little brat had worked real hard to lose the accent, except for an occasional slip like that.

Betsy looked puzzled at first, then said, "Oh, yes. Down this way."

Back at the counter, Billie took out 22 cents to pay for the iodine, but at the last moment said, "I think I only need the small one."

Betsy moved to get it for him.

"Don't bother, miss. I can get it myself."

Matt craned his neck, trying to see without drawing attention to himself. Billie took a wrong turn down one of the aisles, grinned boyishly at Betsy, before cutting across to the other side — right past the caps. Even knowing what he was up to, Matt almost missed it.

Billie came back to the counter and managed to confuse the difference in price with all the skill of a flim-flam man. Which was pretty much what he was, the way it looked from where Matt sat.

Matt sighed, stretched himself out of the creaky chair and followed him out of the store. Halfway down the block, he dropped his arm around Billie's shoulder. "Man needs to keep his ears warm out here, that's for sure."

He felt the kid stiffen under his touch, knew he was about to make a run for it. He closed his fist on Billie's upper arm.

Billie kept his eyes on the dirty snow. "Wouldn't know."

"No?" Matt pulled the toque out of the pocket of the shabby coat. The boy finally slid a look in Matt's direction. Betsy had been right; the gold shade of the hat matched his eyes. They stopped on the boardwalk and Matt let Billie look him over from head to foot, watched him try to remember where they had faced off before.

"Name's Edwards."

"Yeah? So what?"

"Yeah. We talked a bit on Christmas Day. Over at the train station."

Recognition widened Billie's eyes before the brass drained right out of him, leaving him looking a lot younger than he had a minute ago. Still, he had some survival instinct left. "Aren't you supposed to be in a uniform? You can't take me in 'less you're in a uniform."

"Good try, Billie, but I sort of invent my own uniform every morning. All that braid—just a pain to take care of."

Billie didn't seem to know what to make of that much honesty. "Aw, *blimey*," he said finally, his shoulders slumping.

Matt couldn't help grinning. "Let's just wander back to the store and see if we can replace anything they're missing. Think you can do that, Billie? Slick as you got it out, think you can put it back so as not to embarrass Miss Gregson? Or yourself?"

Billie eyed him suspiciously. "Why you letting me off that easy?"

"Because if I turn you over to the town constable, I have to do a bunch of paperwork. I really hate paperwork. I'd rather have a cup of coffee and a good long talk. So that's what we'll do. After you've returned that toque, we'll go somewhere and have a long talk."

Billie kicked a clump of snow down the street in front of them. "Shit," he said under his breath.

"How do you like your coffee, Billie?" Matt asked amiably. "Lots of sugar, I think. Sweeten you up a bit."

"You could be really good if you'd just try."

"I don't want to be good." Jane turned away from Tina's sulky face and jerked the chamber open, expelling the spent cartridge along with the metallic smell of gunpowder. She knew she sounded as childish as Tina looked.

"If you're going to learn how to use a gun, learn properly. Otherwise you'll just be a damned hazard to yourself and everyone else."

Jane refused to react to the vulgar language. It was only midday and they were already getting on one another's nerves. She reloaded, sighted down the barrel until the "San" in "Chase and Sanborn's Fine Coffee" came into focus, then gently squeezed. The pop came a split second before the tin jumped off the log and plopped into the snow. According to the calendar over the water pail inside, it was the 25th of February; she had been practising for over a month.

"See?" Tina said without interest, staring off to the west, toward The Crossing. She turned back to the house. "The wind is picking up. We should go in now."

The wind was not only picking up, it also brought an onslaught of snow with it. It had been a bit breezy when Benny left for The Crossing at the crack of dawn, but there had been no trace of snow. Now Jane felt an ominous change in the air and a tingle along her spine. She cradled the rifle in her elbow and made her way down the path.

The interior of the house grew dark as the storm gathered force, robbing the day of its short ration of sunlight. Jane warmed herself before the stove, then sat on the chair nearest the window to try to read a two-year-old copy of the T. Eaton Company catalogue by the thin light. The wind slammed against the glass, rattling the panes and sending a cold draft down the back of her neck. She shoved the catalogue aside and picked up a deck of cards.

On the other side of the table, Tina set some dried apples to soak and tossed the ingredients for pastry into a crockery bowl without measuring anything.

Jane watched at first, thinking she might learn something, but quickly lost interest. She shuffled the cards and dealt a hand of solitaire. They had more baking than the three of them could eat, and no one had stopped by for weeks.

"Will Benny be on his way home by now?" Jane asked.

"Of course he will." Tina sprinkled flour onto the table and smacked a wad of pastry dough into the middle of it. She punched the dough hard, then her shoulders sagged. "No. This storm is coming from the northwest. They would have got it at The Crossing hours ago, before he started out. He will have to stay put for the night."

Ah, Jane thought. So she's known all along that he wouldn't be home. That's why she's so edgy. Jane stretched her legs under the table and her hands over head. She had a sudden inspiration. "Let's have another bath."

Tina looked at her with what Jane had come to think of as *that* expression—a haunted look that Jane felt was totally out of character. A resourceful woman like Tina should not be so fearful. Jane stood with resolve, desperate to have something to do—to move before she screamed.

"I suppose we could," Tina said without enthusiasm. "But we should do the chores before we lock ourselves in for the night."

"Of course," Jane said with take-charge cheerfulness. "Let's do the chores."

But when they stepped outside, the wind snatched the door from Jane's hands, smashing it against the wall. Her breath was torn from her throat, forcing her to turn her back to the storm. Drifting snow filled the paths and erased their footprints as soon as they lifted their feet. The ghostly outline of the barn wavered somewhere in front of them.

"Stick together," Tina yelled over the wind, "so one of us doesn't get lost."

Daunted, Jane did as she was told. Inside the barn, she struggled to keep her pail upright under the stubborn cow that swished her tail in irritation. "Miserable beast."

Half-wild barn cats ventured out of the dark, cold corners, stiff-legged and blinking. A battered tom with torn ears and scarred face yowled, setting up a cacophony of howling cats. They slopped some of the milk into old fish tins for the cats and spilled a bit more into the trough for the pigs, before leaning into the wind to get the milk into the house. Outside once more, Tina loaded the bronze tub with wood and Jane filled two pails with snow before staggering in for the night.

Tina bolted the outside door, lifted the rifle down from the hooks over the wall and laid it on the end of the table. Her nervousness made Jane all the more impatient and she dumped the wood from the tub into the wood box with a clatter, scattering cats in all directions.

Tina put the pie into the oven. "Maybe we'll want it later." She went to peer out the window, fingering the curtains, sighing like a lost child.

They lit the lamps early and picked at some leftover stew in silence, waiting for the water to heat. Without a word they washed the dishes. As Tina put them on the shelves, Jane ran her fingers around the rim of the tub. "It's a marvellous tub," she said to break the tension.

Tina finally smiled. "I love it. We brought it with us and it has a million good memories."

"What kind of memories does a tub have?"

Tina ran her fingers over a dent near the handle. "Every mark has a story to tell."

"Well then, what does that dent mean?"

"Oh, that isn't very exciting," Tina said. "A horse kicked it. We had a little farm down near the South Saskatchewan River and we had to haul water for the horses. We didn't have a watering tank at first so we used this." She patted the rim.

They sloshed water into the tub, where it sparkled on the bottom and lapped up the sides, steaming their faces and wilting their hair.

Jane looked at Tina's strained face and said, "You go first this time."

Shivering, Tina doffed her clothes and slid into the tub.

Jane lowered herself into the rocker and propped her feet on a chair, determined to find something to talk about that wouldn't cause more strain. "The nick on the handle, there. What story does that have to tell? More horses?"

"No, that's Luc's fault."

"Luc used this tub?"

"Yes, when he ran into a skunk once. But he didn't dent it when he was in it. He lost it off the wagon when we were moving from Medicine Hat. I didn't notice it was gone until we stopped for the night. Then I made the men go back down the trail until they found it. I wasn't very popular that night, I can tell you." Tina chuckled fondly from the depths of the hip bath. She climbed out and wrapped herself in a towel.

Jane added hot water, stripped her clothes from her body with barely a tremor in her hands and sank into the water. Tina hurried into her nightclothes, then went into the storage room, returning with a dusty jug of homemade wine. Jane heard a glug before a hand appeared in front of her face with a nearly full tumbler of thick, purple wine.

"I don't drink spirits," Jane said.

"It's not spirits. It's just wine I made from chokecherries. It's good for a person, especially in the winter when we don't get enough fresh fruit. That's all it is, really. Just fruit juice."

"I don't know."

"Take it. Maybe it will improve your disposition. You've been so restless lately."

Jane held the glass between her thumb and forefinger, tipping her head back and letting some of the sticky stuff run over her tongue. She found it oddly astringent and overly sweet at the same time, like too-strong, sugary tea. "Odd stuff," she said.

"Mm-hm," Tina said, taking a generous drink of her own wine. "Feel better?"

"No. I still feel like I'm going to explode."

Tina curled up on the lounge and lit her pipe, the smell of tobacco blending with those of the pie and the scented soap. "Well, this may be as good a place as any to explode."

Jane let that pass until she could think about it without a glass of wine in her hand. "The problem is, I'm not doing what I set out to do. I feel responsible for Billie, but more so for Suzette. I think Sergeant Edwards is right; Billie is capable of taking care of himself. But Suzette?"

"What about Suzette? I only know that she is, or was, young and innocent. And in the family way."

Jane took a deep breath and let it out noisily. "The home placed her with an invalid, a woman with two grown sons. Suzette was supposed to be a companion, do light chores and go to school, at least half days. One son forced himself on her. Again and again. He denied it, said she had seduced him. And of course the mother chose to believe her son."

"How old did you say she was?"

Jane almost didn't hear the question, it was spoken so quietly. "What? Oh, she's 15."

"And where is she now?"

"In a residence for wayward girls. Sharing her life and living quarters with some very hard, loose women if the ones I met are any indication."

"Daughters of Eve."

Jane set her empty glass on the floor. "Suzette was the daughter of a very respectable woman in Somerset. A soldier's widow, who was forced to take a job as a housekeeper to feed herself and her daughter. But as Suzette became older and prettier, her mother realized she might not be safe with the young men of the household. She'd heard that our mission offered children a good Christian home and an education in Canada. That's all she wanted for her child. We gave her everything her mother had feared and more."

Jane stepped from the tub, feeling a little unsteady, but she was past caring. She towelled herself roughly. "Merciful heavens, what's wrong with grown men who can do things like that to a child? Can you tell me that? Can you?"

Jane held the towel closed at her chest and jabbed her empty glass toward Tina for more wine. She saw revulsion and horror in Tina's white face and glazed blue eyes. "Dear God, Tina. I'm sorry. What have I said?"

"Daughters of Eve," Jane thought, as she wrestled herself into her nightclothes. Was that what Tina had said? How on earth had she come up with such an expression? Jane realized that the wind had stopped and the house had descended into a deep silence. The quiet was not calming. She glanced at the clock and saw that it was only a little past six. Even time had become twisted in this strange world. She poured more wine for both of them and sank into the rocker.

Tina stared at the wine for some time, before she spoke. "Do you remember very much from when you were little?"

Jane nodded. "Quite a lot, actually."

"I don't remember much before I was 15 or so," Tina said and then fell silent again.

Desperate to fill the void, Jane said, "I remember being hurt when I was about four years old. We were playing in the gardener's wheelbarrow and I got a nasty cut on my bottom. I think I still have a scar."

Tina smiled a little. "You think?"

"It's not an easy spot for me to see. The good part was that I got a lot of attention. They even sent for a doctor."

"And did your father give you lots of attention?"

"My father? Heavens, no. When I was a child my father noticed me only once or twice."

"Because you were bad?"

The lamp began to smoke, so Jane turned the wick lower. "No, I was never bad. I recall one occasion when he paid heed to me. My mother was still alive and we were on our way to the sea — Brighton, I think. My father rarely participated in things like that but this time he did — I'm not sure why."

"But he fussed over you?"

"Fussed? Not exactly." Jane laughed self-consciously. "He called me Joan all during the trip. Finally my mother reminded him that my name was Jane."

"What did he say?"

"He said, 'Are you sure?'"

It didn't seem funny anymore and Jane wished she hadn't started the whole, silly story. "I've never mentioned this to anyone before."

Tina tapped her pipe in the ashtray. "They only called me daughter."

Jane wrapped the brown knit blanket around her shoulders. "Pardon?"

"'Be good, daughter,' my mother used to say. 'Then he won't hurt you.' But I could never be good enough."

Jane knew that she didn't want to hear what was coming.

As though she were talking to herself, Tina continued. "Then I tried to be so bad that he would stay away from me—maybe even send me away. He threatened many times to send me to the kind of home you say Suzette is in. He called it a home for *fallen* women. Did I mention he was a pastor?"

"A pastor?" No wonder she hates everything to do with churches, Jane thought. And has little use for missionaries who work with churches.

"Daughter of Eve or Daughter of Satan. Either way, I couldn't do anything right."

"But your mother? Where was she?"

"As I said, she told me to be good. Looking back on it, I think she was relieved not to have to put up with him herself."

"Dear God."

Tina snorted. "God turned his back on me years ago, and I'm

happy to return the favour. We always had to live in the shabby little houses that the church provided. Other families had lived in them before and left bits of their belongings behind. That's how we came by the tub, although we were never allowed to use such a 'depraved' thing.

"It hung by its handle from two big spikes in a shed full of old harnesses. No one ever seemed to go there except me. I ran there to hide one day when he was in a rage and discovered I could ease the tub out from the wall, crawl inside and it would hold me like armour. He could never find me in the tub. It was as though it was invisible to him."

Jane found herself sitting beside Tina, wrapping them both in the brown blanket, sharing her warmth.

"I haven't told many people about this."

"I'm sure you haven't. How on earth did you survive?"

"I don't think I would have. But Bjarne found me there one day. He was apprenticing to be a blacksmith in our town and my father had told him he could come and get an old harness in the shed any time he wanted. He came after I—that is, after an especially bad time."

"How did Bjarne know you were there if no one else did?"

The slim shoulders shrugged under Jane's arm. "He was digging around for a harness. But he seemed to sense I was in the tub."

"That's incredible."

"I was a bloody mess, my hair all wild and everything. I was 15 and quite small still. Bjarne cut a leather thong from some of the harness and tied my hair back and tried to clean me up." Tina drew in a shaky breath and laughed. "I was in love."

"I should think so."

"Have you ever been in a situation where you thought you would die?"

Jane nodded. "At the lake, when the two drifters attacked me. I really thought, before Gaston showed up, that I would die."

"I know," Tina said. "He beat me so badly sometimes I don't remember most of it. We left that night, with the tub, and we've been on the move, more or less, ever since. Bjarne gave up his apprenticeship, and we both gave up our country."

"I don't understand."

"I was 15 and Bjarne was 22. No one would speak out against my father—he was a pastor. By running off with a young girl without her father's permission, Bjarne was the one the law was looking for. And they were looking for us—*he* saw to that. So I cut off my hair and dressed like a boy, and we made our way to Winnipeg by travelling at night."

A cat yowled to go out. Jane rose to open the door for her and felt the room sway. "I'm dizzy. I'll make tea, and I think we should have something to eat. The pie, maybe."

Tina came to the table with the blanket around her shoulders. "Everyone thought we were brothers and hired us as farm help."

Jane put the pie on the table, took plates from the shelf. "When did you stop being brothers and get married?"

For the first time that evening, Tina's voice took on a teasing tone. "The night I turned 18. We stopped being brothers, but we never did get married."

Jane sat with a thud. "Never?"

Tina shrugged. "Nah. It didn't seem to matter after a while. We didn't want to do anything official, like apply for a wedding certificate, in case they were still looking for us."

"Kristina Holte? Like Uncle called you that day."

"Legally, that's my name. I don't think of myself as that person anymore. Well—when I'm alone—you know—I worry—and then I feel like that little girl again."

Jane plunked a slice of pie onto each plate and got up to pour the tea. "Yes, well, that's all understandable now. How did Uncle know your name?"

"I don't know. He's always wandered back and forth across the border. He may have heard something. Or he just got one of his strange old medicine-man kind of messages from somewhere. I don't worry about it. No one takes his ramblings too seriously."

Jane raised her brows. "Maybe they should."

They talked on, about home and family, and it all seemed easier somehow. They scraped the sticky apple filling from their plates and rose to clear up.

"I suppose we should empty the tub," Tina said.

So they bundled their coats over their nightdresses, pulled on their moccasins and dipped buckets into the tub. Jane felt the room tilt. "How much wine did we drink?"

Tina giggled. "All of it."

"No! The whole jug?" Jane slipped in a puddle of water, falling against the table and setting the cups a-clatter.

Tina doubled over in laughter. "I think we should take our drunken selves off to bed."

"No, no." Jane said, seriously. "We have a job to do here. I always finish a job I start." Then she burst into laughter. "No, I don't."

Staggering into one another, howling with laughter until Tina said she had to go to the outhouse, they slopped their way toward the door with two buckets each. Outside, Tina was the first to fall, then Jane. The wind had gone, the night was deathly silent and they were both of sound enough mind to know they were being foolish.

"We'd better leave the water for morning," Tina said.

They made a quick trip to the outhouse, trying without success to stay on the narrow path, then returned to the house, cold and covered with snow, and locked themselves in.

"We should get our drunken selves off to bed," Tina repeated.

"It's only eight o'clock," Jane said.

"I know. You should add your mark to the tub. You are now a part of its lovely history."

Jane was delighted. "What kind of mark?"

"Why not your name? Jane. Remember, your name *is* Jane. Here," Tina said, and found a small nail in a tin of odds and ends. "Scratch it in with that."

Jane did as she was told. They stood back and admired the letters.

"Now we can go to bed," Tina said.

Jane laughed. "It's only five past eight."

"We can go to bed and talk. Come into bed with me and we can keep one another warm and talk all night."

And they did. Talking well into the night, about things that made Jane blush even under cover of darkness, laughing like two schoolgirls.

illie sat on the frozen ground in the tent and felt fear rise up in him in a way he had never felt it before. The storm that had whipped the tent for hours had died down, leaving the cold to sneak in like an invisible monster. Even George and Jake were quiet, braced as though waiting for something worse to happen.

He was going to freeze to death here in the middle of nowhere, Billie felt sure. The men at the livery stable had warned them about the storm, but this bunch didn't listen to anyone. So here they were, a day's drive out of Edmonton, lucky to find some bushes for the horses to hide in, and luckier still to get one of the tents set up.

Vlasek cuddled down into his side, trying to get warm, and Billie didn't even bother to push him away. They might as well die together. If he had it right, today was Thursday. Thursday was the day the train came to town. He should be on it, but here he was instead and it was all because of that copper—that, and he still didn't have enough money in his tobacco tin.

A terrible anger filled his chest when he thought about the

day Edwards had made him take the hat back to the store. He'd asked lots of questions, about the Dook and where they lived and who paid the bills and all. It had tickled Billie to look the nosey bugger right in the eye and tell him the Dook had lots of money. It felt strange, coming out with the truth like that, and he didn't care if the cop believed him or not. But then Edwards started asking about George and Jake, and Billie had clammed up tight. He didn't have any liking for those two, but he wasn't going to make anything easy for the cop. Besides, George got meaner by the day. Billie had managed to stay out of the way of his fists so far, but he wasn't about to give the bully more excuses to pound on him.

What Edwards really seemed to want to snoop into was the business with Hobson. Billie had never told anyone of the things he'd seen and heard that night and he never would. He just stared the cop down over the cup of coffee until Edwards said, "All right, kid. I'll write to the folks over there and find out for myself." Then he had said something real odd. "You know where to find me if you need me, Billie."

Billie tried to imagine what a goldfield looked like—that's where they were supposed to be headed, after all. He knew what a field looked like, but a field of gold? Not even the Dook was foolish enough to believe that. Jake now, he'd believe anything George told him. As for himself, he believed in trains.

They all shared one tent, even though the Dook had bought two. They also had two wagons, four horses and more food and shovels and stuff like that than Billie had seen in his life. It had not taken long for the Dook to go through all the money Billie had boasted about to Edwards.

Next to him, Vlasek snuffled in his sleep. Did the kid even know where he was going? As far as Billie could figure out, Vlasek thought only of his next meal and keeping his filthy pack safe. He had an old sack that he kept bits and pieces of rubbish in, like his worn-out boots and some other rags. Beyond that, it seemed as though thinking was too much work for him.

Billie's belly growled. They hadn't bothered with a fire or food or anything. He tried to get comfortable, with his tobacco tin digging into his hip. The Dook said they would "return to the south by sea" once they'd been north and got rich, so Billie had dug up his stash and brought it along. Jake started to snore. If Jake could fall asleep, maybe they weren't in as much trouble as he thought. He wrapped his blanket around his head and fell asleep, listening for a train whistle that never came.

Jane rose before Tina and Benny, as she often did. She carved a slab of ham and put it between thick slices of bread, then filled a jar with water. She stuffed her lunch into a canvas bag and slung it over her shoulder, took the small rifle and let herself out as quietly as possible.

The weather had warmed slowly over the past week. She wandered in and out of the creek bed and roamed the hills until she came to the rock she and Tina had sat on weeks ago. With her face turned into the wind and eyes closed, she inhaled deeply the hint of better things to come.

She opened her eyes to the flat, colourless light of day. A silver sun hung in a pewter sky, and in the distance, the faint hint of dark green marked a stand of firs. Nearby, a touch of burgundy in some rosehips looked like drops of dried blood against the snow. Unable to sit for long, she got up and pushed herself hard, feeling a slight dampness of sweat between her shoulder blades. Finally, she turned toward the Bulls' camp.

Julie came to the door. "Jane! Will you read with me today?"

"Maybe. But first, look what Tina gave me from the quilt she is making." She held up two long strips of red-and-white checked cotton.

"Red cloth?"

"Almost ribbons. Now that your hair has grown longer, I thought you could use them for ribbons in your hair."

Her face lit up. "Look, *Maman*, ribbons! Can you fix my hair?"

"Later," Louise said. "What do you say to Jane?"

"*Merci, merci, merci!*"

Louise put the kettle on for tea as Jane and Julie read from the battered exercise book and Kokum dozed in her chair. When the tea was ready, along with biscuits and jam, the door opened and Uncle bent his long frame through the door.

"Miss Jane Priddle," he said.

She smiled and regarded him with more interest than before. Old medicine man, Tina had called him. Maybe he had a potion that would quiet her busy thoughts, ease her restlessness.

"You carry that big gun with you?" He pointed at the little rifle hanging out of reach of the children.

"I do."

He sat ramrod straight on a backless chair. "You scare away all those coyotes?"

"They don't seem to be interested in me anymore. They just play together in the snow. I guess they're used to me."

"Mating season," he said simply. "They have better things to do."

"Oh," Jane said, and hoped she wasn't blushing. "When is, uh, mating season?"

"Now." He heaped sugar in his tea.

Louise laughed. "March, sometime. Is it March yet?"

"Yes, I believe it is."

Jane left earlier than usual. At the edge of the meadow, she loaded the rifle out of habit. She had accepted that the coyotes meant her no harm, and quite enjoyed their company. But today, it seemed, they didn't want her company. Uncle was probably right and they had better things to do. She straightened her shoulders, lengthening her stride.

She didn't see him come, had no idea how he appeared in front of her. He stopped in the middle of the trail, head down, limbs trembling. It was the big one, the male, the one that usually hung back. Jane glanced around but did not see the female. There was no mistaking the confrontational stance of the one in front of her. Is this how they behaved in mating season? Uncle should have warned her.

He really was a beautiful specimen, as big as a large dog with thick, sleek fur that ran from rusty brown on his forelegs to a creamy white on his belly. The hackles quivering on his shoulders were grey and black. Jane slid the rifle off her back, but she did not want to have to use it. He circled away from her, then came back onto the trail and faced her again. There was a fine intelligence in his yellow eyes, a question in his upturned lips. Again, he trotted off the trail to the left, again he came back.

Finally, Jane had a flash of understanding. She stepped off the path to the left. He crouched a moment, then trotted farther before stopping to watch her approach. He was leading her to the creek, to a sharp embankment that dropped about eight feet to the ice.

How foolish was it of her to follow an animal into the woods? Even Red Riding Hood would have more sense than this. Checking the chamber of the gun, she eased it into a more accessible position. The coyote spooked, scattering snow, watching her with an accusing air.

"It's quite safe. I won't hurt you if you don't hurt me." Merciful heavens. Now she was talking to him. But he didn't seem to mind. He just kept leading her down the embankment. She grabbed some brambles to get down the bank. "This had better be important."

He became more nervous and agitated and even barked a sharp, short yip that startled her. But it wasn't Jane he was talking to.

Jane skidded to a stop. "Oh, no."

The snare was bigger than anything she had seen Gaston use and the result more sickening. The little female lay on her side, exhausted, her pretty buff coat smeared with blood and her own excrement. She stretched her head back in the fouled snow and looked at Jane with a pleading that was impossible to ignore.

"Oh, my dear. What have they done to you?" She tried to approach but the male stepped between them. Did wild animals behave like this? What would Tina do? Benny? The answer to that flashed through her mind in a split second. They would raise the gun and put this poor creature out of her misery. But the male seemed to expect something more from her.

As she stood surveying the carnage, trying to think of what action to take, the little coyote pulled herself into a squatting position and started to gnaw around the snare. Suddenly, Jane realized what she was doing, why there was so much mess. She was sacrificing her foot in order to live.

"God help me. I need help." She spoke directly to the male, not thinking for a moment that people didn't speak to animals.

But he didn't understand. He just slumped back on his haunches and watched her go, his head hanging, his ears laid back.

She scrambled up the bank, ignoring the thorny rose bushes that tore the mitts from her hands. How could she persuade Tina and Benny to help her save the coyote? She left the bushes on the run and crashed right into Luc Langevin.

Luc grabbed her wrist above the rifle and pointed it away from both of them. "Is that damn thing loaded?"

"Oh! I'm so glad you're here." He felt the rush of her breath on his throat as she grabbed the front of his coat.

"Glad I'm here?" He held her away from him and looked her up and down. She didn't seem to be hurt.

She looked him right in the eye, no sign of her usual shyness. "Can you help me? Please?" She started to back away.

All he could think of was the talk he'd had with Matt an hour ago at The Crossing. "They're on the move. The Englishman has partnered up with those drifters who attacked the missionary woman up at the lake."

She looked at the gun and his hand on her wrist. "Yes, it's loaded but it doesn't need to be."

"Maybe it does, maybe it doesn't." He stuffed his mitts into his pocket so he could unload the gun and prop it against a bush.

"Hurry. Please." She took his hand and pulled him toward the creek.

What the hell could get this woman so riled up? At first her hand was cold in his, but as she led him down the bank he felt a warm stickiness. He dug in his heels and turned her hand over. "What's this?"

She looked as surprised as she sounded. "I must have scratched myself. It doesn't matter."

"Doesn't matter?"

"It's not me that needs your help." She skidded down in front of him.

The only tracks besides hers were some coyotes'—fresh tracks. He was still trying to figure out what had her so worked up when he heard a sound that raised the hair on the back of his neck. His head snapped up.

"Jesus Christ, *Anglaise*!" He wrapped his arms around her middle and hauled her back up against his chest, his rifle useless on his back.

"They won't hurt us," she said.

Luc kept his eyes on the male, who prowled under the bushes behind his mate, his lips peeled back from his teeth.

"What do you mean they won't hurt us?" Her warmth soaked through the sweater into his hands and he'd held enough women to know that she didn't have any corsets on.

The female watched them but kept on gnawing, as though she knew she had nothing to lose. Her face was filthy with her own gore and the hot smell of fresh blood hung in the air. Luc absorbed the woman's shudder when they heard teeth scrape on bone.

"I don't know what to do." Her hair caught in his beard as she turned to look at him and he searched her troubled eyes thinking, Damn it all, she wants me to fix this.

"Yes, you do."

She turned back to look at the animals. "No," she said, and put her arms and hands over his as though she wanted to make sure he couldn't reach for his gun.

"She might bleed to death or she might starve to death," he said. "I've heard it both ways."

"If we could just cut the ..." she began, then seemed to realize what he had said and turned to look at him again. "Did you do this? Is this your snare?"

"No." It was the truth and he was surprised at how relieved he was to be able to say that, because it could have been. And she knew it.

They stood there, understanding one another, her ribs rising and falling under his hands. Why hadn't she gone home months ago?

"If it isn't your snare, why are you here?" she asked as she turned back to the mess in front of them.

"I was looking for you," he said absently.

"What do you want with me?"

He looked down at her, at the rim of the long johns that showed at the neck of her sweater. I don't know what I want with you, he thought, and then heard a high-pitched yelp, almost a scream.

They both shuddered this time. The female had left her paw, from the first joint down, in the snare. Shreds of flesh and fur were tangled around the wire. She ran after her mate, stumbling and pitching face first into the snow, flopping from side to side, not yet able to understand her loss. Each time the bloody stump of her leg hit the ground she cried and fell, only to get up and run again. It occurred to Luc that he'd never seen such a thing in all his years of trapping. Heard about it, but never seen it.

Jane sucked in her breath with the first scream and held it. She flinched each time the coyote cried and moaned when it fell.

Luc gave her a gentle squeeze around the middle. "Breathe," he said.

"Do you think she will live?" The animals disappeared, leaving only footprints and a bloody trail in the snow.

"Maybe."

"How will she hunt?" She had visions of the coyote dying on a lonely hillside. She hadn't even thought about the starving part until Luc had mentioned it. "Will she really starve to death?"

"Maybe not. If she doesn't bleed to death, he might feed her."

"Really?" She heard the childish hope in her voice and turned away from the macabre mess. He made no effort to lower his arms, so they stood in a loose embrace.

"*Oui.* They try to take care of one another. That's the coyote's way of doing things."

Jane searched the blue eyes that reflected the grey of the sky, looking for some hint that he just wanted to make her feel better. But no, that was not his way of doing things. She would have the truth from this man, whether she liked it or not.

"Come on. We'd better get moving." He pushed her up the bank ahead of him, his hand on the small of her back, pausing to pull his grey mitts off the branches where she had lost them.

"Wait," he said when they were at the top. He took her scraped hand and washed the dried blood with clean snow before putting the mitts back on for her.

His coat was open over the red flannel shirt he had worn at New Year's and his own rifle hung down his back, but he was watching her closely and she anticipated the next question.

"How did you happen to find them?" He handed her gun to her.

Jane started to walk, her head down, trying to think how to tell him. There was really only one thing to do and that was to return his honesty with the truth.

"This pair of coyotes seems to have taken a liking to me," she began.

They walked side by side as she told the story of her encounters with the animals. When the trail narrowed, he followed behind her, not saying a word so she didn't know if he believed her or not. When he could, he walked beside her, their shoulders bumping.

"After that first time, Tina decided that I should know how to use a gun."

"Do you?"

She dared to look at him, but he was serious. She walked on.

"Yes, I know how," she said. "And no, I haven't used it. I couldn't use it today and I don't think I ever could."

He didn't respond to that. Just let her keep talking. Her voice faltered when she told him about the male coyote stopping her on the trail, and when she got to the part about following the animal into the bushes, he took her arm and said, "What?"

She stood still and repeated it. He didn't grin or tease her, just appeared to puzzle over what she had said.

"I was going to get Tina or Benny when I ran into you." She relaxed a little. "And I must thank you, Mr. Langevin, for putting up with my hysterics."

He shook his head. "*Hystérie? Non,* I don't think so," he said, still looking thoughtful. "And my name is Luc."

She took a deep breath and smiled. "Luc."

That smile, Luc thought. It drew him to her every time. The light was starting to go, but he could see relief with the smile on her face. It seemed important to her that he understood what she had done. And he did. It was the kind of thing children do, trying to rescue hurt animals, even if it meant putting themselves in danger. She wasn't a child, for sure, but some of the things she did made her seem young.

She started to walk ahead of him. "Now, tell me why you were looking for me."

"I talked to Matt earlier today. He's been keeping an eye on Thomm and that Englishman. He thinks they are headed this way, may already be here."

"How is Billie? Did Sergeant Edwards say?"

"Still the same, I guess. Matt didn't say, one way or the other. That's not what he's worried about. They're travelling with those two drifters. You know, from the lake."

She turned in her tracks and stared at him. "I don't understand."

"The Englishman has hired them to help him get up north. Spent a lot of money on supplies and they're striking out to look for gold."

"Oh," she said.

They walked on in the dusk, talking about what that useless bunch might be up to, until they saw the outline of the Stopping House in the distance. As the house drew closer, their steps became shorter and slower. They lingered together, and Luc remembered that as a child he had stretched out his playtime in the same way.

Finally, their feet dragged to a stop in a little hollow just below the house. He touched her gun, still thinking about the two men who had hurt her. "I think you should keep that thing loaded."

She nodded. "I think you're right."

"Ah." He remembered that he had the cartridge he had taken from it. He dug in his pocket, but when he tried to hand it to her, she couldn't take it with his big mitts, so he pulled open the breast pocket on Benny's old mackinaw and slipped it in. Then, of their own accord, his hands stayed on her jacket, pulling the sides closed so she would be warmer.

She held her breath again, and this time he had to grin.

"Breathe," he said. "All the time, I have to tell you to breathe."

With a little laugh, she let the air out of her lungs and turned toward the light. Then she stopped and looked back. "You're not coming?"

"*Non.*"

"But it's late — nearly dark. And Tina will have supper ready. There's always enough for one more." She walked back to him in the twilight, her face a pale oval.

He took a quick step back. "My cabin is not far from here."

She stopped dead still. "Well, I'll go by myself, then?" she asked.

He knew better than to answer that. He wondered if there was a crazier man anywhere in the world. "Go home," he said.

"I will," she responded, and he could tell by the little break in her voice that they both knew he didn't mean the Stopping House.

n that grey time at the end of the day, when everything looks flat, like a picture in a book, Billie hunkered behind the tent, listening to voices through the canvas wall. He held his breath, afraid someone might hear him. George was getting meaner and meaner. Even Jake had got a kick in the rump when he'd let the fire die down last night.

Bad feelings crackled with the sparks from the blazing fire in the centre of the small, open space where they had their camp. Something in the air sent prickles down Billie's back. Hard to say exactly what it was, but he'd felt things like this before, in the alleys, when something nasty was about to happen. He could almost taste it.

Even Vlasek seemed to feel it, because he stayed off by himself as much as possible. Billie glanced at the boy where he sat with his dirty pack, playing with the cans of food, stacking them up, then taking them down again. Well, it kept him out of George's reach.

The Dook was the only one who acted as though he didn't

know things had started to go sour. Maybe he didn't. But he should have known when he hired the likes of Jake and George that he had to watch his back at every turn. The ferret had crawled inside Jake and George's tent a few minutes ago, trying to smooth things over. That's what Billie was listening to.

He heard Jake's whiny voice. "We got one lame horse. How d'ya think we're goin' to get anywhere with a lame horse?"

"It's like I bin tellin' ya," George said. "The trails is covered with gold rushers, all with good horses an' good equipment. We don't git outta here now, there's no sense in even tryin'. Gold'll be all gone."

Only a deaf man, or someone really stupid, could miss the fact that George was at the end of his rope.

In that superior way he had, the Dook started talking before George even finished. "Now, now. It's all just an adventure anyway. I clearly stated that at the onset. We can wait until the little mare is healed and the weather will be better, too. I don't mind admitting that last cold snap had me a trifle worried."

"Trifle worried?" George bellowed.

Jake added his tuppence worth. "The weather's never better in this country. Yer just tradin' snow and cold fer mosquitoes and flies. Ever try to take a leak with flies and skeeters buzzin' around yer ..."

"Shut yer mouth," George said. "We're not talkin' about mosquitoes."

Billie shrank down even further. They'd been at it for a while now, and were getting nowhere. If the Dook didn't see that he had to give in to these two now and then, he was even crazier than he looked. But what Billie knew, and George didn't seem to have figured out yet, was that the Dook didn't care about the gold at all, didn't believe in the stories of gold lying around for the picking. Frederick Smythe wanted to play cards and take everyone else's gold.

"... perfectly safe here," the Dook said for about the tenth time. "In this little hollow, surrounded by a nice grove. And *I've* provided plenty of supplies."

Earlier today, Billie had made his way into The Crossing and back easily, even though they had told him to stay put with Vlasek. He just followed the tracks Jake and George had made over the last couple of days and it had only taken 30 or 40 minutes.

Billie had to lean into the canvas to hear what George said next. "The way I got it figured, the three of us could make a go of it on the good horses. Dump most of that shit you bought an' pack light. Head out across country and hook up with the rest of the gold rush."

Billie strained to hear every word. What little light had been left in the day faded completely.

"... not stickin' around here because of those two brats. Dump 'em in the river under the ice and let 'em wash downstream with the spring runoff." George's words came hard and low.

The Dook finally had enough brains to get scared. "I'll have no violence, do you hear?"

So that's the way of it, Billie thought, his heart pounding. The horses wandered nearby, pawing to get at the dead grass under the snow. He'd never had much liking for horses and they offered little comfort now. Billie had heard enough about George around that railroad town to know he truly was as likely to throw Vlasek and him into the river as not.

"Something else to consider," George said like an important businessman. "Ever notice that Imperial Bank? It's jest a shack — old trapper's cabin most likely."

"What ya' sayin'?" Jake asked.

"Can't be too secure now, can it? The window is near rotted out an' the door's no better."

"I fail to see …" the Dook began.

"Everyone goes to bed soon's it's dark," said Jake. Even he had caught on to where George was headed.

"We could do it," George said. He sounded real sure of himself. "But same deal as I mentioned—jest the three of us. On horseback. Git out real quick."

"Absolutely not. I am not a common thief. Now I'll have no more of this nonsense, do you understand? I will not attract the attention of the authorities. There will be wealth enough for all when we get to the goldfields."

The authorities. Billie had hightailed it out of the settlement today because of the authorities. Edwards and his partner had been hanging around, talking to people, asking questions. And if that wasn't bad enough, one of the people they talked to was the big Frenchman. Billie thought he'd seen the last of that one in Calgary.

"Get some supper ready now, my good men," the Dook said, as he left the tent. "Be patient. We will accomplish what we set out to do, if you'll just be patient."

"Yeah, we'll rustle up some grub. Have it your way then."

Billie stayed low, his mind churning, listening to the slush of boots in the snow as the Dook walked the short distance to the other tent. The river they had mentioned was only a stone's throw away and George was up to no good. Billie needed to hear more.

Jake started to say something, but George shut him up. "Wait until he's in his own tent." Finally, George spoke very quietly. "Why should we bother with that damn sissy? He'll jest slow us down. Leave him here with his little boys."

Jake snickered. "I was thinkin' the same thing my own self."

"An'," George went on, thinking out loud, working his way through his plan. "We kin take all three horses an' use one fer a pack horse. Take some supplies. Still be able to move fast an'," he said louder, "we'll head south. The sissy'll tell 'em we're headed north to the goldfields."

"How much you think is in there?" Jake asked.

"More'n we got now, don'tcha think? Never mind that. Jest keep your mouth shut and we'll get this jackass his grub and then wait fer them to get to sleep. Act like nothin's changed. Kin ya do that?"

"You bet, George. You bet."

Billie had no way of knowing how much time had passed as he lay straight and stiff, staring at the roof of the tent and listening. Past midnight, probably. Making a run for it was something Billie had done many times and it had never stumped him before. But out here? Still, he had to try, had to fight down the panic that choked him so that he could hardly swallow. How could he catch one of those horses and get out of here as long as Jake and George were still awake, waiting to do the same thing themselves? Only they wanted to rob a bank; Billie just wanted to get back to the train.

The thought of just staying with the Dook and Vlasek entered Billie's mind, but he knew that the north was even wilder than it was here and he'd had enough of the wilderness. Everything Billie owned was stuffed into his pockets or the lining of his coat, so he wouldn't have anything to slow him down.

He dreaded leaving Vlasek with the Dook, but lying here for hours, he'd dreamed up a plan of leaving a note for Edwards. He'd tell the cop that Vlasek wasn't safe with the Dook and where to find him. In his mind it was a grand plan, and even a little funny, getting back at the copper by disappearing and leaving him with the brat instead.

Vlasek snuffled. "Go pee," he said.

"I'm coming, too," Billie said quickly, as they crawled past the snoring Dook. And it was as simple as that. Should have thought of it himself. There were a few stars and part of a moon. The black smudges Billie saw moving near the trees could be the horses, or they could be Jake and George. He was almost beyond caring. He put a hand on Vlasek's sleeve. "Come over by the bushes to do that. There's enough mess around here."

Billie thought he heard a grunt from the other tent as he groped for a bridle. Maybe that was good. Now they knew there was still someone awake and would wait longer. As Vlasek relieved himself, Billie walked up to one of the horses and prodded it to make sure it wasn't the lame one. He fumbled with the bridle.

"You take horse?" Vlasek asked.

"Shut up." Which way was up or down on the stupid bridle? He tried to forget how scared he had always been of horses, because right now his biggest fear lay in a tent a few yards away.

"Billie, don't leave me."

"Billie, don't leave me." It could have been Denny talking, calling out to him in the dark. Of all the things for Vlasek to say, and in perfect English for once. Why did he have to say that? They were the very words Denny had used the night he died.

There should be a strap under the chin of the bridle. The whole thing could fall off if the strap wasn't done up. The horse whinnied a little, impatient with his fumbling, but they had worked their way into the trees so maybe no one heard them.

"You go now, Billie?"

The words carried a kind of hopelessness that Billie recognized immediately. Hadn't he felt the same way himself, many times? His brain hurt from trying to think what to do and his heart pounded nearly out of his chest. It was a big horse, meant for pulling wagons; it should be able to carry both of them.

"Aw, shut up and get on," he said.

They struggled under the trees, pushing and pulling one another to get on. Then it happened—George's voice ringing across the dark clearing. "What the hell's going on out there?"

"Hurry." Billie fought the tears building in his throat and his nose started to run. Oh, bloody hell. He was going to die under the ice of a frozen river in this awful country and no one would know or care.

"Git outta bed, Jake. Git out here. Somethin's wrong."

There was a pause and Billie could imagine Jake stumbling around trying to figure out what was happening. Billie kicked the horse in its barrel belly but the stupid thing kept turning back.

"Ah, Jesus Christ!" George's voice strangled with fury. "One of the horses is gone. Jake, git yer goddam hide out here right now."

Billie tried to remember the words to use with horses. "Get up. Giddy up." He kept thumping his heels into its ribs and Vlasek did the same. It moved a few steps, grunted to a stop and whinnied to the other horses.

"It's that goddam kid. That thievin' little bastard. I'm gonna kill him fer sure now."

Moaning out loud, Billie fought with the big draft horse as it started to plod back to camp. He held both reins in one hand and tangled his other fist in the mane so the trees didn't brush him off.

"Not worry, Billie," Vlasek whispered. Wrapping his arms around Billie, he took the reins and separated them, holding them wide. "Team horses. Drive different." He yanked hard on the right rein and the horse obediently turned right, then he handed the straps back to Billie. Next, Vlasek reached into the trees, tore off a switch and smacked the stubborn creature on the rump. The horse lunged forward, then broke into a trot, heading into a ravine with enough bushes to offer some hiding places. They hung on for dear life, sliding this way and that on the broad back, their teeth jarring each time a hoof hit the ground.

Behind them, all hell broke loose.

"Let the sons a bitches go. They ain't gonna talk to the law. Git the other two horses and let's git to that bank."

Then the Dook, in his high-pitched squeal. "What's going on? You can't do this. Horse thief! Horse thief! Stop at once!"

Billie didn't know if the ferret was yelling at him or the other two, but Vlasek had started to mutter something in his foreign jabber. Sounded like he was praying.

They heard more yelling and swearing, then Jake shouted, "Let go of the horse, you silly old bastard. We're goin' whether you like it or not."

"No! I paid you for your services. You do as I say."

The horse under them kept crashing through the trees so it was hard to hear what they were saying, but there was more shouting. The last he could make out was the Dook screaming and screaming, on and on. Enough to make his blood freeze in his veins.

It was hard to tell what pounded harder, the horse's hooves or his heart. The sounds behind them faded and then became still. Billie tried to wipe his nose on his sleeve, steer the horse and stay on, all at the same time. Then Vlasek reached around him and held on to the mane with both hands, steadying both of them. Billie felt something hard press into his back and realized that Vlasek still had that stupid pack with him.

Shivering and clinging to one another, they kept the plough

horse trotting, heard the hooves thumping in the wet snow and felt branches pull at their arms and legs. They hung on and kept moving. That was as far as Billie could think right now. Just keep moving.

nineteen

 few minutes after Benny left for The Crossing, Jane couldn't sit still any longer. "I'll take the little gun. Do you mind? The big one is over the door."

Tina was still in her chenille robe. "Away you go. I'll be fine."

The air was even more gentle than it had been the day before. Without thought, Jane followed the creek, careful to avoid the rotting ice. South-facing hillsides had begun to turn brown and there was a pungency to the air that held some hint of returning life. Back home, daffodils would be awash in spring showers. Jane couldn't remember the last time she'd felt a good steady rain on her face.

Before long she found herself on a familiar part of the bank, staring down at trampled snow. The indentation where Luc had placed her rifle, and where she returned it now, had been enlarged by the sun.

The dainty paw lay tangled in the snare, just where the coyote had left it yesterday. There was probably too much smell of blood and humans for other creatures to come near. Jane approached slowly, a plan settling into her mind. The sun had thawed some of the flesh, but the limb itself was stiff in her bare hand. She had to tug it free.

So small. She cradled it in her palm, not closing her hand. At the top of the bank, she looked around for a decent place to bury it. The snow had melted from the fork of a large poplar root, leaving a mouse-nest-sized cup of dark earth. Using a stick, Jane scraped until she had a tiny grave for the paw, then covered it over with cold, wet soil.

She went back down the bank one last time, to where the snare lay tangled on the ground, and tore at it with all her strength, trying to get it loose. She yanked and cursed and called it names and, in the end, only hurt her hands because she didn't know any names bad enough and because it was meant to hold fast and kill. Puffing and disgusted with her tantrum, she strode on, skirting the Stopping House, heading northeast.

Lost in thought, Jane tramped farther than she realized, into terrain she hadn't walked before. It must be midday, she thought; she was feeling hungry and hadn't brought a lunch. She turned back over the unfamiliar territory and wove her way through the coulees until she saw the Stopping House. Two strange horses were tied behind the house, instead of at the hitching rail at the front. Something about their hanging heads and wet flanks sent little threads of alarm through her. Tina was alone.

Jane slanted off to the east, coming at the house from the back, sliding her feet soundlessly into the snow. Probably just gold seekers strayed off course and looking for directions. Or homesteaders, riding ahead of the family, wanting eggs or milk.

Muffled words came from the front of the house. Men's voices with a hard edge froze her to the log wall, where she breathed high in her chest, afraid to attract attention.

"All alone, eh?"

There was something familiar about that voice. Jane shook her mitts onto the ground and winced at the soft plop they made. She reached into the breast pocket of Benny's jacket for the cartridge Luc had put there.

"No, please." It sounded like a child. It was Tina.

Jane slid the chamber of the gun open soundlessly and blessed Benny for keeping it clean and well oiled. Bringing the rifle to hip height, she crept along the wall until she could peek through the living-room window. Empty. Then she heard a scuffle from the storage room at the front.

"C'mon, George. We was jest wantin' grub an' we got it. Now let's beat it."

Jane placed the voices. The petulance she had felt as she tore at the snare was nothing compared to the fury she experienced now. Cold, clear, uncluttered with reason, it filled her body and soul with a hatred so powerful she knew she was capable of anything. It was these two who had destroyed her assured frame of mind months ago, and they now became a sharp and well-defined focus for her anger.

"Her ol' man's in town. Deliverin' *eggs*." George managed to make an insult of Benny's honest labour.

Inching her way along the wall, Jane made it close enough to the open door to see in. Jake was kneeling, stuffing tins and packages into a burlap sack. George had Tina sprawled on the floor near the wood box, sitting back on his heels, looking her over as though trying to decide what to do with her.

"Might be, she has some money around. Got money on you somewheres?" He ran his hands over her body, her breasts, up her leg to her crotch.

Tina whimpered.

"Them Mounties'll be close behind us. The way we messed up that damned bank. An' fer what? Nothin'," Jake said.

"Git over here," George laughed. "Have a feel for yerself. You bin sayin' how you bin missin' a good feel. Now's yer chance."

Jane let her breath settle into her chest as she watched Jake obediently poke two fingers at Tina's breast, continuing to complain.

"We gotta git outta this territory. Not jest because of the bank, that sissy, too ..."

George cuffed his partner on the side of the head. "Shuddup. She ain't deaf, ya know. You jest shuddup."

It was the distraction Jane needed to step into the room, taking two long strides to come up soundlessly behind the two men. Tina's eyes grew round, but Jane shook her head abruptly. With more purpose and concentration than she had ever felt in her life, she slowly brought the barrel of the gun up to George's bent head, just where the oily scalp and the grimy neck met, the small indentation looking vulnerable, even on a piece of human waste such as this. Jake froze with his mouth hanging open.

Power buzzed in Jane's head, blurring the distant sound of more horses approaching. She saw the skin twitch under the cold barrel.

"Is this close enough, Tina?" Jane asked conversationally. "You said it was best to be close to a man to kill him with this rifle."

"What the Christ?" George tried to sit up.

Jane pressed the barrel harder, forcing his chin onto his chest, then ruffled the dirty hair with it, like one of the obscene caresses he had given Tina.

"Pull the trigger," Tina whispered. "Pull the trigger."

Everyone in the room knew Tina meant it, wanted these men dead. Jane was probably the only one who realized she was capable of it, that she was on the brink of shooting this man in the back of the head. One false move and she'd have no choice, because they were all aware that he would make short work of the women if he had a chance. She felt a thrill start somewhere down deep in her groin and run right through the top of her head until everything took on a clarity that she had never experienced before.

"Hello again, George," she said. "It's me. The uppity bitch. Remember?"

Jake forgot Tina for a moment and moved slightly toward George. "What d'ya want I should do?"

"Don't do nothin' 'til I straighten this bitch out."

It gave Tina time to inch her hand along the floor and for her fingers to come in contact with a length of stove wood. Jane calmly watched her friend pick the wood up quickly and bring it crashing down on Jake's head. He slumped with a grunt.

"Now, Tina?" Jane asked quietly, dragging the gun a slow inch up and down George's head.

Tina knelt across from Jake, but it was Jane she stared at. Tears filled her eyes. "He was going to—you know."

"I know. He tried to do it to me, too. I don't think we should let him do that to any other women, do you? Maybe now is the time to put an end to his miserable life."

From somewhere very distant, she heard Benny calling Tina's name, and Matt Edwards quietly saying, "Stay back, Benny, stay back."

"Please, Jane," Tina said.

"Of course," Jane assured her, as she stroked her thumb back and forth over the hammer, letting it click softly, once, twice.

The head under the gun shook uncontrollably. She heard a splatter and looked down in time to step back from the puddle of urine that drizzled between George's knees.

"Is that thing loaded?" The voice at her neck was quiet, curious. An arm in a red coat lightly glided over hers, gently took the rifle and released the hammer. Jane felt a terrible sense of loss and disorientation.

"Oh, Bjarne." Tina threw herself at Benny.

Then somehow, Jane was outside, sitting on the end of Benny's wagon, alone and shivering. She turned sideways to lean against the side of the wagon for support. No, she was not alone. Stretched out beside her, with boots sticking out from under a bloody grey blanket, was the body of a dead man, gone to eternity with his right hand frozen out from his body and pointing straight at her heart.

"Maybe we should throw some straw in the bottom for them to sit on," Matt said. "They don't deserve it, but it's a three-day drive back. And tell Luc thanks for the use of his spare rig. I'll see he gets paid for it."

"I will," Benny said. "He was wondering how he would get it to Edmonton anyway."

Matt figured he would just dump the two prisoners in the wagon with the dead man. He'd let them bounce around with the corpse for a few days and maybe it would jar the truth out of them. It sure looked as if they had done the man in, but there were still two missing boys, and one of them had a bad reputation hanging over his head.

Matt and Gibbs stayed long enough to have a cup of coffee and for Gibbs to listen to Tina's shaky account of what had happened and to painstakingly write down every word.

Before they left, Matt said, "One more minute, then we'd better make a start."

He found Jane in the barn with her arms around the neck of Luc's big gelding, stroking the black mane. "You going to be all right?"

She nodded. He could see her hand shaking as she tucked the mane under the halter. Tina would cry on Benny's shoulder and he would hold her awhile and eventually she would get over it. But this woman wasn't going to cry. Cool as a cucumber with that .22, fighting right this minute to stay calm and controlled.

"Tina told us her story. Do you have anything to add, anything we don't know?"

"I don't think so. I came home in time. They would have taken any money or valuables that Tina and Benny have in the house, too."

"I know. You saved Tina from—well, you know what. It was brave of you."

"No." She spoke so softly he hardly heard her.

He stepped closer. "No?"

"You don't understand." She perched on the manger and squeezed her hands between her thighs, bent over as though she had a stomach ache.

Matt squatted in front of her, looking up into her face. "You sure you're all right?"

"No, Sergeant Edwards." Her voice broke and she wouldn't look him in the eye. "I'm not all right. Something is terribly wrong with me."

"What? Did they ...?"

"No. It's me. Something inside me. When I stood there with that gun and they were, uh, molesting her ..." She looked over his head, squirming on the manger.

"You knew better than anyone what they were capable of. You were scared, that's normal."

"No! Listen to me." Now she looked him straight in the eye, her own eyes wild. "I wasn't frightened, don't you see? I should have been. Afraid or sickened or something. But I was *glad* to be there, to have that loaded gun in my hand, to stand over that animal and …" she trailed off.

"Ah." Matt got up and sat close beside her, taking her cold hands between his own and rubbing them. "I see."

"No," she started again in exasperation.

"Yes, Jane. Look at me." When her troubled eyes looked into his, he said, "You wanted to pull that trigger."

She slumped with the relief of not having to say it out loud. "I did. God help me, I did. Does that make me as bad as they are?"

"You know the answer to that."

She shook her head. "No, I don't," she said desperately.

"Did you have time to pull the trigger?"

"Yes, but …"

"But you didn't. What do you think either of them would have done if the tables had been turned?" When she didn't answer, he went on. "Most of us have felt like that, or something close to it, at one time or another."

"Really?"

He could see how badly she needed to believe him. He grinned. "Would I make up something like that?"

She took a deep breath and even managed a shaky smile.

"Now," Matt said. "I want you to come back to the house and get something to eat. Don't stay here by yourself." He nudged her out the door and up the path. "Talk it all out with Benny and Tina. You'd be surprised how much it helps just to talk. And, Jane?"

"Yes?"

"Don't *ever* let me see you pointing a gun at someone's head again."

"But, he had Tina, and Tina …"

"I know about Tina. That's why I'm letting you off with a warning."

There would be plenty of time later to let her know that the boy was mixed up in another murder and on the run again. On the run or frozen somewhere, like the poor old remittance man in the back of Luc's wagon. Nothing she could do about it right now anyway.

twenty

ane calculated the dates and came to the conclusion that, if she made the right connection in Halifax, she could be home by the first of May.

"So, if you can be ready in two days' time, Miss Priddle, we'll be happy to stop for you." Mr. Gallagher sat ramrod straight at the head of the table.

"I can," Jane said. "Thank you. I'm glad the warmer weather allows for more travel."

A steady stream of visitors had come and gone from the pine table in the two weeks since the bank had been broken into, and the Gallaghers were no exception. Robbery and murder were nearly unheard of in this part of the world and everyone seemed to need to hear more or to add an anecdote of their own. The two Mounties were heroes, having run the culprits to ground at the Stopping House before carting them off to garrison headquarters in Edmonton. And through it all, the central players in the drama kept their silence. Neither of them would reveal the true happenings on the day they would sooner forget.

Mr. Gallagher slurped his coffee and continued with the gossip. "Had two youngsters with them, I hear."

Jane tried to look interested. "Oh?"

"Completely disappeared. Edwards came back with some young troops to search their camp and ask questions. No trace of them. Could be dead, too, for all we know."

Jane played with her spoon and stared idly out the window. She had learned that much, and more, from Matt when he had stopped in two days ago. Jake and George had lied and bluffed all the way to Edmonton in the hope of casting blame elsewhere. They said that Billie and another lad had stolen a horse and hightailed it out on their own. Whether this was before or after the Englishman had died was hard to know.

"Beat about the head," Dora Gallagher said in hushed tones, titillated by the gruesome details.

Jane fiddled with her cup. Billie might be dead. And Suzette, the child-mother? Where was she and did she still have her child?

"Well, at least they didn't get much from the bank. Not much in there, from what I hear," Benny said.

Vera broke her cookie into ladylike pieces. "We were congratulating ourselves, weren't we, Mr. Gallagher? We left our money in the bank in Edmonton."

"Yes. That's what this trip is about, Miss Priddle. Going into town to buy material for our new hotel. We'll start building as soon as we get back," Mr. Gallagher said.

By early afternoon the next day, Jane's bags were packed, and her navy travelling costume brushed and hanging on a peg on the wall. She had one more task to perform, and that was to say goodbye to Louise and the rest of the Bulls. After an early lunch, she set out alone, feeling free and unfettered. She hadn't lifted the .22 since her escapade with George. Surely there were no more criminals in this part of the world, and her coyotes had disappeared, as was to be expected.

Spring rot had set into the camp. Snow melted away from a winter's worth of refuse, leaving it to swim in stagnant puddles or drain down to the creek in muddy rivulets. Jane sat on the end of a broken-down cart, watching Louise gut a scrawny prairie chicken. Uncle joined them, sitting on his heels as comfortably as another man would sit on a chair.

"Jane is leaving," Louise told him, swinging a stick at the pack of mongrels as they slithered on their bellies to get closer to the smell of the freshly killed bird.

He nodded. "Uh huh."

"She thinks it's time to move on."

"Time for everyone, maybe," he said.

"Where do you go in the summer, Uncle?" Jane asked.

"Oh, not so far anymore."

Louise threw a stick at the dogs and they backed off a short distance. Beyond the bushes, with their burgeoning pussy willows, Jane heard children playing. She leaned back against the splintery cart, soaking up the sun.

"Heard about those coyotes," Uncle said.

Jane nodded lazily. "I didn't think wild animals would come so close to a person."

"Sometimes. Different things happen, sometimes."

Louise went inside to start cooking the bird. Unchecked, the dogs pounced on the entrails of the prairie chicken. The noise of the children lessened and Jane looked up to see two strangers enter the camp with the curious children trailing behind.

They were beyond thin. The skin on their cheekbones was stretched shiny and tight, their eyes had a sunken, haunted look. This was starvation, then.

Their clothes were in tatters and one man even had cardboard and rags tied on his feet instead of moccasins. Lurking behind them were three of the ugliest dogs that Jane had ever seen, even out here. She slid over on the cart, closer to Uncle. Gaston walked slowly in their direction.

Uncle stood and mumbled some quiet words to the strangers, then said, "Go, Gaston, and ask your mother if she can spare anything to eat."

Gaston turned toward the house.

Julie left the group of children and came toward Jane, holding stubby braids out on either side of her head. "Look, Jane," she called.

"You have your ribbons in your hair." In some part of her mind, Jane heard the low rumble of the three dogs and the answering snaps from the local animals bent on their feast. She realized that the little girl, intent on her hair, was skipping across the space between the two packs. Jane raised her hand to motion Julie back, but the patch of grimy snow erupted into a nightmare of growls and snarls. And screams. Jane froze in horror as she saw the child caught up in the melee, her hands useless over her head.

Without thinking, Jane waded into the battle, kicking and beating at dogs with her closed fists. "Gaston," she yelled. "Help me, Gaston!"

How could something so terrible happen so fast? Within seconds, Gaston and Uncle had scattered the dogs and Jane knelt by the twitching form of Louise's little spirit child. The tiny girl sprawled, face down in the mud, her hands still raised over her head. Jane hesitated to touch her. Was she hurt, or just paralyzed with fear? Gaston fell to his knees and scooped his little sister onto his lap.

As long as she lived, Jane would never shed the image of the bloody mess that had been Julie. Jane pulled away from the agonized moans that came from Gaston. Julie's clothes were torn, her body covered with gouges and teeth marks. But her face—her face was nearly gone.

Jane pushed herself to her feet and felt something sticking to her palm. She looked at her hand to see a bit of frayed ribbon, then raised her gaze to see Louise coming straight toward them.

Jane spread her arms and placed herself in the way. "No, Louise. Don't go."

Louise stared hard at Jane for a second. "Move," she said quietly.

Jane closed her arms around her friend and leaned into her, futilely trying to hold her back. Her feet skidded in the mud.

"Get—out—of—my—way."

Nausea overcame Jane. She stumbled into the trees. The heaving started deep down in her belly, tearing over her ribs and through her chest as though her body and soul needed to throw off what she had just seen. From far, far away, she heard Gaston screaming in French and Cree. Other voices tried to calm him. Spasms cramped the arches of her feet as the heaving continued. She swiped at the mucus that dribbled from her nose.

The first crack and yelp made her cry out, too. She whimpered, her mind not able to comprehend more violence. After the second shot, she realized what Gaston was doing, and that the other voices had stopped trying to prevent it. She gulped for air and counted four more shots. Carefully she scraped soil and twigs over the mess she had made.

The bubbling scrap that had been Julie hung stubbornly

onto life for hours. Crouched in the old cart in the darkness, Jane heard a change in the keening wail that Kokum had kept up and knew the little girl was dead.

It was Uncle who took her home, Uncle who led her through the dark, keeping up a soothing patter that she sometimes understood and sometimes didn't. She heard moaning and thought the wind must have come up and then realized the sound came from her own chest. She walked through an alien landscape with no lights and no buildings, where no one spoke her language. Sometimes a moon floated out from under clouds and during one of those moments of brightness, Jane saw that she was escorted not only by an old man, but by two coyotes as well.

The smaller coyote limped close behind Jane. The bigger one circled them at a distance, like a sheepdog protecting his flock. The old man talked to them in strange tongues and when Jane thought she heard the animals answer, she knew she was close to madness. The coyotes stayed by them until near the Stopping House when a lantern dipped and swayed into sight. Benny and Tina had come to find her.

Jane spent the rest of the night in the kitchen, sipping chokecherry wine that turned to vinegar in her stomach and trying not to hear Uncle, in his gentle monotone, tell Tina and Benny every single detail of what had happened.

An hour after the sun had spilled across the pine table once more, the Gallaghers came to take Jane to South Edmonton and she had to listen to the heartbreaking story again. She sat in a stupor, her clothes stiff with mud, feeling no warmth from the sun.

It had been a long tiring night for everyone; Benny left to drive Uncle home and Tina went to do the morning milking. Jane walked the Gallaghers to their wagon, wanting them gone so she could stop answering questions.

"You really shouldn't miss this chance to get back to the train," Vera said. "You don't need to feel you have to go to that child's funeral, just because Mrs. Lindstrom is going. She's known these people for years, but they're nothing to you. They're always dying off like flies. It's just not possible to keep up with the funerals."

Jane watched the woman's lips move, followed the words carefully and tried to sort them into some kind of sense. "I will go to the funeral."

The older woman smoothed her black, watered-silk dress over her corsets, tugging to get the wrinkles out of the middle. "Well, you're making a mistake if you think there will be a respectable couple going to the train anytime soon. But I'm sure you think you know what is best."

"I do."

"And, since we are being so frank with one another, I must tell you that women in men's trousers are not attractive at all. I've told Mrs. Lindstrom the same thing, many times mind you, but she doesn't listen."

Jane stared at her blankly, then looked down at her dirty clothes. "Yes, I will have to wash them."

Mrs. Gallagher frowned, shook her head with a clucking sound, then hoisted herself into the wagon.

Having done her duty by advising Jane, she settled complacently onto the buckboard. "Well, perhaps I'll see you in Edmonton or South Edmonton. Although I'm sure I don't know how you'll get there." She waved cheerfully as the wagon pulled away.

Luc came as soon as he could, topping the knoll in time to see the back of the Gallaghers' rig as it headed east. A gopher stood stiff-backed on the side hill watching him approach, then scampered across a soggy patch and disappeared down its hole.

Luc was not interested in gophers or any other varmints. He was not feeling the softness of the air on his freshly shaved chin, nor seeing the feathery white clouds scuttle across a sky the colour of bluebells. He was feeling a great sadness for his friend Louise and all the grief she had suffered in her life. Her husband and three of her children had died too young.

He was also feeling a heavy responsibility for the Englishwoman. He sloshed through trickles of water that ran down to the creek without enjoying the earthy smell, because he couldn't get over something Uncle had said about her, just now when he had passed him and Benny on the trail. "Her spirit has gone from her body."

In the yard, a tired Tina said, "Jane's out with your horses. She says the smell of horses is the only thing that reminds her of home. They are the only 'constants' in her life, she says."

Luc headed to the barn. It sheltered a comforting peacefulness, solid and permanent. He thought of all the times he had puttered in one barn or another over the years, doing just what she was doing now, working through all the hard thoughts and sore feelings that life kicked into a person's face. Lobo dozed with his big head hanging, one foot tipped up in a resting position.

She sat balanced along the polished log that formed the top of the manger, lost in thought, bathed in a shaft of sunlight with her heavy hair in one long braid. Her legs were crossed at the ankles, and her hands were folded in her lap. Lobo gave a little whinny.

Luc took a step closer and ran his right hand under the horse's mane. Jane turned her head to look at him, the rest of her remaining still. As Uncle had said, the life seemed to have gone from her. His heart reached out to her a split second before his arms did, and she slid off the manger and stepped right into both. She dropped the burden of her head onto his shoulder and wrapped her arms around his waist.

"I'm going to the funeral tomorrow, then I'm leaving for Edmonton, if you want to come," he said.

She tilted her head and breathed her response somewhere in the direction of his open shirt collar. "Thank you."

"I have to make a couple of stops on the way, so it will take a few days longer than normal. I usually buy furs from a few people and take them to the Hudson's Bay Company. Saves them the trip."

"I don't mind."

He tilted his own head so their temples rested against one another. "We'll be alone. I don't know anyone else going."

"I'll be grateful for the ride."

Luc gave himself the gift of the feel of her, the whole length of her, enveloped as they were in the earthy smell of horses and the protective hush of the barn. He sighed, and reminded himself that she had to go home, that she was lonely and heartsick and fed up with the cruel life out here. The only decent thing for him to do was to get her back to South Edmonton and put her on the first train east.

Jane stood close to Tina, once again straining to understand what was being said. A squirrel chattered in the lone spruce that stood sentinel in the tiny consecrated patch on the windy hillside. Father Benoît let tears stream down his brown face and fall on the prayer book, ignoring the squirrel, communing one on one with God, asking for Julie's protection and salvation.

It's too late, Jane wanted to scream. It was hard to follow the words, so she concentrated on the squirrel instead. He was making as much sense as anything else. The wind whipped her navy skirt around her legs and her feet felt stiff and cold in her cracked boots. The cloth coat was no match for the spring wind. She tried to pull her kid gloves on, but her hands shook so badly she couldn't.

The squirrel nattered in a frenzy. Jane's head throbbed and all she could think of was finding a way to calm the squirrel. Once again, as happened many times a day now, she wondered if she had lost her mind. Finally, they moved away from the dark hole in the ground where Julie was supposed to find eternal peace. Did anyone believe that?

They had tea and cookies at Louise's cabin, where Kokum sat on the floor, looking smaller and more shrunken than ever. Jane let the smell of smoke, tanned hides and tobacco wash over her for the last time, then went and squatted beside the chair that Louise sat on. She opened her mouth, searching for something to say, at a loss for words for the first time in her life. Louise stroked the hair back from Jane's forehead, the way she had done for Julie hundreds of times. No words passed between them.

Gaston stood at the door. She touched his arm as she left. "Thank you for coming," he said.

"Goodbye, Gaston," she whispered.

Luc was filling the back of his wagon with bundles of furs, paying people from a wad of cash. Jane's belongings were tucked under the wagon seat.

Tina waited in the mud to say goodbye and again, words failed Jane.

"I'll miss you," Tina said. "I put some supper in the wagon for both of you."

Jane nodded. "I'll miss you, too."

"It's good you're taking the long way back. Spending some

time in the mountains. I always sleep like a baby in the mountains," Tina said.

"Mountains?"

"Yes. Didn't Luc tell you? He's buying furs on his way back. He'll go by the Whitford place in the mountains. You'll like the Whitfords."

They left the quiet, subdued camp, squinting into the afternoon sun. The runners on the sled had been changed to wheels, so Luc had to pick his way through the patches of mud, looking for dry ground. With only the wilderness in front of them, Uncle stepped out from behind a tree and bowed in his courtly way, just as he had the first time Jane had seen him. Luc brought the horses to a stop.

Uncle reached up to shake her hand, and Jane thought her face would crack as she tried to smile.

"You are going to the mountains?" he asked Luc. "Take her to the healing waters up that way. You take her there."

"I'll try," Luc said.

"It was good to know you, Miss Jane Priddle." He held out his hand again and this time she felt something smooth and warm in her palm. He spoke a few more words to Luc that she didn't understand.

As they drove on, Jane opened the leather pouch he had given her. She lifted out a small wooden carving of a coyote, sitting back on its haunches as though howling at the heavens. She turned it over and over, running her thumb along its smooth surface.

"She's very pretty," Luc said. "You can wear her around your neck. That's what the long cord is for."

Jane slipped the thong over her head and opened her coat so the pouch could fall on her chest. She looked back to wave at Uncle, but saw nothing except their own tracks. She looked ahead and saw nothing there either.

t was a long, hard drive over bogs, across swollen streams and through clouds of mosquitoes. There was no trail to speak of, although Luc had been this way a few times and knew that the easiest route was to follow the Athabasca River as much as possible. They faced a warm southwesterly wind that dissolved the rest of the snow and put colour in their winter faces. Flocks of geese headed north in waves of thousands at a time, nearly blocking out the sun. All told, it was Luc's favourite time of year, but he kept thinking of his friend Louise, and wondering if he was doing the right thing by the silent woman beside him.

The day before, they had turned straight west onto the Jasper Trail, deep into foothills and forests of spruce and lodgepole pine so thick they formed a solid wall on each side. Splashes of gold tamarack stood out against the dark green, along with an occasional bare poplar. Spring came a little later this high up.

They were five days into their trip before the Rocky Mountains loomed over the trees with white-topped peaks, their shades of blue and purple shifting constantly with the movement of the clouds and the wash of sunlight. By the time the sun started back down toward the west, they were surrounded by towers of granite. Moulting mountain sheep dozed on slivers of shale, chewing their cuds and soaking up the sun.

They stopped early to rest the horses and ease their own stiffness, camping by a small lake that lay deep and quiet in the pure, sharp air. Jane, back in her pants and a blue shirt since the first day out, took the horses down to the lake for a drink while Luc started a fire and pitched the tent. He sliced some salt pork into the frying pan and opened a can of beans. She'd tried to cook the first evening and cut herself opening a can of corned beef, then burned a perfectly good frying pan. Her coffee was so weak he could see the bottom of the mug. She was happier taking care of the horses and even Lobo was docile at the end of a day's work.

They sat by the fire, listening to loons on the lake and watching the stars pop out over the peaks. "Ever seen mountains like this before?" he asked.

"Yes. In Switzerland."

"Ah, Switzerland." She had a whole other life on the other side of the world and this was the first time he'd ever heard her talk about it.

"Joseph," Luc said. "He's been to Switzerland."

"Joseph?"

"My oldest brother. I have two brothers and three sisters."

"Yes. Louise told me."

He leaned back on his elbows. "Which are better, the mountains in Switzerland, or these?"

She leaned back, too; it made it easier to look up. Their shoulders were only a few inches apart. She'd adjusted quite well to being in close contact, both in the tent and on the wagon. He liked it himself.

"We arrived by train in the Alps at night and got up the next day and they were there," she said. "Very picturesque. But these mountains, well, they seem to have been watching and waiting for us. Becoming more imposing every day."

Luc turned his head to look at her. "Imposing?"

She looked at him then, and thought for a moment. "Imposing. To me it means they are very grand—*magnifique*. Would that be a fair statement? The mountains will have their own way whether men or animals like it or not?"

He nodded slowly. It was good to hear her talk, and to know she was thinking of something besides little Julie. When he had asked why she didn't sleep, she'd said that as soon as she closed her eyes, all she could see was Julie and a scrap of red ribbon. He had told her that sort of thing happened and that it would go away, but he wasn't sure she believed him.

They spent the next night with Peter and Muriel Whitford. Luc arranged to borrow two mountain-wise saddle horses and packs from Peter, then had the old mountain man draw him a map to the mineral springs.

"Take her to the healing waters," Uncle had said. Luc didn't know if they healed anything, but she had shown an interest in the mountains and it would take her mind off things for a day or two. That would be good enough for a start.

"We'll only have room for a change of clothes and something, you know, to bathe in."

She nodded.

"Can you ride a horse?" He thought he knew the answer to that, had seen her handle horses enough to know the ability had to have come from somewhere.

"Yes, but it's been a while."

"Me too. We'll take it easy."

229

They were on their way early the next morning, just as the rising sun reflected back from the eastern slopes. The weather did what it rarely did in the mountains: it stayed fine as they rode almost straight uphill. To get to the mineral pool, they picked their way along a narrow trail beside a canyon that was punctuated with a series of crashing falls, staying well back from the steep banks that could send them plunging 50 feet or more to their doom. Strands of sulphur steam drifted above the water and then disappeared.

The best campsite was a small meadow just below the hot pool on a green shelf cut into the side of the mountain. The thin air was pungent with the resinous tang of the forest and the mist from the mineral soup that boiled up from the bowels of the rock. A musical stream trickled across the east side of the clearing where they pitched their tent. They watched the sun set behind the mountains as they ate the last of their venison and drank water from the stream—water so cold it hurt their teeth.

When it was fairly dark, Luc said, "A good soak in the pool will get the sore spots out from the ride."

She looked toward the pool and then back at him.

"Can you swim?"

"Yes."

"That's good, but you won't need to if you're careful. Peter said it was only about five feet deep at the middle. Get your towel and, uh, whatever you want to soak in."

He led the way the short distance through the few saplings that formed a screen between the camp and the pool.

Still she hesitated, staring at the simmering water that had turned navy as the sun disappeared. It was about 20 feet across. Thirty feet from the bank in front of them, there was a tangle of trees and rocks that had caught in the mouth of the falls as they plunged into the gorge.

"It's not dangerous, as long as you stay back from the edge over there. And watch where you put your feet. Some of the rocks may be sharp."

She stared at the water as though in a trance.

"I'll go back to the camp and wait until you're done. Then I'll come have a soak."

At dusk the next evening, Jane lifted her soggy, cold shift from the bushes where it was supposed to have dried and headed toward the pool. She stared at the blank surface, unable to see into the depths of it. Like her mind, she thought. Too dark and miserable to go into. She pulled the pouch from around her neck and stuffed it into her pocket.

Her bottom still hurt from the ride yesterday and she knew it would help to go into the water. She liked the pool, liked the way it had of draining her body to the point of weakness; on the other hand, her nipples were as sore as open wounds, rubbed raw by the stiff, wet shift she had worn twice already today for her morning and afternoon soak.

Behind her, Luc chopped wood to keep the fire going. He had seemed content to laze the day away, talking a little about his family and sleeping most of the afternoon. She wished she could fall asleep as easily as he did. At nights, in the tent, he no sooner lay down than he was snoring. Even on the rockiest ground.

Jane sighed and pulled her sweater over her head. "Only 15 minutes," he'd said. "Otherwise you get too weak." She skimmed out of her trousers, then her drawers and camisole. Holding her breath, she dropped the cold shift over her head, holding it out from her chest, and waded into the water. She was amazed again at the heat. She sank lower and lower until the water came to her chin.

And so she sat, watching the steam gather in clumps and spill over the edge of the falls to drift down the gorge like a spirit, riding the echo of the water. She wished she could just send her awful memories of Julie over the falls along with the steam.

She had heard Uncle say that her spirit had gone from her body. Well, she wanted her spirit back. Wanted her memories to float away, not her spirit, wanted to sleep soundly at night and think straight during the day. She sat and let her fancy run away with her. She decided that, since it was her mind that seemed to have lost her spirit, and her mind was apparently in her brain, then it should be her head that she was soaking, not the other end. Tightening the bun on top of her head, she sank lower into the water. The heat burned her eyelids. How long did it take to heal a mind? She kept her mouth closed tight and held her breath, knowing she wouldn't be able to stay under for long.

Jane felt, rather than heard, a splash, and was about to come up for air when hands grabbed her roughly under the arms and she was jerked to the surface a lot faster than she had planned.

"What the hell are you doing?" Luc was yelling at her and dragging her backwards over the rocks, bruising her heels.

"Ow." She sputtered and wiped the water out of her eyes. The cold air instantly glued the shift to her tender breasts.

He flopped the towel around her shoulders and pushed her ahead of him toward the camp. "You could drown. Is that what you want? To drown?"

It was just too much. Her senses had been scattered to the wind by the sight of Julie's bloody face, the satiny feel of a trigger under her finger, an old man carrying on a conversation with coyotes and now Luc looking at her as though she really was a madwoman. "My clothes," she said.

"I'll go back and get your clothes."

She tried to pluck the shift away from her breasts, making two snowy peaks on her chest. Then she stubbed her toe on a root. "Ouch!" The burning heat she felt on her eyelids had nothing to do with the mineral spring.

"Don't move." He went back for her clothes and handed her moccasins to her. "Put these on."

At the campsite, he shoved her into the tent and crawled in after her. She sank to her knees and, even though she tried to stop them, felt tears spill down her face.

"Look ..." He squatted beside her, raking fingers through his messy hair. "Look, *Anglaise* ..."

"My name is not *Anglaise*!" She threw her clothes into the corner of the tent, rose to her knees and, using two hands, pushed Luc Langevin over, screaming at him like a fishwife. "I have a name. My name is Jane!"

Luc propped himself up on his elbow. She hit me, he thought. Well, not hit really, pushed was more like it. Her sobs came from somewhere deeper than he thought possible.

"I know what your name is," he said.

He watched her helplessly; she was shaking with cold and something a lot more powerful, and she kept tugging at her shift.

"What hurts?"

She flapped her hands vaguely at her chest. "My—from the wet shift and the cold."

"You have to get out of that thing. The cold air is dangerous if you're wet."

He dug into his own gear and came up with the red flannel shirt he had worn at New Year's. "Put this on. I'll be back in a minute."

He left the tent and stripped out of his own wet clothes, laying them near the fire. He found his dry suit of underwear and pulled it on, picking his way to his saddlebag and back to the tent in his bare feet.

She sat on her haunches with his shirt on, but she was crying and shaking so hard she couldn't get the buttons done up. He took the lid off a tin of ointment and held it out to her.

"I brought you something for, you know, your, uh, sore places."

"What is it?"

"Well, I use it for saddle sores, mostly. But it works on people, too." How could anyone cry so hard? He had some dim memories of Felicity's tearful sighs, but then she had cried over a broken fingernail.

He held the tin closer. "I've used it myself. It's just—how do you say it? Vaseline?"

She struggled with the buttons and shivered so badly he started to worry. "You're freezing. Let me help. What were you doing under the water anyway?" He moved in behind her and cradled her hips between his knees.

She didn't answer.

"You scared the hell out of me." He took a glob of ointment and a deep breath, slid his hand inside the shirt and did what she didn't seem capable of doing. There was a sainthood in this somewhere, he thought.

"Don't do that." She put her hand on his and tried to draw it away. He resisted her efforts easily, then did the same thing on the other side.

"You need to get under the covers as fast as you can." He helped her with the buttons, pulled her moccasins off and handed her a pair of his wool socks. "Put these on."

"I was just trying to heal my mind," she said. "Like Uncle said."

"Aw, Jane. You can't believe all those old stories."

"He's right."

"Maybe. Partly. Mostly, time is what heals your kind of hurt. Believe me."

She got under the quilt but still shivered so hard Luc's own body ached. He spread his bedroll over her, but that didn't help. There was only one more thing he could think of. He crawled under the blankets and turned her on her side. Making spoons, they used to call it when he was young—three little boys on cold Manitoba nights. He pulled her back tight up against his chest and rubbed her shoulders hard. Sainthood. For damn sure.

uc sat by a dying fire in the full light of day under a sky made impossibly blue by its contrast to the dark mountains and verdant timber. It was the kind of day, with air like champagne, that almost made him believe in God, or something almighty.

He threw a stick onto the fire, then stared into the open flap of the tent. Was she ever going to wake up? She sprawled on her stomach with her right hand curled toward her face like a child. But she wasn't a child. If he wasn't sure of anything else in the bold light of day, he did know that much. And he couldn't blame the air, or anything else for that matter, for his feeling lightheaded. He was 33 years old. He should have known better. He'd been sitting here for hours, waiting for her to wake up, rehearsing what he would say. This wasn't supposed to have happened, and for sure, he wasn't going to make it as a saint.

Last night he had held Jane for what seemed like hours, waiting for her body to stop shuddering. Eventually the shivering and crying had worn themselves out and the tent had become still in that black time of night before the moon is up. He had loosened her hair from the knot on top of her head and spread it out to dry, wondering if he would be able to hold that memory the way he was holding her, knowing that it would be all he had for the rest of his life.

Now, he smelled something scorching and looked at the pan of biscuits he had made for breakfast hours ago. They were all dried up so he tipped them into the fire. Maybe he should go look at her again. *Non*, he'd already done that a half-dozen times. To see if she was breathing.

He'd felt certain she was asleep last night before he tried to slip out from under the blankets. He wouldn't have got any sleep if he'd stayed. He would have been all right, just taking a blanket out by the fire, but as he was leaving, she rolled over and spoke, quietly, but clearly enough to be heard.

"Please don't leave."

He still should have known better. He looked at the sun high overhead and back at the tent. She hadn't moved. He stomped over to the saddlebag, found some line and hooks and marched off upstream, knowing he could trust her. That's what she had wanted to tell him last night. That he could trust her not to do anything foolish, like drown herself.

She hadn't said anything about her being able to trust him. He drew back his foot and kicked a rock as far as he could, then swore as he hobbled on.

Jane awoke feeling hot and sticky, unsure of where she was. She was hot because she had too many blankets on and the sun was glaring through the white roof above her. She rolled onto her back, took a deep breath of clear air; she was sticky because — merciful heavens.

Gathering her scattered clothes in her arms, she peered out of the tent. The camp was empty, the horses hobbled in the meadow grazing industriously. At least there were still two horses, so he hadn't gone very far. If she had ever needed a good soak it was now. She picked her way carefully to the pool in her bare feet, noticing for the first time that the juniper was a lot darker than the spruce. Little strawberry blossoms peeked out along the path. She tossed the wretched shift aside, took a quick look around before dropping the flannel shirt and waded into the water naked. Was he watching again? What did it matter now? Last night, however, she had desperately wanted him to know that he didn't have to watch her all the time.

"Please don't leave," she'd said. It had been so dark she couldn't see him, but she had gone on, "I don't want you to think I can't be trusted. You know, that you have to see to me every minute."

"I've been worried about you," he'd said.

"I know, but I'm all right. Or at least I will be. I'm sorry I worried you, and I'm sorry I shoved you."

"Bigger, meaner folks than you have shoved me. You're the only one who knocked me down, though."

It seemed to have started when he leaned on his elbow and said, "I'm sorry I called you *Anglaise*. I don't like to be called Frenchie, either."

But his work-roughened hands had been tangled in her hair. He'd tried to brush it away, lifting the strands from her face and smoothing them over her shoulders.

"Jane," he said.

"What?"

"Your name. It's Jane." His accent gave the J a soft touch, somewhere between Jane and the French name, Jeanne.

"You make it sound pretty."

"It is pretty," he'd responded.

She jerked herself out of the water. Fifteen minutes were up. She pulled her clothes on quickly and realized that she was very hungry, for the first time in weeks, and would have to go back to the fire and try to find herself something to eat.

Jane was just down at the pool. Luc forced himself not to go check on her. Instead, he dropped four small rainbow trout into a pan with a chunk of bacon and put it over the fire. The fish started to sizzle immediately and a couple of minutes later, he flipped them as he saw Jane coming back to the camp.

He watched out of the corner of his eye while she hung her towel on the bushes. Her face was pink, but then she'd been in the hot pool. She wore a pale blue shirt with the sleeves rolled back to the elbows, tucked into the trousers. When he stood up to face her, she did what she often did—surprised the hell out of him.

She offered him the tin of ointment on the palm of a hand that shook only a little. "Thank you."

"Uh, why don't you keep it? In case you need it again."

She put the tin in her pocket and offered him a little smile.

"Do you like fish?" Was that the best he could come up with?

"Very much." She had a hard time looking straight at him, but she managed better than he did.

He slid two of the trout onto a tin plate and handed it to her. "We have to eat it with spoons."

"I can manage." Sitting cross-legged on the ground, she balanced the plate on her knee.

"About last night," Luc said, as he watched her try to eat with a spoon. She gave up and used her fingers. He sat down on a log, wondering how to say these things.

"Last night?"

"It shouldn't have happened," was all he could think to say.

She plucked a tiny bone from the tip of her tongue with her fingertips, then looked at him steadily. "No, it shouldn't have happened, but you mustn't feel obliged."

"Obliged? What the hell does that mean?" He got a tight feeling in his chest, knew his voice was rising.

"You know what oblige means. Oblige, *être obligé*. It means the same thing in English and in French." She concentrated on picking the last bits of flesh from the fish bones.

Now she was correcting him in both languages. "Can you stop eating for one damn minute?"

"I guess I have to. It's all gone." She looked at the scraps on her plate, then directly at him with an exaggerated shrug and the small smile with one dimple.

He stretched across and slid one of his trout onto her plate. That earned him two dimples and the nicest little speech he'd ever heard in any accent.

"Let's just keep last night as a very pleasant memory and not talk about it anymore."

He'd have to go fishing more often.

Jane concentrated on the trail, mindful of loose footing. It took them the better part of what remained of the day to arrive back at the Whitfords', tired and hungry. Their hosts, starved for company, were content to do all the talking.

The next day, the mountains watched them leave. The wagon was full of furs and, with the days growing longer and hotter, there was no time to lose. Most of the furs were well dressed, but as Peter said, "Some of them might be crawlin' before too long."

By the fifth day from the Whitfords', with the mountains a hazy memory over their shoulders, Jane had fallen into the rhythm of walking more than riding in the wagon. She had developed a long, easy stride that matched Luc's, and a quiet strength grew in her, along with the muscles in her arms and legs. Her hands and forearms turned brown like his and she supposed that her face and neck had, too, but she washed each morning and night in cold water from a stream or lake without benefit of a mirror. When her hair wouldn't stay up in the wind, she left it in one long plait down her back, like Uncle.

She had long, unbroken hours in which to think. She thought of Julie—Julie laughing and playing, Julie cuddled up to her side in the cabin, practising her letters on a greasy old piece of brown paper, because that's all they could find. She thought of Billie and Suzette, but she didn't worry. She'd know what to do for them when the time came. There didn't seem to be anything she couldn't deal with anymore. Except, perhaps, Luc Langevin.

He ranged ahead of the horses, as much a part of his world as the moose and deer that stood quietly by the trail and watched them pass. At the end of each long day, they worked easily together, setting up camp and tending to the horses, but never touching. At night they crawled into their bedrolls with few words and no contact. Jane was pretty certain that she was the one to fall asleep first.

The foothills gave way to rolling parkland, the hollows trimmed with bright green aspen and glittering ponds, the air sweetened with the blossoms of wild fruit bushes.

"Saskatoons," he said. "And those are chokecherries."

"Like the wine?" she asked.

"They make good wine, for sure. You like chokecherry wine?"

So she told him of her tipsy encounter with the brass tub and chokecherry wine, and he laughed.

A day out of Edmonton, they stopped at noon on a warm hillside overlooking a small, tree-rimmed slough. They unhitched the horses and watered them, then tied them under the trees in the shade. They ate cold meat from a tin and biscuits left over from the night before. Luc rolled onto his stomach and folded his arms under his head. Jane knew that he would be sound asleep in seconds and would awake in an hour as easily as he had fallen asleep.

She stretched onto her back and closed her eyes. "Don't snore too loudly," she said.

"I don't snore."

"Yes you do. You keep me awake at night. You're worse than Tina and Benny."

He was quiet for a long time, then she heard him move and opened her eyes enough to see him, up on one elbow, looking down at her. "Tina and Benny snore?"

"Uh, I don't think so." She squinted up at him.

"You said I make more noise than Tina and Benny."

"I did?" She got up and started gathering their dishes.

Devilment danced in his eyes. "You listened to Tina and Benny at night?"

"I didn't *listen*. I couldn't help hearing. The wall was paper thin, and my heavens, they never stopped."

He rolled on the grass, his laughter echoing over the hills.

Jane knelt for their mugs, her face burning. "It's not funny. All winter, night after night …"

He howled all the more, drawing his knees up to his belly.

"We're finished here, if you're not going to sleep," Jane said stiffly. "Let's clean up."

"*Every* night?"

"Stop it." She bit her bottom lip, then smacked him on the shoulder.

That seemed to be all the encouragement he needed. He wrapped his arms around her middle and rolled with her partway down the knoll. They came to rest in a mauve and silver bed of crocuses, their cheeks stiff from laughter. The sun soaked into Jane's bones and she went limp with the pleasure of it all, drugged by the smell of the moist, rich soil rising back to life, seasoned with a bit of last year's decay to give it a good start. Like yeast to an earthy loaf.

"You're heavy," she said, all traces of laughter gone. The sky disappeared.

At some point she had enough sense to say, "We can't do this out here, in the light of day."

"There's no one else for 30 miles," came his muffled reply.

By then she didn't care. And later still, "Get up, let me get my clothes on."

In a near whisper, he said into the hollow of her throat, "Stay with me, Jane."

She went very still. "Just—stay? Like Tina and Benny?"

He raised himself and looked into her eyes. "You know about Tina and Benny not being married?"

She nodded. "Chokecherry wine—brass tub."

"I have to get some of that wine."

"Get up. You're heavy."

"You didn't answer me."

Stay. Could she let herself imagine such a thing? "I have responsibilities."

"Responsibilities," he said, and rolled off her. The sun had lost all its warmth.

Jane fumbled with her clothes as Luc headed off to get the horses. She clattered the dishes into the pack without worrying about how clean they were, then noticed a lone rider coming directly toward her.

"Luc?" She ran her hands over her clothes to see that they were done up.

"I see him," Luc said.

"Thirty miles," she hissed between clenched teeth. "No one around for 30 miles?"

Luc looked at her intently, differently somehow, and pointed at her shirt. "Do the top button, *mon amour*."

He tied the horses to the tailgate and walked toward the stranger.

Jane cupped her hand over her eyes to stare at the two of them, thinking, I know this man. She scrambled through her memory to try to attach a name. There was something familiar about his features, and when he slid off his sway-backed nag, she recognized the loping walk. Not a speck marred his black broadcloth clothes and shiny boots. He had a blue-and-red sash wrapped around his middle, a sash exactly like the one she had worn on her dislocated shoulder.

Then he and Luc were face to face, shaking hands and patting one another on the back. With a jolt of disloyalty, she realized that she was looking at a perfect version of Luc. They turned as one to stare at her. She dropped her hand, resisting the urge to fuss with her hair.

"Jane," Luc said. "Miss Jane Priddle. This is my brother, Joseph. Father Joseph Langevin."

"Good God!" Her knees turned to pudding.

Father Joseph raised one aristocratic eyebrow toward a black clerical hat. Even with all his hauteur, he nearly took her breath away. God has a sense of humour, she thought, to call such a well-favoured man to the priesthood. It was too soon to have to come back to earth. They had a right to one more day, at least, before having to face the music.

And Father Joseph was only too happy to provide the music. "How long have you two been travelling together?"

"Weeks," Luc said.

Joseph looked askance at Jane, but spoke to Luc. "Weeks? The two of you, alone? How did you plan to get into town?"

"I know how to get to town," Luc said.

Jane untied the horses and backed them into the traces. Luc came to help her. She felt a headache begin behind her eyes.

With an exasperated snort, Joseph went on. "Have you thought of the gossip, the repercussions?"

Luc wondered if he could keep the horses on the trail a few hours longer. He had thought about how he could get Jane into town without causing her more problems, but the best he could come up with was to wait and go in at night. That wouldn't be foolproof—if anyone saw them in the middle of the night it would be even worse.

Luc tied Joseph's horse to the back of the wagon and climbed into the seat beside his brother. He glanced over his shoulder at Jane, perched in the back of the wagon, and winked at her. She gave him her little worried smile. Then he looked at Joseph's profile and thought, will he never look his age? He's 45 years old, has studied in four countries and served his church in three more.

"Where have you been today?" Luc asked, to change the subject.

"Out to the Dufresnes'. I didn't see them all winter."

Luc turned to Jane. "Joseph's work takes him many miles." He waved his arm in a full circle. "Almost the whole territory— like Matt."

Joseph spoke over his shoulder to Jane. "And you? What has brought you to visit this country?"

"She rescues things," Luc answered.

"What do you mean, she rescues things?" Joseph asked suspiciously.

Luc shrugged. "Oh, coyotes, kids, her friends." He turned sideways so he could see her in the back. "Tell Joseph about your kids, Jane," he said.

So she did. In an even voice, she talked about Billie and his beatings, and of the little brother who had died in England. After a couple of minutes, Joseph climbed into the back with her, so he could look her straight in the face. Luc checked to see if she was all right with that, but she just kept looking off over the fresh green hills and talking, this time about a little girl called Suzette. She poured it all out, like sour wine from an uncorked bottle, and a lot more of her own feelings went into the telling than Luc had heard before. Must be that white collar across from her.

In the end they pressed on for three more hours, 11 in total, and they walked onto the ferry as the sun sank on the western horizon. The horses stood on the wooden deck with their heads hanging.

Jane leaned against the railing, trying to pin her hair up. "I thought we'd stop somewhere. I would have liked to change into something suitable." Her eyes were bloodshot from the sun and dust, but Luc couldn't get enough of looking at her.

"I'm sorry," he said. "I thought the best thing would be to get this over with."

"What's that around your neck?" Joseph asked.

Jane's hand went to the leather pouch. "It's a carved animal. A coyote that Uncle gave me. He's an old man with ..."

"Yes," Joseph said. "Uncle Charles. Charles Sparkling Eyes. Full of pagan nonsense. I hope you didn't listen to his stories."

Jane's eyes widened and she looked at Joseph in the steady way that Luc had come to love. "Uncle has a name?"

"Of course he has a name."

She smiled with all the dimples. "Sparkling Eyes? That's perfect."

The smile worked on Joseph, too. They both chuckled. She looked from one to the other and said, "My goodness, you even laugh the same." Then, "Tell me everything you know about Uncle. Is he really as old as the hills?"

Finally, Joseph seemed to get into the spirit of it all. He leaned toward Jane and said, in a secretive kind of way, "He may be. You know, he told me once that his first recollection was of crawling out of a badger hole."

Jane drew back and looked at Luc and he could see she didn't know whether Joseph was fooling with her or not.

Luc nodded and kept a straight face. It was like old times, only they were not teasing a sister. "I heard that, too."

"A badger?"

"Yes," Joseph said. "A badger is an animal ..."

"I know what a badger is. We have badgers at home."

"Well, he claims to have crawled out of a badger hole." Joseph lowered his voice all the more. "No clothes on, nothing. Hungry, though, and looking for food. So he has always believed that he was born of the earth, you see."

"You can't expect me to believe that."

The ferry docked with a thud and Luc untied the horses. They started climbing up the steep bank.

Joseph strung his story out a little more. "Ah, but years ago the local tribes often fought amongst themselves, trying to claim the best hunting grounds. Or sometimes they fought just for the fun of it, I think."

Jane knew she presented quite a spectacle as they paraded down the avenue, covered in dust. She was so tired she had to pay close attention to picking each moccasin up and setting it down. But Joseph's tall tale was irresistible, another priceless memory to take home. "What does that have to do with Uncle being in a badger hole?"

Joseph spread his arms as though giving his favourite sermon. "It was very clever, really. The mothers hid their babies until the fighting was over so they'd be safe. Only this time no one came back for baby Charles. So he crawled out of the hole and has been looking after himself ever since." Joseph nodded wisely and looked at Jane out of the corner of his eye. "People claim he can still disappear back into the earth whenever he wants."

"He does, you know. I've seen him disappear myself," Jane said, before she became aware of curious faces, all staring at her; even the grimy newspaperman who had run her advertisement in the paper spat a brown cigarette stub onto the ground and gaped. He nodded respectfully to Father Joseph and said, "How-do, Luc."

The noise and congestion closed in on Jane, leaving her with a feeling of suffocation the like of which she had never experienced before. She wanted to disappear, to hide, to find a badger hole of her own.

In the distance she saw the Princess Hotel, remembered the jugs of hot water and clean white sheets. If she kept her attention fixed on the upstairs window, she would be fine.

Too late. Two women stopped dead in their tracks not 20 feet away.

"Jane? Is that you, Jane?"

Then Jane wondered if her mind was leaving her again. She stared at the women, unable to believe what she was seeing.

"Dear, dear Jane. Is it truly you?"

For the second time that day, Jane took the name of the Lord in vain. "God almighty."

Joseph sucked in his breath.

Cousin Caroline floated toward Jane in a gossamer yellow frock, her straw hat decorated with a matching fabric flower. "My dear Jane. Look at you!"

Aunt Evelyn, tightly corseted and sensibly fashionable, clung to Caroline's arm, her face a mask of shock. "Where—what? I can't countenance this, I truly ..." She sputtered to a stop.

Jane glanced at the two men, tried to see her relatives through their eyes. Luc stood with his weight on one leg, watchful but silent. Joseph had a wary, "Now what do we do?" look about him.

"Why are you here? When did you come?" Jane asked.

"We came to find you, silly thing." Caroline let go of her mother and swooped at Jane with her arms dramatically spread as though to hug her, then stopped at the last minute and took a hasty step back. The glitter of curiosity in her baby-blue eyes turned to disgust and then pity.

"The smell is just from the furs," Jane said. "We've been hauling furs."

"Furs?" Aunt Evelyn's chubby fingers massaged her handful of temperance tracts. "The nuns have furs?"

Jane could not follow her aunt's reasoning. "Nuns?" The sisters were as far from her present situation as these two women, who stared at her like a specimen in a bottle. Then she remembered her manners. "Aunt Evelyn, Mrs. Webb, I'd like you to meet Luc Langevin and his brother, Father Joseph Langevin."

Aunt Evelyn gave Luc a dismissive glance and offered her

hand to Joseph. "Father Langevin. How good of you to bring Jane from the mission."

Joseph pounced on her aunt's assumption and turned on a practised charm. "Madame. Luc has come to the Hudson's Bay Company with furs so we rode with him today."

Not exactly a lie, Jane thought.

"And now we must move on." Joseph began unloading Jane's luggage.

"Where are you staying?" Jane asked her cousin.

"We've rented the most rustic little cottage, just down this road." Caroline pointed to a side street. "The hotels are all booked. The village is full of men looking for gold. Fancy something so foolish. Gold." She reached for Jane's battered cases.

Aunt Evelyn bent to drag her little trunk. "We must get off the street at once, before anyone of consequence sees us. The cottage is just referred to as the old Hawthorne place." She turned back to Joseph. "I must thank you for your assistance, Father. That awful Sergeant Edwards was no help whatsoever. He said Jane had taken the long way home from the mission, whatever that means. He even said Jane was in good hands. Now, I ask you, does she look like she's been in good hands? Well, she's not my daughter, but I try to do my best."

And so the criticism goes on, Jane thought, as though it had never stopped, as though she had not been away from this woman for almost a year. If Matt were to show his face right now she might be tempted to give him a hug.

She turned to Luc who raised an eyebrow but didn't speak. In good hands, Matt had said. Surely it would be acceptable to shake hands. She offered hers and he wrapped his around it, rubbing his thumb over her knuckles.

"The old Hawthorne place," she said quietly.

He nodded, wouldn't let go of her hand, then grinned and mischief twinkled back into his eyes.

"Merciful heavens, don't start anything now," Jane muttered. "We've got enough problems."

twenty-three

"Y ou don't have to stay here," Jane said. "You can go back to Halifax and wait for me there, or all the way home if you like. I can cross the Atlantic by myself, as I did last year."

"We've been here an extra week as it is."

"Well, as I said, you and Caroline can go on without me."

Aunt Evelyn stood in a shaft of sunlight on the worn linoleum floor in the tiny kitchen, her hands on her hips. "You sound as though that is exactly what you would like us to do."

"Don't be silly."

She flapped a damp tea towel at Jane. "And that's another thing. Since when do you tell me I'm silly, young lady?"

"I'm not young, Aunt. You've pointed that out often enough. I am willing to pay the rent on this cottage for another week. Or two, if necessary," she added.

"You really are getting high-handed. I brought the earnings from the inheritance your mother left you so that you would have the means to get home. Not so you could waste it on this shack."

Jane looked through to the cozy sitting room with its horsehair furniture, then toward the stairs that led to two small bedrooms under the slanted roof. "I rather like this little house. And if you think I shouldn't spend my income on the rent, I can always find work. Teachers are scarce out here."

Caroline wandered into the kitchen in a blue silk robe. "You two must stop arguing. You woke me up."

"It's past noon, for mercy's sake," Jane said, her eyes on her aunt's pink face.

"So that's the way of it? You'll have us linger in this dreadful place so you can look for work?" the older woman asked.

"No. I don't want to work so much as I want to wait for Suzette to arrive so I can help her."

Caroline circled Jane slowly. "Is that a new dress?"

Jane looked down at the leaf-green organdie print. "Yes, I bought it from a dressmaker on the other side of the river. I needed something cooler."

"Never mind the dress. Which is much too young for you, I might add. Not at all suitable." Aunt Evelyn wadded the towel into a ball and threw it onto the faded oilcloth on the table. "You're going to take a teaching position so you can bring that little — hussy — out here? And Caroline and I are expected to wait around for you to humiliate us more? Haven't you caused enough of a sensation?"

Caroline blinked at Jane. "Do you know a hussy? Where on earth did you meet ..."

"Caroline, do shut up, please," Aunt Evelyn said.

"You don't have to wait anywhere. But I've had a letter from Suzette and she's already on her way. I'm going to see that she's settled and that may take a few days. If all else fails, I'll take her home with me."

Aunt Evelyn collapsed onto a spindle chair that complained

with the strain. "You'll do no such thing. What would your dear father say, if he heard his Jane talking like ..."

Jane snorted. "He'd say, 'Who's Jane?'"

Veins stood out on her aunt's forehead. "Don't be sarcastic."

"It's the truth," Jane said steadily.

"The truth, Jane Priddle, is that you have become altogether too wrapped up in these—these—strays. I don't know what you hope to accomplish by pampering them. They've had every good opportunity, and if they choose to ..."

"Suzette," Jane said quietly, "did not choose to be in her present circumstances. Billie did not choose to have his teeth knocked out of his head. John did not ..."

"John, I neglected to tell you, has up and abandoned the kind people who took him in. He has gone to work in a foundry in Toronto, the ungrateful wretch."

Jane smiled for the first time that day. "Good for John."

"Don't be so naive. People like that, why, they create their own circumstances. They draw trouble to themselves at every turn."

"People like who? You've never even met any of these children."

Aunt Evelyn chose to ignore Jane. "That's why we try to help them, although, hard as we work to raise the money for their passage and new clothes, there are going to be some who make a mess of things. Could you see any of us getting into such scrapes?"

Jane opened her mouth to relate some of her own scrapes, but her aunt ploughed on.

"Of course you couldn't. And don't you see? Their experiences build character. That's why we sent them here, to learn something, to build character, to make them resourceful adults. It's not your job, Jane, to be responsible for them now. It's their job to take care of themselves." She smiled smugly, pleased with her line of reasoning.

Before she lost her temper completely, Jane grabbed her bag and plunked her sailor hat on her head. "I'm going to the bank. May I get you anything from town?"

"No, thank you," Aunt Evelyn said cheerfully. "We have a meeting at the church this afternoon. If we think of anything, we'll get it ourselves."

"Very well," Jane said, and was out the door before her aunt could start harping on about anything else. She walked in a temper for the first block, then slowed to enjoy the lilac blossoms that hung heavy on the bushes. Bees hummed and two kittens played around her shiny new boots. The cats reminded her of Benny and Tina. Tina would be one of "those" people, and—so would Jane. How easy it was for her aunt to categorize and dismiss people with impunity. But character and resourcefulness? She may have hit upon something there. Character was something Tina had in abundance, and Billie was nothing if not resourceful.

Leaving the bank, she turned east and picked her way across the railroad tracks to the tent camp. It looked much the same as it had in the fall, although one or two patches of grass had turned green, and there were more tents. It was a simple matter to find the Baldwins' sprawl; if anything it had spread, like a patch of nettles.

"Well, lookee, lookee." Ruth Baldwin sat on her backless chair with her dress sagging between spread legs, a baby flopped over her lap. "Look who's here. And a pretty sight for sore eyes, I must say."

Jane's mood lifted with the corners of her mouth. "Hello, Mrs. Baldwin. Is this your newest?"

"Yup. Another boy. An' just call me Ruth. Let me get the tea on here, then set yourself down and tell me about your winter. Never did expect you to last the winter, an' that's a fact."

Ruth shoved the soaked infant at Jane and turned to her stove. Jane held the child away from her new dress and took a closer look. "He's a fine big lad."

They sat in the mess and the heat with the swarm of children quarrelling at their feet, slurping their tea with relish. "Quite a little talk you stirred up, getting stranded last winter."

"So I've been told."

"Ah, well. Good thing about these little places, there's always somethin' new happenin' to take folks' minds off last week's talk. They've probably forgot about you already."

"I hope you're right."

"An' did you find the boy? As I recall, you was lookin' for a boy. Tied up with that remittance man what got himself killed."

"I doubt that Billie is even in the territory anymore. The two men who killed the remittance man will be up for trial soon, and he might have been expected to give testimony. Billie has an ability to disappear when attention turns in his direction."

"Well, don't look so down in the mouth about it. You done your best, I'll wager. You can go home with an easy mind."

"Not really. There's another child, Suzette, who needs help, and I need your advice."

Ruth Baldwin sat up straight and put on her no-nonsense face.

Jane filled her in on Suzette's story. "So, you see, I will need to find her a job and a place to live."

"A job? An' a place to live? For a 15-year-old with a new baby?" Ruth asked with obvious disbelief.

Jane's heart sank. "There must be something for her. She was placed as a companion and housekeeper previously. She could do that again."

"Well, first off, not many folks hereabouts can afford to take on a young mother and child, even if she's a willin' worker. They got enough to do, feedin' their own."

"No one? Not even one of the more successful businessmen?"

"*Men*. That's the tricky part, isn't it? If she's as pretty as you say, an' already spoiled goods, the men will be lookin' her over and the women will be sendin' her packin'."

Spoiled goods. "What about a position as maid at one of the hotels?"

"Where will her baby be? Hotels can't have a cryin' baby around to upset their patrons. An' think of all the men passin' through, pawin' at the pretty young thing that's cleanin' their bed chambers."

That thought stopped Jane's—what? Wishful thinking, she had to admit. "What's to be done?"

"Best thing for her would be to hitch up as soon as possible with one of the homesteaders. There must be five or six men to every woman out here—she'd be married off in no time."

"That's ridiculous," Jane said, thinking of the frightened little mother in the soddy where Luc had fixed her shoulder. "She's too young to marry."

"Nah, they do it all the time."

"Well, Suzette won't be one of them."

"Wish I could be more help, but I don't see any sense in tryin' to fool you. It's a touchy situation, no doubt about it."

"It leaves one more possibility. I will take her back with me."

"You goin' back, then? Thought somehow that you might stay."

Stay. There was the word that had been playing around in her mind for days. Return to London for Suzette's sake, or stay for her own? She hadn't merely been taunting her aunt when she said she could find a position. As well, her little bit of money from her mother's estate would continue to come to her, no matter where she was. She would be something of a remittance man, or woman, herself.

Ruth sat placidly in the midst of her chaos. "You can't really do nothin' until the train gets in tomorrow anyways. Sleep on it. Take your time thinkin' it through."

Finally, Jane had to leave, crossing back over the tracks to town, dragging her feet, gazing into store windows. Think it through.

Lost in thought, she was startled when a figure hailed her from the mercantile store.

"Oh, Tina, it's so good to see you."

Shoppers stopped to stare. It seemed that she and Tina shared a reputation for being a bit odd, if not downright fast.

"Jane, you look wonderful. That dress is just the right colour, and those small tucks, all soft—perfect. I want to hear all about your trip, do you have time for a cup of coffee?" The words spilled out in a rush.

"I'd love that. I ran out of the house without eating and I'm starved."

"House? Ran? We have a lot of catching up, I can see." They entered the dining salon of the elegant Raymond Hotel on a trail of chatter, attracting the attention of the other patrons, mostly men. They sat, heads together, over a linen-covered table and talked their way through cold turkey and potato salad.

"And where is Luc?"

Jane shook her head. "I look for him every day. I thought he would stay in touch, but I guess he's given up on me."

"Oh, he's probably just working. He has to take advantage of all the work in the area right now. I'll bet Bjarne could find him for you."

"No, I don't want to cause him any more inconvenience," Jane said, and changed the subject before Tina could press any further. "How is Louise?"

"She's aged terribly. With all the grief she's had, I think losing Julie was just too much. She's on the move again with Gabe. Homesteaders are flocking to the area and they couldn't stay anymore. I'm sure Gabe would rather be wandering the hills looking for game or offering his services as a guide, but he will always take care of his little band first. Kokum hardly says a word now and certainly nothing that makes sense. She's a lot of work, but that's probably good for Louise. It keeps her busy."

"What of Emilie? She must have had her baby by now."

"Emilie has a baby boy, and she and Gaston turn more and more to the old ways. They talk of heading north, as far away from white people as possible. If anyone can manage that, it's those two."

They lingered as long as they could, but Benny finally came to claim Tina. They parted this time with a warm embrace and promises to stay in touch.

illie slumped against a smooth hitching rail outside the barbershop and waited, squinting down the street. She was tall and was wearing a green dress. That's what he'd been told.

He groped in his pocket and found a butt with a few puffs left in it. He spun the spent match into the street and stepped away from the rail. Maybe he'd just wander off. No, he wouldn't get away with it. He looked up the street again. A tall woman in a green dress was walking right toward him. It could be her. Seemed like the one he remembered, the one with that serious look on her face.

When she came alongside, he ground the butt under his heel. "Miss Priddle?"

"Yes?"

Yup. There was that little frown. This was the worried one. "You've been looking for me, I hear. I was told to wait for you, and let you know I was all right." He pulled a tweed cap down over his forehead and shoved his hands in the pockets of his matching pants.

She stared at him. Well, he'd done as he was told. He sidled away. "I'm all right," he repeated.

Then her face lit up and she grabbed him by the upper arms. "Billie! Is it really you?"

Oh, Lord. Right here on the street. He didn't even like to be out in the full glare of the afternoon, never mind stirring up a commotion like this.

"Look at you! But it *is* you. I can tell by the eyes. I remember those eyes."

She's as crazy as that Frenchman, Billie thought, glancing around, expecting to see him. Because he knew he was being watched this very minute.

She looked around, too. "How did you find me? You're so tall now." Then she seemed to see that he wanted to find a hole to crawl into. "Oh. I'm embarrassing you, aren't I? Let's go somewhere quiet. Have you had lunch yet? This Chinese place is supposed to be good." She nodded toward a café beside the barbershop. "I'll buy you lunch."

"Well," Billie hedged. How could he turn down a meal, even if it meant putting up with this woman? He remembered her as being the talkative one from the mission and she couldn't seem to shut up out here on the street. Better to get out of sight. He tipped his new tweed cap back on his head. "Why not?"

"Why not indeed?"

The Chinese place was cool and dark. A couple of old men slouching on stools along a brown counter stopped talking and watched them. Jane marched straight to a back booth and slid in. "It's more private here," she said, facing the door.

"Doesn't matter to me," Billie lied. A dark back corner would suit him just fine.

"I'll have a pot of tea, thank you," she said to the man who shuffled over. "And what is your noon special?"

"Very nice meat loaf. I bring two."

"No, I've eaten. Just one for the young man. I'll have tea."

"Very nice meat loaf," the waiter insisted.

"I'm sure it is. I'll have you bring a glass of milk and the meat loaf—one meat loaf—with bread and butter, if you please."

Billie couldn't help grinning. "You always get what you want?"

She looked surprised. "No. Hardly ever. Now, tell me, what has happened to you these past two years?"

Behind him he heard the door open, saw the splash of sun on the oiled plank floor, then it was gone again when the door closed. The bread and butter arrived. Around a mouth crammed full, Billie asked, "What d'ya want to know for?"

He shouldn't have been so interested in the bread. A buckskin-clad shoulder slid into the booth beside him.

"Aw, shit." He tried to slide under the table and make a run for it, but he had grown too big.

Matt grabbed his collar and hauled him back up. "That's no way to talk in front of a lady, Billie. Just coffee," he said to the waiter.

"We were hoping to have a nice quiet talk, Sergeant," Jane said. "Is there a problem?"

Billie hunkered over his potatoes and meat loaf. If he had to sit here, he was going to eat. He looked from one face to the other and saw immediately that Jane wasn't any happier about the cop than he was. So she hadn't set this up. That made him feel a little better.

With his eyes on Jane, Edwards leaned back and made himself comfortable, spooning sugar into his coffee. Then he took his time opening a little notebook and digging in his pocket for a pencil. "Problem, Miss Priddle? I don't know. Why don't you two just go on talking about whatever it was you were talking about, and I'll think about it."

Jane stirred her tea until it sloshed into the saucer. She wondered if she would go to jail for kicking a Mounted Policeman on the shins. She could tell that Matt had settled in for a long stay. Billie took a gulp of milk, then sucked his top lip around his broken tooth.

"Very well," she said defiantly. "Tell me about your tooth, Billie. Let's see what the law thinks about a child being treated like that."

The potatoes and meat loaf had disappeared, so Billie ate his green beans one at time, using his fingers. "They sent me to a farm out in the middle of nowhere, a farm with a bunch of cows. I don't know anything about cows, but I was supposed to keep them together all day long. I didn't even have any shoes. They took most of my clothes and gave them to their own boys." He shrugged. "So the cows ran away."

"And they broke your tooth when they ran away?" Jane prompted.

"Naw. They ran away *from* me, not to me. I mean, no fences nor pens nor nothing. Nobody can keep them together without fences, can they?"

"Not as a rule," Matt said.

"So the farmer got mad at me."

"He hit you hard enough to break a tooth?" Matt asked.

"He beat me with a piece of wood he was cutting for the stove. So I ran away. Like the cows."

Even knowing the story, Jane's hand shook as she set her cup down.

But Matt barely reacted. "We know you got to Calgary stowed away in a freight car, and cattle drovers brought you north to South Edmonton. Then you got mixed up with a man called Smythe. Would you care to tell us how you came to be with a dead man called Smythe?"

Billie wrapped his arms around his ribs. "No. I wouldn't care to tell you that."

Jane ached for the man-turned-boy who sat frozen across from her. She waved at the waiter. "Does this meal have a pudding? A dessert?"

"Will you tell me later?" Matt asked.

"Later?" Billie looked as though the beans had disagreed with him.

Jane wanted to wring someone's neck, and it wasn't Billie's. She had no stomach for the things these two needed to talk about. Dessert came, much to her relief. It was dried-up tapioca.

"Take this back or put some cream on it," she said in disgust.

The waiter hustled away and returned with a jug of cream. Jane pushed it toward Billie and he poured all of it on his pudding. Then he slid a weak smile toward Matt and said, "She always gets what she wants."

"Miss Priddle is a remarkable woman. You're lucky to have her for a friend."

Billie looked as astounded as Jane felt. "Friend?" he asked, as though it was a whole new idea. He polished off the pudding before asking, "You said once that you'd help me if I needed it. Did you mean that?"

Jane was about to say of course, when Matt answered instead. "I meant it. What do you need, Billie?"

"There's this boy, Vlasek."

Matt nodded. "Where is he? Is he safe?"

All Billie's cockiness returned. "'Course he's safe. You think I'd hurt him?" He licked the back of the spoon.

"It wasn't you I was thinking about," Matt said.

"Who's Vlasek?" Jane asked.

Billie ducked his head. "I protected him from—you know."

Matt nodded. Jane wondered if anyone remembered she was there. She should just leave and let Matt pay for the meal.

"And we didn't hurt that son of a …," he stopped at the look on Jane's face. "We didn't hurt anyone. We just took that horse so we could get away. George said he was going to drown us under the ice on the river. And the horse is with a farmer about an hour out of town. Go see for yourself."

"I'll do that. It was good of you to take Vlasek with you. Takes a real man to look after someone like that."

"I don't mind taking care of someone."

Matt raised his brow.

"He speaks the truth," Jane said, thinking of the little brother. "I don't know as much about Billie as you profess to, but that's the truth."

Billie nodded, and spoke to Jane. "He had this sack with him all the time and he'd sit and play with the cans of food. Lor', that Smythe bought enough food to live on for years. Anyway, when we ran away, Vlasek brought his sack, and he'd put a bunch of those cans in it, you see, so we had lots to eat. The weather was warmer by then, and we made fires and managed pretty good. We got lost a couple of times, but we finally found our way back."

Even Matt looked impressed. "Is that all you wanted to say?"

"I wanted you to know we didn't kill anyone. When we ran away, they were fighting and yelling and talking about robbing a bank."

"I know. Jake pretty much blabbed it all. George was the one who hit Smythe on the back of the head with a shovel."

Jane listened in horror. This was the stuff of penny dreadfuls.

"So—me and Vlasek didn't do anything wrong except take that horse. And we didn't really take it to keep. I hate horses as much as I hate cows. But I can't take care of Vlasek anymore. He's down in The Flats with Coal Chute Bessy. They're sort of the same, if you know what I mean."

"I know what you mean," Matt said.

"I don't," Jane said.

They ignored her.

Billie looked directly at Matt for the first time. "Could you take care of him? Or find someone to take him in? He said he doesn't know where his ma or pa are, and Bessy, well—you know."

"Know what?" Jane demanded.

The two of them grinned at one another and looked at her as if she were a child. Then Matt said, very quietly, "Why can't you look after him anymore? You going someplace?"

Billie looked cornered again. "I told you, we didn't hurt that stupid Dook. You said yourself he was ..."

"I want to go back further than that. To another dead man called Hobson."

Jane was furious with Matt. This was what he'd wanted all along. He knew Billie didn't have anything to do with the death of Smythe.

"What do you care about that for?" Billie demanded. "It's got nothin' to do with you, and I'm thinking no one over there cares if he's dead or not."

Matt sighed. "I have an unfinished report on my desk, Billie."

"I'm glad he's dead," Billie said, his mouth and face twisted so that Jane barely recognized him.

"He hurt your little brother?" Matt kept forcing the subject, digging at the wound. "Took him—where? To do what?"

Billie slid Matt a bitter look. "If you know so much ..."

"And you went to find your little brother and found Hobson instead?"

With one violent sweep of his hand, Billie shoved his plate furiously across the table. Jane caught it before it could hit the floor. "He deserved to die. Denny," Billie's voice broke, "was so little."

"Letter I got says Hobson died from knife wounds. You carry a knife, I believe. Care to show it to me?"

Billie dug into his pants and tossed a penknife onto the table. "Why don't the police talk to those swells that buy little boys? That's who they need to talk to, but they won't on account of they all have important fathers."

Jane swallowed the bile that rose in her throat.

Matt opened the blade and measured it with his fingers. "This is it? Not big enough to do much harm, is it? Do you have another knife somewhere?"

"Only knife I've ever owned," Billie said blithely.

Jane knew without a doubt that he was lying.

So did Matt. He was too good at his job to accept what Billie had said. He just looked long and steady at the boy.

Billie poked his hands over his head. "Want to search me?"

And Matt did, groping into Billie's pockets and patting down his limbs, to Jane's astonishment and the amusement of the men at the counter. To no avail.

"Where's the rest of your gear?"

"I don't own nothing, 'cept what I wear."

Matt sighed, stretched and stood up. He turned and rested his palms on the table. "You don't, eh? Well, Billie Thomm, I don't want you disappearing again until I say you can. I want that report done and gone in the next day or two. And then we have a trial to think about. Can you tell the truth long enough to speak before a judge?"

Billie shuddered.

"Uh huh," Matt said. "You stay in town where I can find you night and day. I'll tell you when you can leave. I'll even put you on the train myself."

"Where would I go?" Billie asked, all innocent.

Matt snorted. He leaned closer to the boy. "Understand? I'll take care of Vlasek and you'll stay right here."

Then he stood and patted Jane on the shoulder. "Sorry to spoil your reunion. Give Luc my apologies."

"What?" She stared at his retreating back.

Billie edged off the seat. "I'll be going too, miss."

Jane dropped 50 cents on the table and hurried after him. "Wait, Billie. There are other things *I* wanted to talk to you about, then I'll let you be on your way." She followed him outside. "I have to know, Billie. Would you like to go home? I'll help you get back if you want."

He looked dumbfounded. "Home? You mean back," he waved his arm, "across the ocean?"

"Yes. Back there."

"Lor' no! You in on this with Edwards? Looking to send me back to the coppers over there?" Then a truly horrified look came over his features. "Or that Distributing Home in Manitoba? Not on your life, miss! I'm not going back there. They beat the ones who run."

She shook her head and steered him down the street. "No, I'm not going to send you anywhere you don't want to go. I only wanted you to know I would help you with anything you needed. Do you need money?"

He pondered the temptation of money for a moment or two, a sly grin passing over his features. "Naw, miss, I can take care of myself," he said with noticeable pride. "I got a bit of money of my own—hid away, like." He looked around and lowered his voice. "That horse? The farmer handed over a pretty sum of money for it."

"You *sold* the horse you *borrowed*?"

He shoved his hands into his pockets and grinned, the ragged edge of his front tooth showing. "Anyway, why would I want to go home? This is a great country, innit? I mean, that farmer who took the horse? He gave the money over without asking me why I had a horse nor nothing. I wasn't thinking of anything except to get rid of the thing, but I sure wasn't about to say no to a packet of money, now, was I? I got myself these clothes and I have a nice piece of change left over."

"Well, if you're sure you want to stay?"

He lifted his shoulders and made to disappear again. "I like it here now."

"One more thing, Billie."

He looked pained. Not as pained as you're going to be, Jane thought as she led him into the medicinal smell of the dental parlour two doors down.

Dr. Robson sat in his own dental chair reading a newspaper.

"Good afternoon. I'm Jane Priddle and this is my friend, Billie Thomm."

The doctor looked from Billie's shaggy hair to Jane's crisp dress. "How may I help you?"

Jane shoved Billie forward. "My friend has a broken tooth that is very painful. Can you help him?"

Billie backed away. "Now see here, miss ..."

"You can't go on with it like that. It'll become septic and make you sick. And it will never stop hurting, isn't that true, Dr. Robson?"

"Well, I'd have to have a look at it."

"Let me do this for you, Billie," Jane pleaded. "Then you can go to Vancouver without any worry or pain."

Billie eyed the doctor nervously, lifted the corner of a snowy towel on a tray and looked at the instruments with a cringe.

Dr. Robson smacked his fingers. "Don't touch."

"Let the doctor examine you," Jane said.

"Who's going to pay for this?" the dentist asked.

"I am," Jane said.

"Cash?"

"Cash. Now, before I leave."

They talked Billie into the chair and the dentist pried his mouth open.

"I think I can fix it. I won't have to pull it. Fixing it will cost more, it will be expensive, but it should serve him well. How old are you?"

"S'teen," Billie said around the man's hand.

"Sixteen? How can that be? Two years ago you told me you were 12." Jane said.

"I lied."

Dr. Robson looked all the more uneasy.

"Shall we stop the hurting, Billie?" Jane said before either Billie or the dentist could change their minds.

He squeezed his eyes shut and nodded.

"Good." Jane paid the dentist and, as she headed out the door, said, "By the way, Doctor, don't let him talk you out of that money. I want his tooth fixed or I want my money back."

The dentist paled and Billie grinned. She couldn't resist going back and giving him a pat on the shoulder. "Good luck, Billie."

"Ta, miss."

She returned to the boardwalk outside and took a breath of fresh air. There was no doubt in her mind that Billie would make it to Vancouver, whether Matt Edwards got his report done or not.

A boot echoed on the walk behind her and a voice at her shoulder said, "So, how much did the li'l bastard take you for?"

She laughed and pressed her hand to her chest. "Just the price of one silver filling." She slipped her hand through his arm. "Will you walk with me, Mr. Langevin?"

Luc stumbled over his own feet before catching himself, enjoying the feel of her hand tucked into his elbow. A woman in front of the Temperance Boarding House went "Tut tut," but Jane didn't seem to care.

"Where have you been?" she asked.

"Not far. Did you miss me?"

"*Oui*," she said quietly. "Day and night."

He stumbled again. "Jane, for the love of God."

"Speaking of God, what's become of Joseph?"

"He's around, I suppose. I told him you would be on the train last week."

She steered them off the boardwalk and down a side street in the direction of the Hawthorne place. "But I wasn't on the train last week."

"*Non.*"

"You found Billie for me, didn't you? Why did you bother?"

"You had responsibilities."

She sighed and looked away. "Yes, responsibilities."

"Can we stop and talk?" A chickadee hopped down the dirt path in front of them.

"Soon. Did you get your money back?"

"What money?"

"The money Billie stole from you. You were looking for him so you could get your money back."

He shrugged. "I never expected to see that money again. Why? Do you need money for your ticket?"

"Would you give it to me if I did?" she asked.

"If that's what you want. Jane, stop for a minute."

She kept her arm in his and pulled him forward, past a honeysuckle at the side of the Hawthorne house.

"Jane." His voice got louder. He didn't want to have to face any of her relatives.

She opened the back door and stepped into the dim kitchen. "Hello? Anyone home?"

Silence. He stepped cautiously into the kitchen as she went into a sitting room and called again. No answer.

Luc looked around. "It's a nice little house," he said.

Jane returned to the kitchen. "I like it, too. That's why I've rented it for the rest of the summer."

Jane spent the next afternoon unpacking her trunk. Downstairs, her aunt's fury had subsided into a hostile silence. She had told her relatives at lunch that she wouldn't be returning with them. "I need time to see what Suzette requires. If she will come home with me, we'll follow you in a few weeks."

Now, Caroline tiptoed into the room and sat on the narrow metal bed that they had shared. "Will you really stay by yourself?" she whispered.

"I won't be by myself." She squeezed her trousers and sweater into a drawer of the tiny chest and placed her moccasins at the foot of the bed. "I'll have Suzette and her baby."

"But aren't you anxious to get home? To have, you know, a *nice* life again?"

With no hesitation, she answered, "No."

Caroline picked up Uncle's pouch and weighed it in the palm of her hand before dropping it back onto the bed. She wiped her hands on her skirt. "I don't believe I know you any more. You seem so different, so—distant. Have you had such a strange time here, then?"

"My experiences have been no stranger than those of the children."

They ate a cold supper in a colder silence. Aunt Evelyn set off for the church to leave her last wad of tracts, saying that she hoped to find someone in this outpost who might listen to her good advice. Jane and Caroline washed the dishes and left for the train, walking alternately through long shadows and patches of glaring light. The evening sun of early summer in the North West Territories lingered until well after 10:00.

They joined a high-spirited crowd on the platform. Drays lined up, waiting for the trade that the train would bring. Caroline looped her arm through Jane's. "What fun. It's almost like old times."

Jane didn't answer. Nothing would be like old times again. They passed Matt and Charlie Taylor, leaning against the station, taking everything in. Both men nodded. A handful of women stood under the C & E Railroad sign, looking very cool and composed in white linen frocks. Men began vacating the taverns, looking forward to the weekly entertainment. A cheer arose at the first sight of the smokestack. Children tore around like wild things, threatening to shove one another in front of the train.

The whistle blew as the train thundered into town and squealed to a stop. The doors opened and a tumble of humanity fell, stiff and stunned, into the prairie wind. Jane strained to see over and through the crowd. She saw Father Joseph, taller than most, helping two nuns from the train, before she was jostled aside. Caroline kept a tight grip on her arm.

In the end, it was Suzette who found Jane, tapping her on the back. "Miss Priddle?"

Jane was at a loss for words. No trace of round cheeks remained in the thin scrap of a girl who stood with sad blue eyes and a bitter recognition of what surely must show on Jane's face. Strands of dull blond hair hung around her face. Suzette still wore the middy blouse in which she had boarded the ship two years ago, now badly stained and tight across her bosom, and a crumpled black georgette skirt that didn't reach the tops of her boots. She carried a small, fussy baby on her hip and an oilcloth bag that reeked of soiled diapers.

Jane recovered. "I'm so glad you're here. Are these all your things?"

The crowd pushed in and around them, men already beginning to stare. The conductor approached them with an exasperated expression and dropped Suzette's box at Jane's feet none too carefully.

"These two belong to you?" he poked his chin at Suzette and her baby.

"Yes, they ..."

"You got no business sending people like this around the country by themselves, lady."

The crowds stopped to stare. Here was the sideshow they had hoped for. Jane's heart sank. "They had their fare," she said as quietly as possible.

"Yeah, well, I had to nursemaid them all the way from Calgary. Every randy pair of britches on the train finding a way to ..."

"Please, not so loud," Caroline said.

Suzette began to tremble, and a little whimper came from either her or her child, Jane couldn't tell which.

"Don't tell me what to do, young lady," the conductor barked at Caroline. "We don't need you bringing in more of this kind of trash ..."

Jane reached for the box and started to drag it down the platform.

"That's quite enough!" Caroline stepped right up to the man, shoving her face near his. "You will not treat us in such a manner. I shall report you to your superiors first thing in the morning. See if I don't."

Merciful heavens, Jane thought, she sounds just like her mother. "Not now, Caroline. Let's just get out of here."

But the beery men were not about to let the moment get away from them. They crowded closer, making rude comments, laughing, bringing their unwashed smell and ugly insinuations within inches of Jane and Suzette, halting their progress. The few women in the crowd sniffed, then retreated quickly before they could be contaminated by the scene. Caroline continued to harangue the conductor, her voice getting louder all the time.

Taking Suzette's hand in one of hers and the box in the other, Jane tried to drag and push her way forward. She felt the box lift and turned to fight for the girl's belongings, but stared straight into the face of a tight-lipped Matt Edwards.

"Get off the platform," he commanded.

"Can't you see we're trying to?" Jane said in desperation.

He put the box on his shoulder and stood straight. "This way."

Jane turned back to grab Caroline, who was now trading insults with the drunks. "Hush. Please. You're not helping," she told her cousin.

The crowds parted for Matt, but they didn't shut up.

"You man enough to handle all of them, Edwards?"

Jane felt certain that Matt liked this kind of demonstration even less than she did. And just when he was beginning to think better of her; he had called her remarkable and a good friend.

The baby whimpered again. Suzette shook so badly she stumbled. The poor girl had been suffering this kind of treatment for months. Jane heard Caroline's shrill voice but had no idea what she said. Then, around Matt's shoulder, she saw the crowds melt away and Joseph came striding through, like a modern-day Moses parting a sea of drunks. He took the baby from Suzette without a word and stepped off the platform into the open back of a wagon.

Matt dropped the box beside Joseph, then lifted Suzette and sat her on it. "Get in," he ordered Caroline, but she was enjoying her first foray into public spectacle. Matt picked her up and shoved her into the wagon ahead of himself.

Lobo slobbered on Jane's neck before Luc said, "Hurry."

She climbed up beside him.

Caroline stood to throw one more taunt. "I'll have the law on you!" Then the horses jerked to a trot and sent her sprawling back into the wagon on top of Matt.

"Caroline. For the last time, stop," Jane said. "You're only making matters worse. We need to get home without any of them following us."

"I'll have the law on them, Jane. I promise."

"Caroline, you're sitting on the law."

They trooped into the house without a sound except for the occasional snuffle from Suzette. Aunt Evelyn charged out of the kitchen. "Caroline, where have you been?" She came face to face with Suzette. And recoiled.

Suzette took a step back, right onto Jane's instep, her head barely brushing Jane's chin.

"This isn't …?" Aunt Evelyn finally stammered.

Matt placed the box on the floor. Aunt Evelyn's gaze flitted to the name in bold white letters: Suzette Merriman. And across the end, in black: Halifax.

"It can't be." The older woman waved her finger at Suzette. "She's so, well—small."

"She's a child," Jane said.

"A child?" Aunt Evelyn's hand fluttered to her bosom. "What do you mean, she's a child?" She looked at the baby fussing in Father Joseph's arms.

"She's a child. They're all children. That's why it's called the British *Child* Emigration Movement."

No one spoke for some time; everyone stared at the grubby girl pressed against Jane, while a new level of understanding settled over each countenance.

Aunt Evelyn's eyes roamed around the room, and Jane knew the blustering and excuses would soon begin again.

Caroline, flushed with excitement a moment ago, stared openmouthed at the baby, then Suzette, obviously appalled. And probably glad it wasn't her, Jane thought unkindly.

Matt, looking at the little girl, had to see Billie as well—a bold and brazen boy, no doubt, but a boy all the same.

Joseph's bright mind would be searching through the acquaintances and connections he had in the community to see if he could help.

Luc was the only one in the room not staring at Suzette. He shook his head at Jane with a resigned expression. "She rescues things." Wasn't that what he had told Joseph?

The baby started to howl in earnest so Joseph passed her quickly to Suzette.

"What's the baby's name?" Jane asked.

"Margaret, after my mother," Suzette whispered.

"We will go home to your mother as soon as you've rested," Jane said. And after you've put on a little weight, maybe acquired some clothes that fit, she thought.

For the first time since she had left the platform, Suzette spoke aloud. "No! Oh, no, Miss Priddle. My mother would be heartbroken to see me brought to this."

"You mean she doesn't know?"

Suzette shook her head vigorously, loosening more hair.

"But ..."

"No! Please! Don't make me do it!" And she started to cry along with her baby, deep heartbreaking sobs wrenching the whole of her thin body.

Jane took a deep breath. "Of course not. Whatever you say. Caroline, would you take Suzette upstairs to feed her baby, please? Then come back and get some warm water so they both can have a good scrub."

"Am I going to have to listen ..." Aunt Evelyn began.

"Aunt, find some food for Suzette and take it to her immediately."

"Food? What food?"

"Whatever you can find. Now, if you please."

Her aunt's mouth opened and closed twice, but she returned to the kitchen, muttering.

Caroline started up the stairs, but Suzette stayed firmly attached to Jane. "Go with Caroline," Jane said gently.

"Miss?" Suzette whispered.

"Yes?"

Even quieter. "Who are they?"

"They?"

"These men."

Jane looked at the three very tall men who filled the sitting room. Of course. Men. Striking fear into the hearts of unprotected girls. Relief at being away from the rabble, and perhaps the knowledge that she had good reason to stay in the New World, made Jane a trifle giddy. She propelled Suzette toward the stairs with a firm hand on her back, and the answer to her question: "The Three Wise Men."

Matt Edwards laughed out loud for the first time since she had met him. It had a nice ring to it.

"Get away, miss," Suzette said, but she stopped crying and a smile trembled at the corners of her full mouth. She followed Caroline up the stairs.

Matt leaned against the station, shoulder to shoulder with Charlie Taylor, watching a few passengers straggle onto the train.

"Quiet morning, isn't it?" Charlie commented.

"Never as many leaving as there are coming."

Two women were hurrying down the platform toward them. Matt motioned to the conductor who was taking up the stool, getting ready to yell, "All aboard."

"Better hold up there," Matt said. So the relatives were on their way back to the Old Country. Jane would have her hands full with her latest stray, but he knew now that she could take care of it. Luc seemed to be content to have Jane around; whether he could handle her do-gooding or not was another matter, but Matt had a lot of faith in his old friend.

The two women bore down on them, nattering at the top of their lungs, struggling under the weight of a half-dozen suitcases. The conductor saw who they were and made no effort to help.

"Not one moment's sleep for two nights," the older one complained.

"I still wonder if I should stay and help Jane," the other said as she started to heave their bags into the train.

"Put that thought right out of your mind, young lady," the aunt said.

Matt saw a tweed-covered arm inside the train reach to help the women.

"Thank you, young man," the aunt said.

The conductor picked up his stool and climbed the stairs. "All aboard!"

Through the open window, Matt saw the women stumble down the aisle and try to find seats. Then, as the train gathered speed, Matt heard the older woman screeching, "My handbag! Where's my handbag, Caroline? Caroline! Stop this train!"

Matt was relieved that the steam engine was gathering speed. Let them deal with it in Calgary.

That's when the fellow who had pretended to help them pushed his tweed cap back and looked out the window directly at Matt. He had a wary look in his gold-coloured eyes, until he realized how fast the train was moving. Then he touched his fingers to his forehead in a jaunty salute and flashed a shiny silver tooth in a big grin.

Matt pushed himself away from the wall, swearing a blue streak. The whistle blew one last time and the train disappeared in a cloud of steam.

Freda Jackson was born and raised on the Canadian prairies. She has a degree in education from the University of Alberta and has completed several post-graduate courses in Creative Writing, Canadian History and Women's Studies. Her travel articles and short stories have been published in the *Edmonton Journal* and *Western Families*. A mother and grandmother, she lives in Edmonton, Alberta.